MEN BEYOND THE LAW
A WESTERN TRIO

MAX BRAND™

SAGEBRUSH
Large Print Westerns

First published in the United States by Five Star

First Isis Edition
published 2015
by arrangement with
Golden West Literary Agency

ISBN 978–1–78541–000–0 (pb)

Published by
F. A. Thorpe (Publishing)
Anstey, Leicestershire

Set by Words & Graphics Ltd.
Anstey, Leicestershire
Printed and bound in Great Britain by
T. J. International Ltd., Padstow, Cornwall

This book is printed on acid-free paper

Table of Contents

WEREWOLF

In the mid 1920s Faust both consulted with C. G. Jung and entered analysis with H. G. Baynes, a Jungian analyst in London. This proved to have an effect on the preoccupations of his Western stories as is quite apparent in "Werewolf" which first appeared in Street & Smith's *Western Story Magazine* (12/18/26) under the Max Brand byline. Christopher Royal finds that he has become a wanderer, a searcher, and it is in the deep fastnesses of the wilderness through the medium of an ancient Indian that he is confronted with the terrors of his own soul and the meaning of his life. He has found love, as deep and abiding as it is ever given to human beings to know, but it is lost to him until his own spiritual odyssey has completed its course, until he has had his spirit vision, confronted the terrifying shadow within, with only the mournful howl of an ancient werewolf to accompany him on this lonely, and terrible, and anguished journey.

CHAPTER ONE

"The New Comer"

All day the storm had been gathering behind Chimney Mountain and peering around the edges of that giant with a scowling brow, now and again; and all day there had been strainings of the wind and sounds of dim confusion in the upper air, but not until the evening did the storm break. A broad, yellow-cheeked moon was sailing up the eastern sky when ten thousand wild horses of darkness rushed out from behind Mount Chimney and covered the sky with darkness. Dashes and scatterings of rain and hail began to clang on the tin roofs in the valley, and the wind kept up a continual insane whining, now and then leaping against window or door and shaking them in an impatient frenzy.

On such a night as this, few men got as far as Yates's Saloon beyond the outskirts of the town of Royal, but nevertheless he was always glad to have this weather, for those who *did* come stayed long and opened their purses with as much freedom as though the morrow was to be doomsday, and as though their souls needed much warming with honest rye whiskey against that great event.

3

Mr. Yates had two rooms. The bar was in one, with a round iron stove at one end where the guests might warm themselves and a row of chairs against the walls, for one of the maxims of Yates had to do with the evils of drinking — while standing.

He was engaged in giving good advice at this moment to a youth who rested one elbow on the edge of the bar and poised the other fist upon his hip — a tall, strong, fierce young man who smiled down at the saloon keeper partly in contempt for the advice and partly in mild recognition of the privilege of white hairs.

"You give me another slug of the red-eye, old boy," said the cowpuncher.

Mr. Yates filled the glass with an unwilling shake of the head. As he pushed it back across the bar and gathered in the fifty-cent piece he said gloomily: "You can't hurry liquor, son. Whiskey is something that can't be rushed. You got to go slow and easy, let it mellow you, treat it with caution . . . and then whiskey will stand your friend."

"All right," said the cowpuncher, tossing off the drink and shoving back the glass. "Never mind the change. Gimme another, will you . . . and then you can talk some more."

Mr. Yates came to a pause.

"I dunno that I ought to let you drink another so quick," he said.

"You dunno?" said the young man. "I know, though. Fill up that glass!"

There were five men in the barroom, their chairs tilted against the wall, and now five chairs swung softly forward, and five heads were raised.

"I tell you, lad," explained the saloon keeper, "that the whiskey which will be a friend to the wise man can turn into a devil if it's treated carelessly. You can't crowd it into a corner. You can't treat it like a slave!"

"What'll it do?" asked the boy. And stretching out his arm with a movement of snaky speed, he wrenched the bottle from the hands of the saloon keeper, and filled his glass with such a careless violence that an extra quantity spilled upon the well-rubbed varnish of the bar.

"What's this stuff going to do to me?"

Mr. Yates did not attempt to protest against the act of violence. But a dark flush spread over his face and he said solemnly: "It'll take you by the throat and strangle you. It'll send a bullet into your back. It'll throw you under the feet of a mad horse. Or it'll kill you with the horrors, if it feels like it!"

The youngster tossed off his liquor again, coughed, and then shrugged his shoulders. "I don't understand what you're driving at," he said, "and I don't know that I give a damn! Is there any writing paper in that other room?"

There was still more contention upon the tip of the tongue of Yates, but he controlled himself with an effort, for words flow more willingly from the lips of an old man than water from a rich spring. He merely said: "There's always paper there, and welcome!"

There was no answer to this courtesy. The cowboy turned from the bar and kicked open the door. His chair screeched as he drew it up to a table, and after that there was silence from the second room, and silence at the bar, also. The five farmers and cow hands smoked their pipes or cigarettes and watched the thoughtful cloud upon the brow of their host.

"And who is he?" asked one at length.

"Him? Didn't you have a fair look at him?"

"It's Cliff Main," said another. "I knew him over in the Ridoso Valley a few years back, and I'm sure it's him."

"Yes," nodded Yates, "it's the same man."

But one of the others said suddenly: "Why, partner, that's the name of Harry Main's brother!"

Again the saloon keeper nodded.

"It's him," he confessed.

This was followed by a deeper and longer silence, and more than one apprehensive glance was cast at the door of the second room. A weather-beaten farm hand approached the bar and leaned against it.

"Tell me," he murmured, "is he like Harry?" And he hooked a thumb over his shoulder.

"You can see for yourself," said Yates solemnly. But he added, forced on by a keen sense of fairness: "No, he ain't a killer, you might say. He's gone straight enough. But still he ain't any lamb!"

The farmer shuddered a little. "What's his game here?" he asked.

"It's that girl up the valley . . . her that young Royal is after."

6

"Which Royal?"

"I mean Christopher."

"It's the Lassiter girl that Chris Royal goes with, ain't it?"

"That's the one. They say that Main seen her at a dance down in Phoenix last year, and it addled his head a good deal. So I guess that's why he's here."

"That would be a thing!" said the farmer. "A Lassiter to look at a Main, eh?"

"Well, I've seen stranger things happen," said Yates. "A pretty girl takes to a strong man, and a strong man takes to a pretty girl. Goodness and badness ain't considered much, and neither is the poor old family tree. But that ain't the point. Georgie Lassiter, she's got one strong man already, and that had ought to be enough! I guess that no woman can ask for more than a Royal, eh?" He leaned on the edge of the bar. "I guess that no woman could ask for more than that," he echoed himself, and he shook his head slowly from side to side and laughed softly.

The others nodded in understanding, as though they were all familiar with the qualities of the family which had given its name to the valley and to the town.

In the meantime the storm had been rising and quickening like the pulse of a sick man's heart, and now the wind broke with hysterical wailing around the saloon. The windows and the doors rattled furiously. The very roofs seemed about to be unsettled, and a contrary gust came down the chimney and knocked a puff of smoke through every crack of the stove.

"What a night!" breathed Yates.

"I'll take another whiskey!" said one.

"And me!" said another. "We'll set 'em up all around. I say that I don't mind a night like this when you can sit warm around a fire with something to keep your heart up. But I could tell you about a night that was a twin brother to this, except that it was in February with ice in the wind. I was back up in Montana, that winter, riding range for the . . ."

The door quivered and then jerked open, and the wind, like an entering flood of water, made every man cringe in his place. With that burst of the storm came a big young man who thrust the door shut behind him with a strong hand and then leaned against the bar, stamping the water out of his soaked riding boots and shaking the rain out of his hat. He was neither beaten nor even embittered by the force of the wind and the rain. It had merely brought a rosy glow into his face and dimmed the brightness of his eyes a bit with moisture.

"Well, Chris Royal," said the bar keeper. "What're you having?"

"Nothing," he said. "I'm bound home, you see, and Mother doesn't like me to have liquor on my breath. I stopped and put my mare in your shed for a feed and a bit of rest. She was fagged by bucking this wind all the way up the valley."

He broke off to speak to the other men in the room and, as he completed that little ceremony and had asked after their welfare, you might have put him down as the son of a great landed proprietor on whose estates all of these men were living, so that their welfare in a way was his. However, that was not the case, even though the Royals had been so long in the valley, had given it its name, and had dominated all affairs in it that they were placed in a truly patriarchal position. There were no political parties in Royal County or in Royal Valley, for instance. There were only the Royal partisans and their opponents. And the opponents were sure to be merely a scattering and spiteful handful. In other ways, too, the family dominated the region.

"It's a sort of queer name . . . Royal," someone had said to a man from the valley, and the answer had been instant: "That's because you ain't seen them. They're all fit to be kings!"

"But look here, Christopher," said Yates. "D'you know that, if you don't drink, you're missing one of the best things in life?"

"I take a drink now and then," said Christopher. "I like it as well as most, I suppose. But it bothers Mother to have me do it. So I don't when I'm going toward her, you see."

"Ah, well," said Mr. Yates, holding up a bottle toward the light, "here's something twenty-five years old that I was going to offer you a sip of, but heaven knows that I'd make trouble between no boy and his mother. She's a grand lady, Christopher, and amazing how well she carries her years, ain't it?"

"Years?" said Christopher. "Years?"

"Well, she's getting on, ain't she?"

Christopher Royal looked rather blankly at his host. "I never thought of that," he said. "She isn't really old, you know."

"No, not old! Not old!" said Yates, smiling. "But when we have white hair . . ."

"Her silver hair," said Christopher, "is beautiful. It's always been silver, you know. As far as I can remember."

"I can remember farther back than that, though," smiled the saloon keeper. "I can remember when she first came to Royal Valley. It was a dark, mean day, and she come in a covered carriage, all made snug. But I had a glimpse of her through the carriage window and saw her face all pink and white and her yellow hair like a pool of sunshine in the shadows of the carriage."

Christopher shook his head. "I can hardly think that my mother was ever like that," he said, smiling in rather a bewildered way. "But you mustn't call her old!"

"Why, Chris, at sixty you can't exactly call her young, can you?"

"Sixty?" exclaimed Christopher. He began to think back. "I'm twenty-five. Duncan is twenty-eight. Peter is thirty. Edgerton is thirty-one. Samson is thirty-five. By heavens, you're right, and she's sixty years old. I should never have guessed that. One doesn't connect years and time with her." He added with a smile to Yates: "And you're one of the unchangeables, too. You've never been any different, have you? Not in my lifetime!"

"Well, lad, well!" smiled Yates, "I do well enough. I just shrink and shrivel a bit as time goes on. I get a little whiter and a little drier, and there's less hair for me to bother about combing, from year to year. But I don't change much. Neither does the old place."

"You've put a new wing on the shed, though."

"You noticed that, eh?"

"Yes. Who did you have do the work?"

"I had the slaves of Adam," said Mr. Yates, and he held out his two hands with a chuckle.

"You did it all yourself?" Christopher whistled. "You're a rare old one. If there were more like you, there'd be no room for the youngsters in the world. You'd take our work away from us."

A door crashed just behind him.

"Are you Chris Royal?" asked a voice, and he turned about and looked into the dark eyes of Cliff Main.

"I'm Christopher Royal," he admitted.

The other stepped up and faced him at the bar.

"I started to find you today," he said. "Then the rain dropped on me and I put in here. I want to have a talk with you, Royal."

"A talk? Where?"

"Well, there's an empty room back here. We might go there."

CHAPTER
TWO

The Locked Room

Christopher regarded the newcomer rather dubiously for a moment, but then he nodded and followed him into the other apartment. The door closed behind Main, and the lock grated as it was turned.

"Hello!" said the saloon keeper, starting around from behind the bar. "I don't like that!"

"What're you going to do, Yates?" asked one of the farm hands, catching his sleeve as he passed.

"I'm going to have that door open."

"Now, don't you do it. You know Main. Don't take more'n a little thing like that to send Harry Main crazy. And his brother looks like the same kind of gunpowder."

Yates paused, biting his lip with anxiety.

"Besides, there ain't gunna be no trouble," said one of the others. "It ain't as though Duncan or Edgerton or Samson Royal was in there. Christopher, he's softer than the rest. He's easier and quieter. He's more like a girl, you'd say, compared to his older brothers. He can get on with anybody. I never heard of Chris having an enemy."

"And that's all gospel," said Yates, going back behind the bar. But he paused, now and again, and shook his head. "I don't like that locked door," he sighed. "I remember once that me and my wife had a bad quarrel. And it started with me locking the door . . ." He broke off with a laugh. "And when I wanted to open that door, I'd lost the key!"

There was general mirth at this, until a sudden uproar of the wind and its loud whistling beneath the door caused the human voices to fall away. The wind itself dropped to a murmur shortly afterward, and everyone in the barroom could hear the voice of Christopher Royal, saying sharply: "I tell you, man, that I don't want any trouble with you! I swear that I've never done you any harm!"

The wind began again, and all the six in the barroom looked mutely at one another, with great eyes.

"It's the whiskey," said Yates suddenly. "I might of knowed it. I told him when he was pouring it down that way. I've seen it happen before. And I tell you that door'll never be unlocked until there's been hell to pay inside!"

He rushed out from behind the bar and tore at the knob.

"Open the door!" he yelled.

There was a sudden sound of thunderous scuffling within, and then a heavy body crashed against the door. Yates, terribly frightened, shrank away.

"Why don't you do something?" he wailed. "Ain't they in there killing each other? Ain't there five of you, big and strong and young, to stop 'em? Why do you stay here with your hands hangin'?"

They looked at one another, these five. Surely they were as strong and as brave as most men, but the sound and the thought of the battle which was raging beyond that door baffled and overawed them. They could not move to help. Perhaps in another instant they would have recovered their courage and been able to act, but the whole duration of the scuffle within the other room lasted only a single moment. It ended with the sound of a revolver shot. Then the key grated in the lock. "May heaven forgive me," said old Yates, "but I'm gunna die with poor young Chris or revenge him!" He picked up a shotgun from behind the bar and laid it level with the opening door, his old face white and tense with savage energy.

The door swung wide — and Christopher Royal stepped out, while a gasp of wonder and relief came from the others in the place. For their sense of suspense had been as great as if they had been forced to stand by while a man was caged with a tiger. And now the man came forth alive.

In the hand of Christopher there was hanging a big Colt with a thin wisp of smoke still clinging to its muzzle like a ghost.

"He's dead, I think," said Christopher, and he leaned against the bar. "I wish that some of you would go and see."

They poured into the writing room. It was half a wreck. One could see that two very strong men had wrestled here, and whatever they touched had given way. Cliff Main lay in the corner on his back with a smudge of blood across his face. There was no reason for a second glance. He had been shot fairly through the brain.

When they came back into the barroom, Yates hastily filled a glass with whiskey and in silence placed it beside the youngster. He gripped it eagerly — and then pushed it away. "She wouldn't like it," he explained. He raised his head and, seeming to discover the gun in his hand, or to remember it for the first time, he threw it on the bar and shuddered violently. He was very white, with a look of sickness in his face, but he was extremely steady and quiet. He said: "Is your telephone working in spite of the storm, Yates?"

"It's working, Chris."

"Then I want you to ring up the sheriff and tell him what's happened out here."

"I'll do that."

"There's nothing to be done for . . . him, I suppose?"

"For Main? No, he's dead, Chris."

"I thought so. But what did you say the name was?"

"Cliff Main . . . Harry Main's brother."

"Harry Main's brother!"

He took the glass of whiskey which was standing on the bar. He tossed it off, and then without another word he strode away into the night.

"Look at him," said Yates, addressing the door through which his guest had just disappeared. "Look at him. And you call him soft. I tell you, even Harry Main wouldn't get any better than his brother, if he should come along to even things up. There's something in the

Royal blood, and it can't be beat, and it can't be downed. Did you notice him when he came out from that room? Sick looking, because it had been a dirty job and a dirty sight at the finish. But like a rock, eh?" He rubbed his hands together. "As for the killing of Cliff Main," he added with a sudden sternness, "you was all here to witness how Main carried on from first to last, wasn't you?"

"We seen it all," said one of the farmers. "They'll never lay a hand on Chris for this. It's only Harry Main that he's got to think about! And I thank heaven that I ain't in Chris's boots!"

CHAPTER
THREE

Dark Thoughts

The wind had changed so that, as Christopher Royal rode up the valley, the rain was volleyed at him from the side, stinging his face until he was forced to cant his head against it. It was an automatic movement. The howling of the wind and crashing of the rain which had seemed terrible enough to him before were now as nothing, for there was a war in his spirit which quite overwhelmed all mere disturbances of nature.

He had killed a man! To Christopher the miracle was that in the crisis, when his back was against the wall, his skill with a gun, built up by many a long year of practice, by many a strenuous hunting season, had not deserted him. When the need came, mechanically the weapon had glided into his hand, and he had shot swift and true, so swiftly and truly, indeed, that Cliff Main had not been able to complete his own draw before the pellet of lead had crashed through his brain.

But suppose that he had known that the name of the man was Main? Suppose that he had known that this was none other than a brother to the famous fighting man, Harry Main? What then?

It made convulsive shudders run through Christopher's body, and in the blackness of the night with the rush of the storm about him he told himself again the secret that no one other than the Almighty and his own soul had ever been cognizant of before: he was a coward!

How, then, could he have come to the age of twenty-five years without having that weakness publicly exposed by the rough men of Royal Valley, where he had spent his life? The answer was simply that his family were all above the shadow of reproach. They had filled the mountains with their deeds for many a year, and this present brood seemed to have improved upon the old stock rather than fallen away from the good tradition. If there were a riding or a hunting or a shooting contest, one could be sure that one of the Royals would be the winner. And when it came to fighting — why, who was apt to forget that the scars on the face of Samson Royal had been received in hand-to-hand battle with a grizzly? And who could fail to know that Edgerton Royal had ridden single-handed into Pinkneyville, when he was deputy sheriff, and come out again herding two prisoners before him — prisoners he had taken away from beneath the eyes of a hundred of their friends? As for Peter Royal, he had proved that he was worthy of spurs on that dire night when the three Mexicans cornered him, and only a year before Duncan Royal had shot out an argument with two men on the Chimney Trail.

So they were all proven, and there had remained only the youngest of the brood, Christopher, to make his name. Yet it had hardly needed making. Men took it for

18

granted that one Royal was about as good as another. There might be little differences, but the world generally agreed that all were lions — pick which you would!

For one thing they all looked alike. That is to say, the smallest of them all, Samson, was a full two inches above six feet, and the tallest of them, Duncan, towered a palm's breadth above his older brother. They had all the same sort of shoulders, filling a door as they went through it. And concerning their might of hand, wonderful and beautiful fables filled the land. How Samson had twisted the iron bar in the blacksmith shop in Royal Town — behold, it still hangs against the wall as proof! And how Edgerton could take two packs of playing cards and tear them across. And how Christopher himself had lifted the entire bulk of a horse!

Such stories filled the mountains with echoes. Since not one of the band had ever been found weak in any manner of physical or nervous test, it was taken for granted that all were of the same true, pure steel. But one person in all the world knew the facts. He knew that Duncan and Edgerton and Samson and Peter were all undoubted heroes with hearts even stronger than their hands. But he knew also that there was one fatally weak link in the chain of brotherhood. That was himself. For Christopher during years and years had felt a weakness in his spirit, and he had waited for the dreaded moment when he should be tested. Or could it be that the family name and fame would shield him effectually all his life?

19

In his school days he had not so much as guessed it. No matter how mighty had been the tradition that his brothers had left behind them in the little white schoolhouse by the river, he had not been overawed. The height of Duncan's jump, and the width of Peter's leap, and the speed of Samson on foot, and the weight of Edgerton's fist had all become proverbial in the school. But young Christopher bided his time and surpassed them, one by one. He was just as strong as they, and in addition he was a little more supple, a little more graceful, a little more brilliantly swift and sure of hand. And other graces had been lavished upon him, as though Nature, who had framed his brothers on so magnificent a scale, had been merely practicing for the moment when she was to create Christopher. So she had made the others big and glorious, but she gave to Christopher the gift of beauty, also. The others were dark. She made him fair. There was a touch of gloom about the others, as there is apt to be with big men, but Christopher she made joyous from the beginning. Altogether, if the citizens of Royal Valley had been asked to select one of the family as the representative of all that was best and finest in them, they would have picked Christopher with almost one voice. There were a few, of course, who were not impressed by his gentleness.

But in this lavishness of hers, Nature had forgotten the prime and essential gift. She had left out the vital spark of courage. And though no man knew it except Christopher himself, he had passed through many a dreadful moment when he stood face to face with his secret.

Now the very secrecy that enveloped the fault was threatened. For, as certainly as lightning strikes, Harry Main was sure to come to avenge the death of his brother. And when Harry Main came, what would Christopher do?

In his desperation he vowed that he would go out to meet the destroyer and in some hidden place, with no man to see, he would fight and die. Yet, in his heart of hearts he constantly knew that he would not be able to meet the great test. When Harry Main approached the valley, Christopher would slink away — and never again dare to show his face among his kin. Somewhere far off he would have to find a new place in the world, a new name, and there live out his wretched destiny.

And when he thought of these things, it was typical of Christopher that he did not think of the faces of his four strong brothers, hard with scorn and contempt, but the picture that rose before him was of two women. One was his mother, and the other was the lovely Georgia Lassiter whose head was always carried so jauntily high. He was sure that the reason she loved him so passionately was not so much for himself, his mind and his spirit, as because of an ideal of manhood which she had conceived and which she had grafted upon Christopher. She loved, not him, but her idea of him. If once she guessed at such a dreadful taint as cowardice, all her love would be replaced by a fiery disgust.

And his mother? When Christopher thought of her, his heart bowed almost to the mud of the road. What she would think and do and say was beyond him, for he knew the sternness which underlay her motherhood, and he knew the iron of her pride in her family.

He reached the turning from the main road and saw before him the avenue of poplars, their heads shaken and bent beneath the fierce hand of the wind. Down the gravel drive he galloped the tired mare and so wound into view of the Royal House itself, with its lofty front and its romantic wooden battlements. From the top of the neighboring hills the naked eye could see Royal House like a great natural landmark of the valley, and from directly beneath it looked rather like a great palace than the residence of a rich rancher.

Behind its wide-flung arms were the sheds, the barns, and the maze of the corrals where the weaker cattle were sheltered and fed through the severer winters. There were the quarters for the hired men, also. Day and night, for all these years, there had never been a moment when smoke did not rise from some chimney in that group of buildings.

Christopher, looking at it all, and thinking of what it meant, felt again what he had often felt in his childhood — that big and strong as all his brothers were, his father who had built these things must have been even to them as a giant to pygmies. And his mother had been the proper wife of such a man. Still she ruled the establishment with a power as firm as it was mild, and even her eldest son dreaded her quiet voice more than the booming of a cannon.

Christopher had been a little different. He had been the baby of the family. He had been the petted one. For having raised so many sons so well, even such a woman as Marcia Royal could afford to relax a little and favor her youngest child.

He thought of this bitterly now. For, if he had passed through the same stern school as the others, might he not have developed, like them, the same iron core to his spirit? Might he not have grown, like them, into a hero of heart and hand also?

He gave the mare to a stable boy. Then he turned to the house, and, as he walked, he wondered how he should tell the story. And what would the others say? He decided that he would say nothing for the time being. So he went into the living room and found them all, except Samson, gathered in easy chairs near the fire on the open hearth.

He changed his clothes, and, when he came down again, he found that his mother had a cup of hot coffee waiting for him. She stood behind his chair, with her hands on his shoulders, while he drank it.

She spoke quietly: "Christopher, dear, you shouldn't have come out on such a night. You know that."

"I tried to telephone from Wooley's, but the line was down in the wind, I think. I was afraid you'd worry if you didn't hear from me. So I came on out."

"And why not telephone from Yates's place? And stay there the rest of the night?"

He did not have a chance to answer, for just then Samson came in and fixed his dark eyes instantly and firmly upon the face of his youngest brother, so that Christopher understood that Samson knew all that had happened.

23

CHAPTER
FOUR

No Assistance

There was something so unusual about Samson's air that the others noticed it instantly. For that matter, the oldest brother of the Royal family was always so direct, so fiercely sincere, that it was not usually difficult to understand what was going on in his mind.

He came across the room after a moment and stared down at Christopher, who stirred uneasily beneath that glance. Afterward, Samson went before the fire and stood with his back to it, until steam began to rise from his wet clothes.

"Now what is it, Sammie?" asked his mother.

Samson was the only member of the family that dared disregard for an instant a direct remark from his mother. In place of answering he suddenly put back his head and shook with silent laughter.

"Samson!" cried Mrs. Royal.

At this, he came to himself with a start.

"What on earth is the matter with you?"

"Nothing, Mother."

"My dear, you must tell me at once. You make me nervous."

24

Samson allowed a broad smile to spread over his face, while he stared straight across the room directly at Christopher. "Look there!" he commanded.

"There is Christopher, of course," said the mother. "You are really rude, Samson. Now, what about Christopher?"

"I don't know what you mean. What should there be about him?"

"Don't beat about the bush, Samson!"

He sobered down at that, but still there was a suppressed exultation in his eyes and in his voice. "You haven't heard. He wouldn't say anything about it. He doesn't want to shock you!" And the laughter broke out again, not mirthful, but savage. "I'll tell you what," said Samson, "this old Christopher of ours, whom we've always thought so gentle and all that, he's a lion under the fleece! I've always guessed it. And tonight he's proven it!"

Mrs. Royal turned on her youngest son. "Christopher, what have you done?"

Christopher stirred in his chair and tried to answer, but he could only shake his head and murmur, "I can't talk about it!"

"It was too much," said Samson with a grim satisfaction. "Nasty business. He doesn't want to talk about it. Doesn't want to at all! Well, I'll tell you what happened. I came up the road to Yates's Saloon and got there just after Chris left. I heard what had happened, and I saw!"

"What was it, Sammie, in the name of heaven!"

"Why, I'll tell you what it was! I found there the proof that Chris is your real son, Mother!"

"Have you doubted that? Did you think he was a foundling?" asked Mrs. Royal, looking fondly at her youngest son.

Samson went over to her and dropped his big hands on her shoulders. "You understand, Mother, that it was always easy to see that Chris was like you in one way . . . like the gentler side of you . . . but we didn't think that he had your iron."

"Am I iron, Sammie dear?"

"You may smile at me, Mother, but you can't fool me. Yes, you are iron, in the time when iron is needed. And if you hadn't been a woman, you would have made as hard a man as ever stepped!"

"That needs some explaining, foolish boy."

"Well, we all remember the time that the Crogan dog went mad, and tried to get at us, and how you stood it off with your walking stick!"

"That was a horrible day," she said.

"No, you liked it! I'll never forget how your eyes shone as you stood up to that wild, foaming beast!"

"Tush, Sammie. But I want to hear about Christopher."

"Well, about darling Christopher," murmured Samson, and he turned his powerful, homely face toward him. "I'll tell you. But watch him squirm. Watch him wriggle while I talk."

"Don't be too ridiculous, Samson. Just tell me the facts."

"There were several facts. To begin with, Chris was at the Yates place this evening. And so were several others. And one of them was young Main."

There was a sudden stiffening in the attitudes of all of the family.

"You mean Harry Main's younger brother?" asked Duncan, the giant.

"Yes."

"A ruffian, like his brother Harry!" exclaimed Mrs. Royal.

"Look at Mother's eyes shine," nodded Samson. "She's gentle . . . no iron about her." He stopped to laugh with a savage satisfaction again.

"Samson!" cried Christopher hoarsely. "I don't want to hear any more of this!"

"You can't help it, Chris. You simply can't help hearing it."

"I can, though, and I shall!"

And Christopher strode hurriedly from the room.

"Now will you tell us before we all go mad?" said Mrs. Royal.

"It was like this . . . Cliff Main had come to Yates's place, poured down some stiff whiskies, and then gone into the next room to write a letter. Then Chris came in. He wouldn't drink, not when he was riding home to his mother."

He paused and grinned.

"My darling Christopher," smiled Mrs. Royal.

"He's a darling," nodded Samson. "A perfect lamb. Wait until you hear the end of this yarn, though."

"I want to hear it, if you'll only get on."

"Main come out of the other room and found Christopher . . ."

Here the door opened suddenly and caused everyone to start. It was Christopher coming back — a pale and shaken Christopher.

"Samson," he said, "I want you to stop making such nonsense over what happened."

"Well?"

"I'll tell them myself exactly what happened, since they have to know the truth about the miserable affair."

"Go on, old man. Of course, we have to know."

"Cliff Main made me leave the barroom with him. We went into that other little room. The moment we were alone, he grew insulting. And after a time, when he saw that I wanted to be friendly and keep out of trouble, he grew overbearing . . . horribly so! And finally he said that he happened to be interested in Georgia Lassiter, and that that was reason enough for me to stop paying attention to her."

There was a stifled exclamation from Mrs. Royal. Christopher, his eyes closed, rested a hand against the wall. He said slowly: "I couldn't quite stand for that, you know. And I had to tell him that the thing would not do."

"And then?"

Christopher did not speak for a moment. He was recalling that moment over again — the sinking of his heart and the sickness of his spirit, and the manner in which he had felt that he was slipping into a sea of darkness. Another instant and he would have begged for mercy. Another instant and he would have tried to flee from the room. But that instant was not given him by the brutal Main. There had been a flash of a hand toward a gun. And he instinctively had moved to make his own draw — and made it first!

"And then," said Christopher faintly, "he started for his gun. And I had to start for mine . . ." He paused, breathing hard. "The bullet passed through his brain." Christopher sank down in a chair. He was overcome by horror.

His mother was suddenly beside him, her arm around him. "Chris, my dear boy. I know. No matter what a brute he was, he was a human being. But now that you've done this thing, there'll never be any need for you to do another. You detest bloodshed, and having proved that you're a man who cannot be tampered with safely, the others will be sure to leave you alone! Dear boy, how my heart aches."

He did not answer. He could not look at her. She thought his horror was because he had had to take a life. But it was not. It was horror at the knowledge of how close he had been to a nervous collapse, to a complete hysteria of cowardice.

"But you're wrong, Mother," said Edgerton Royal, the logician of the family. "You're quite wrong. Before the week's out there'll be another gun fight on Chris's hands."

"What do you mean?"

"Think for yourself. Will Harry Main allow the man who killed his brother to get on without another fight?"

"Harry Main! That murderer! That gunfighter! No, you will all band together and prevent him. You'll all meet him and crush him!" cried Mrs. Royal.

"Wait!" said Peter Royal, for he was the judge of the family. "Wait, Mother, and tell me if you yourself would allow other people to fight your battles if you were a man?"

She hesitated. Christopher, his face buried in his hands, waited breathlessly. Then he heard her saying slowly: "No, I couldn't. And not a one of you will be different. Not a one of you will want to help poor Chris, though every one of you would die to avenge him! But oh . . . what a dreadful trial for my poor Chris. Such a man as Harry Main."

Samson was speaking, Samson the mighty, the ugly of face, the steely hearted. "Chris'll beat him! Let these gentle fellows get the taste of blood and they're worse than the worst of the gunfighters that are born hard and mean. I'm a prophet. You wait and see what happens. For a million I wouldn't be in the boots of that fellow Harry Main!"

Harry Main? To Christopher, it was as though he had been thinking about a great tiger rather than a man. Harry Main? He would as soon stand up to a thunderbolt as to that destroyer. What was Cliff Main compared to such a devil of a man?

He waited. A pause of solemnity had come in the talk of the room. And in that solemnity he knew that every one of the stern and strong brothers was resolving that the battle must be fought out man to man. So his last hope was thrown away.

CHAPTER
FIVE

Words for the Weak

Sleep came to him that night as a most unexpected guest. And the morning dawned and found him twelve hours nearer, not to death, but to his humiliation. For all thought of standing for the trial of courage against Harry Main had left him. But, knowing that in the crisis he would not be present, he was able to put on a smile when he went down to breakfast. The others greeted him with a forced cheerfulness that made him feel they already thought him as good as dead. Only his mother did not smile but sat very sternly erect, her eyes looking far away. What schemes might be passing through that formidable brain of hers, equal to any man's?

After breakfast, Peter called him to one side. "Here's that Winchester of mine that you've always liked, Chris," he said. "I want you to have it."

Peter hurried away, leaving Christopher more thoughtful than ever. For his brother, Peter, was a great hunter, and this was his favorite rifle of which he had often said that the gun had a will and a way of its own in shooting straight to the mark. Such a gift meant a great deal. It was more than a rifle. It was as though

Peter had parted from some of the strength of his very soul.

To be sure, Harry Main was as apt to fight with a rifle as with a revolver. Various stories of his prowess passed through the mind of Christopher. He remembered that old tale of how the four Brownell brothers had gone on the trail of Harry Main and shot him from behind, and how he had dragged himself from his fallen horse to a nest of rocks and bandaged his wound, and fought them off through all of a hot, windless day among the mountains. Three of the Brownell boys he killed outright. And Jack Brownell, with a bullet through his shoulder, rode fifteen miles to get to a doctor. As for Harry Main, he had needed no doctor but cured his own hurts.

That was one eloquent testimonial to the skill of Harry with a rifle. And Christopher's face contorted a little in unwilling sympathy as he thought of the injured man dragging himself about among the rocks and firing at some momentarily exposed bit of an enemy among the adjacent rocks.

However, though rifles were a possibility, revolvers were far more likely. And as for the examples of the hardihood of Main with a Colt, there were a dozen to select from, each well-nigh as incredible as the other. Perhaps none was quite so startling as that tale of how, when he was little more than a boy, he had followed three Mexican cattle thieves who had raided his father's little ranch — followed them over a thousand miles, until the trail crossed the Rio Grande, and on the other side of that famous river had encountered them in broad daylight, unexpectedly, at a bend of the road. All three had opened fire. But Harry escaped without so much as a wound, laid the three dead with three bullets, and then turned and began the long march back toward the ranch, driving the lean cattle ahead of him.

That had been revolver work, and upon a revolver it was most likely that Harry would depend now. So Christopher took a pair of Colts and a loaded ammunition belt. He went back behind the house to a quiet little dell where the poplars walked in their slender beauty along the banks of a winding stream. It was an unforgettable spot in the mind of Christopher, because at this place he had first told Georgia Lassiter that he loved her, and she had said so frankly and joyously that she had always loved him.

It gave him seclusion now. With his heavy knife he sliced a blaze on the faces of six posts and then, at twenty paces' distance, he walked rapidly past those posts and put a shot in each.

He examined them afterward. A bullet had cut through the heart of each white spot except for one, where the pellet had torn through the margin of the blaze. But even so it would have touched the heart, had that post been a man.

He was infinitely pleased with this exhibition of skill. Not that it determined him any the more strongly to remain and wait for the coming of Harry Main into the valley, but, because he had worked for so many years to make himself expert with weapons, there was a meager satisfaction in seeing to what a point his skill had attained.

He went on to other little bits of marksmanship. He would select a tree, mark it with a blaze, and then turn his back upon it, close his eyes, and, whirling rapidly around, look and fire all in an instant. It was terribly trying work. He missed the blaze three times out of four, but still he always managed at least to strike the tree trunk.

Then he had another little exercise of skill which he often worked at. If you knock a man down with your first bullet, he may still shoot and kill you while he lies, bleeding and sprawling on the ground. So he marked trees with a double blaze, one head-high and one against the roots, and he began to fire his shots in pairs, and the sap oozed from the wounds that he made in the tender saplings.

He changed from that to picking up bits of wood, or stones, and tossing them high in the air — then whipping out a revolver and firing at the flying target. Once in three times he hit with his first shot. And half of the remainder he managed to smash with a second shot. But one in three fell to the ground untouched. However, such shooting could never be made perfect. It was just a wonderful test and training for speed and accuracy of hand and eye combined.

Three times in succession he tossed high into the air a stone no larger than his palm in size, and three times in succession he blew it into a puff of powder with a well-planted bullet. As the last bit of sandstone dissolved in the sunshine into a glimmering mist, there was a little burst of hand-clapping from the side of the meadow, and Georgia Lassiter rode out to him on the little white-stockinged chestnut that he had given to her the year before.

She was the last person in the world he wanted to see. All the rest he could give up and endure their loss — even his mother. But Georgia was different.

She swung down from the saddle and into his arms, and she stood there, holding him close and straining back her head a little from him to look up into his face.

"You'll beat even Harry Main!" she declared. "You can't fail. It really isn't in a Royal to fail, Christopher."

"Mother has told you, then?" asked Christopher gloomily.

"Your mother didn't need to tell me, because everyone in the valley is talking about nothing else, and last night the telephones were simply humming with the news. Everyone says the same thing, Chris . . . that you'll beat him! Because an honest man is stronger than any scoundrel and thief."

"Is Harry Main a thief?" he asked rather blankly.

"He is! He is!" cried Georgia, who never failed to defend her opinions with vehemence. "A man who picks pockets is a thief when he only takes away a watch or a wallet. Then what about a villain who uses his greater training and cleverness to steal the lives of other men? Isn't he a thief . . . a murdering thief?"

"He always uses fair fight, Georgia."

"I know, and there's something grand and terrible about Harry Main. But still . . . when I stood there and

35

watched you practicing, Christopher, I couldn't see how any man in the world could safely face you."

"There's a difference between target practice and practice at a living target, you know."

"You seem so pale and gloomy, dear."

He looked vaguely at her, like a child, hardly seeing her, and yet keenly aware of details, such as the depth of tan in the hollow of her throat, and the trembling in the wind of the cornflower at her breast.

"I'm not very cheerful," he told her anxiously. And he waited, to see if that would make her guess anything. She was merely a little irritated.

"There's Lurcher, too," she said, "looking as if you'd just beaten him!"

Lurcher was a melancholy crossbred hound, a very ugly beast that had strayed down the road to the Royal ranch and stayed there, adopting Christopher as his particular sovereign deity. But he would never follow Christopher farther than the limits of the ranch, which he seemed to know by a peculiar instinct. Even when there was a hunt, he would not follow a trail beyond the borders of the Royal estate. Lurcher had passed through many a dreadful trial, it seemed, in his earlier life, and he was fixed in his determination to remain as much as possible on the soil where he had found freedom from persecution. Now he skulked in from the edge of the meadow and lay down in the shadow of his master, raising his mournful eyes toward the girl.

"I never beat Lurcher," explained Christopher, a little hurt by her tone.

"I wish that you would," she said in one of her petulant moods. "It might do him good. It would stop him from thinking so much about his troubles by giving him something to worry about."

"He's not a bad dog," said Christopher. "He does things, you know."

He drew his hunting knife and threw it dexterously so that it stuck in a poplar trunk thirty feet away. "Get it, Lurcher!" And the hound trotted obediently over, worked the blade from the trunk, and came back, wagging his tail with joy to lay the knife at his master's feet and then raise his sorrowful eyes in worship toward the face of Christopher.

"Without cutting himself!" cried Georgia.

"You see, Georgia, he's not such a bad dog."

"But he's a coward, Chris. I never could understand how a Royal could endure any cowardly creature near."

This was pressing him very close, and he winced from the thought. "He's not cruel or treacherous or unkind or bullying or underhanded or disloyal, Georgia," he argued. "You have to admit that's a good deal to say for any character."

"Is it?" She shrugged her shoulders and then burst out: "I'll tell you, Chris, it really doesn't amount to anything. What's the good of friendship that doesn't dare to fight for the sake of its friend? What's the good of love that won't die for the thing that's loved? Can you answer me that?"

CHAPTER SIX

A Woman of Steel

He went back to the house with Georgia at his side, sitting lightly in her saddle.

"All the rest seem to think that it's the same as sure death to have Harry Main go on the trail of a man, but I don't feel that way," said Georgia Lassiter. "I know that courage and the right have a force in the world. I thank heaven for that faith. And . . . I want to have our engagement announced tomorrow . . . before anything can happen to you."

He caught at the bridle of her horse, but she reined the chestnut dexterously out of his reach.

"Georgia! Georgia! Do you mean that?"

"Why, of course I mean that, silly."

"And then . . . suppose that something happens . . . ?"

"Something may happen to you, but that won't kill my love for you, dear. You don't suppose that because a bit of a bullet might strike you down, Chris, it would strike down my love also? No, I laugh at such an idea. I've no fear of myself! And once I've let the world know that I love Christopher Royal and intend to marry him, I'll never change my mind. Nothing can change it. I tell you, Chris, that I'd be as true to your ghost as to yourself."

She said it with a fiery enthusiasm, her nostrils dilating a little. He thought that there was something rather more knightly than womanly in her bearing. It seemed odd to Christopher that his mother and this girl, both so deeply in his life, should have such a strength between them. And he such a weakness!

"Georgia," he breathed, "I wish . . . I wish . . ."

"What do you wish?"

"I wish that there didn't have to be any change, but that the two of us could just go on like this forever . . . no tomorrow . . . no yesterday . . ."

"You'd get hungry after a while," observed Georgia.

"That's the way that the gods live," said Christopher. "Always in the present, with no sorrow for what has been and no dread of what is to come."

"Chris, you're talking like a pagan priest."

"To be like this, Georgia dear, with you on your horse, within the sweep of my arm, and I walking here beside you, and the good rich yellow sunshine pouring down on us both, and the face of that river always silver ahead of us . . . don't laugh, if you please!"

"I won't laugh. You frighten me when you talk like that."

"Frighten you? You?"

"Do you think that I can never be frightened?"

"Yes, I've always thought that."

"I'll tell you what, Chris. If something happens . . . oh, why should I beat about the bush? I mean . . . suppose that Harry Main actually kills you, I'll have to go the rest of my life like this . . . I mean, with my back turned on what's around me and always looking away on the times when you and I were together and alone. There aren't many of those times. I suppose that I'll begin to wonder why I didn't spend every moment with you while I had the chance, and why I didn't beg you to marry me quickly, and why I didn't have a baby to keep after you. And . . . I'm getting so sorry for myself that I'll be crying in another minute!"

Christopher could not answer, for such a coldness of dread and of sorrow had grown up in him that he felt the very nerves of his knees unstrung, and a horrible weakness of spirit passing over him. "Georgia, you'd better go on home."

"No, I want to talk to your mother first."

"There's no good in that. You understand? I don't want to talk about Harry Main. I don't want to think about him . . . until I have to."

She swung the chestnut closer and dropped her arm over his shoulders. "I know," she said. "That's the right way . . . not to worry about the game until it has to be played. But heaven won't dare to let Harry Main win."

He looked up to answer her. She kissed him, and then galloped the chestnut away. He watched her across the fields. Lurcher, who had followed the galloping pony to the first fence, stood up with a forefoot resting on the lower rail and looked after her with a low whining which was the nearest approach to a voice of any kind that people had ever heard him use.

There was something wonderfully touching, to Christopher, in the dumb excitement and grief of the dog. He called Lurcher back to him, and went on into the house where he found the letter that laid the last stone in the wall of his misfortune.

It came from Harry Main, and it said simply:

They've brought me news about how Cliff died. I'm coming down into your valley as soon as I can. That ought to be by about Thursday. I suppose that you'll want to meet me somewhere around Royal Town. Wherever you say will suit me fine. I'm coming to Yates's Saloon to talk to old Yates. And you could leave a message with him for me.

Yours very truly,
Harry Main

It was all so very quietly written, and so rather gentle in a way, that Christopher could hardly believe that the quiet words which he had been reading could have flowed from the pen of the man whose terrible guns had brought him such a crimson fame throughout the land. But, after all, Christopher knew perfectly well that the loud-mouthed and cursing heroes are of a very inferior breed compared with the silent and workman-like gunfighters who build their fame by actions rather than by boasts.

He read and re-read that letter, and then he showed it to his mother. She read it with care, as though it were a much longer document.

"I'm sorry," said Mrs. Royal, "because I'd hoped that you would not be destroying such a thorough man as this letter seems to be from. I'd hoped that you would simply be facing a vagabond and a bullying scoundrel. But it seems that Harry Main is not that sort. It's a very good letter, Chris. Don't you think so, dear?"

He could nod in answer to this.

"One feels so much assured strength and self-reliance in it," she went on. "And no cursing, and no boasting, and no threatening. In fact, it's just the sort of a letter that I would hope to see *you* write, Chris, if you were in a similar position!"

He said, "If one of my brothers were killed, would you want me to ride down to murder the murderer, Mother?"

He was curious, and listened to her with a sort of detached interest, although he knew her answer beforehand.

"No," said Mrs. Royal, "I shouldn't expect you to do anything like that . . . not trail until your older brothers had ridden out first, I mean to say!" She added this as a sort of afterthought.

"But suppose that they all went down, one after the other . . . ?"

"Oh, of course, you would go! Why do you ask such a foolish question?"

"Because in some parts of the country they think that the law should be left to handle such work as this."

"In some parts of the land," she replied, "the law is a grown-up force, but it's not grown-up out here. It's simply a child. And one poor sheriff has less chance of keeping order among the wild men of these mountains than a single little boat would have of policing the seven seas. So that's why there's a different code. And there has to be. Manhood is the mainly important thing. Just sheer manhood. That's what we have to worship out here."

He could see that there was no use trying to persuade her into another viewpoint, for she had lived so long in this land and had grown so inured to its strange ways that she could not feel or think in any fashion other than this. She believed in the lynch law for cow and horse thieves, for instance, and there was on record a case when she masked herself and rode with the mob to see justice done. And yet there was very little of the iron to be seen in her face. She was rather a small woman, delicately made, and her hand was smaller, indeed, than the hand of Georgia Lassiter's. Her carriage was as daintily erect as Georgia's, too, and her laughter had almost as young a ring in it. Youth might wear a different face in Mrs. Royal, but its heart was not greatly altered.

"There are still forty or fifty years for growing old," she loved to say, "and I'll never use them all."

"What do you mean?" someone would always ask her.

"One of these bucking horses will finish me one of these days. Or else, one of our enemies will creep up and shoot me. I only hope that it's not in the back. I only hope that I can see my death coming straight before me. I don't think that I'll flinch."

That was not an affectation but the actual state of her mind and of her desires. She had lived like a lady all her life. But she wanted to die with her boots on, like a man.

"I don't know that my granddaughters will have much use for me," she also used to say, "but I want all my grandsons to be able to look up to my memory."

Which was the reason why Christopher, hearing her speak in this fashion, could not help wishing that some of the "manhood" which she worshipped, and which she also possessed in such a degree, could be stolen away and placed in his own heart. But he saw that for the first time in his life he would be able to draw no comfort from her. For the way she saw the matter was far closer to the manner in which Harry Main was seeing it than it was to the viewpoint of her own son.

He went up to his room and sat there in a brooding silence. He could see that there was no cause for changing his earlier decision. If he could manage to slip away from the house that very night, he had better do so, because there were only two days left before the announced date of the arrival of Harry Main, and before that time he must be far, far away, leaving a small track to be followed, as followed he must be.

CHAPTER
SEVEN

Flight

He made himself quite jolly through that evening, because he knew that he was making his last impression save one upon his family. And in the course of the evening Peter Royal could not help breaking out: "I wish that I had your fine nerve, Chris! To stand up to the music like this while every minute is bringing that devil closer and closer."

Christopher, when he was alone in his room, brooded over this, sitting by the window and looking into the dark, deep face of night that lay outside. He was called down to the telephone, then, and Georgia's voice came sweetly to him.

"I had to speak to you again today, Chris. I've had a dreadful feeling all the time, as though you were slipping away from me. No, it's not prophetic. It's only fear. It's only fear, Chris! But, oh, I wish the thing were over with!"

He said good night to her hastily, for the sound of her voice had sent a thrilling weakness through all of his veins, and he felt that he had hardly the strength to get back up the stairs to his room.

He turned out the lights and lay down to rest a little, if he could, but the blackness swirled above him and stifled him like the beating of wings of enormous moths. Time dragged on miserably until at length the house grew quieter, then silence, and he knew that he alone was awake — or should be awake. He made up his pack for the trip. He made it small, consisting of the barest essentials, so that it could be done into a tight roll inside his slicker. He had in mind the horse he would take. It was the flea-bitten roan which Samson had given him as a birthday present the year before. The gelding would never tire at his work, wherever it led.

When he had completed the preparations, he remembered that he had forgotten Peter's rifle. That was just the last thing in the world that he wished to leave behind him, so he reached into the closet to find it. Pulling it out, the old bamboo fishing rod swayed out and tapped its slender stem against his forehead. He stood for a moment in the darkness, gripping it, and remembering with a sudden rush a thousand things out of his boyhood, when he had first learned to use that rod. He saw again the windings of the creeks, and the creaming surfaces of the little rapids, and the broad, brown faces of the pools, where the fish would be lurking beneath the fallen logs along the banks. He saw himself once more trudging home with the rod on his shoulder and the dangling fish snapping their lank tails at the dust, and he heard his voice raised with the voices of his companions, proclaiming lustily what

46

manner of men they should be when they grew up. Ah, there would be no cowardice in them surely!

He remembered the day that a wave of scorn ran over the boys in the school when they heard how a forgotten outlaw had walked into a bank in broad daylight and had held up the cashier and three or four others, made them open the safe, and shovel the contents into a sack, which he then carried away with him, mounted his horse, and cantered cheerfully and unharmed away from the city. Ah, how the schoolboys had raged when they heard of it! Had only a few of them been in that town of cravens, they would have upheld the law in a more fitting manner! But they had not been there, and little Christopher Royal, lying awake in his excitement at night, had dreamed long and wildly of what things he should accomplish when he grew older.

He thought of this as his hand closed around the narrow shaft of the fishing rod, and then he turned sadly away and closed the door. For he felt gloomily that he had shut away one part of himself in that closet, and all his hopes of what he might be were confined with the old toys in the dark of the closet.

Then he hurried from the room, opening the door with care, lest some squeaking of the hinges might betray him. But, as he stepped out, he tripped and stumbled heavily over a form which lay in the hall just outside his door. It was Lurcher, who now came cringing to him and licked his hand by way of apology.

He cursed the dog in a whisper, for the noise he had made might have caught the attention of his mother, who was a very light sleeper. But, after listening a moment and finding all silent in the house, he went softly down the stairs to the lower floor. The side door creaked badly, so he did not attempt that, but spent a moment sliding the bolts of the front door gently back and then turned the big key slowly, without making the slightest whisper of sound.

After that, he slung his pack over his shoulder and turned for a last look at the old house. As he did so, he saw a glimmering form on the lowest landing of the stairs. And then he made out his mother's face as she watched him.

It was characteristic of her that she had not cried out to him, but there could be no doubt that she understood. The pack at his back, the rifle in his hand, and the hour of the night could mean only one thing. So he stood confounded before her, and she came finally down to him.

She said: "Then we were all wrong, Christopher. After all, you couldn't stand it?"

"No, after all, I couldn't stand it."

She sat down and drew her white dressing gown closer around her, because the night air was chill, and, though she did not speak, her eyes never moved from his face, and he knew that her stern heart was breaking.

"Will you say something, Mother?" he begged.

"What can I say, Christopher? I know that your own heart has said all of these things to you before me."

He nodded, dumb with shame and remorse.

"What are your plans?"

48

"To go somewhere far off. I don't know where. And take a new name and try for a new life."

She shook her head. "Someone from this part of the country would be sure to find you and tell what you had done."

"I suppose that there's a chance of that."

"And then?"

"Then I'd have to move on again."

"Oh, Christopher, a man can die only once!"

He bowed his head.

"And if you stayed, and if you fought, heaven wouldn't let you lose. It couldn't. And you've already won once!"

He could not lift his head to answer. He began to tremble from head to foot.

"And Georgia?" she asked suddenly.

He did raise his head then. "I've thought of Georgia every minute!"

"Why, if that thought doesn't stop you, then I suppose that I've no influence whatever. And still I can't help talking. I wish . . . oh, I wish that I could disguise myself and pass for you. How gladly I'd take a gun and face him! Oh, how gladly, Christopher, if that would save you!"

He felt the lash and winced.

"Christopher, you've already met one of them and beaten him. Do you think of that?"

"I didn't know who he was," said Christopher, "not till afterward. And even before a stranger that I didn't know, I was in a blue funk. And when Samson and the rest hear what I've done . . ." He struck his hand across his face with a groan. And then he looked out at her and found her watching him with a cold eye of agony.

"It's the fear of death?" she asked him. "It's not knowing what will happen after death?"

"No, it's not death. I don't think that's what tears me in two. But there's a dread feeling in standing up to a man who actually wants your life, and seeing his eyes turn to fire, and a grin like a beast on his mouth. It's seeing a man turn into a beast, and then being filled with a horror of the thing that he's become. And . . . oh, what's the use of trying to explain? Because it's cowardice, and I know it, but you don't. You've never really felt such a thing, and you never will!"

"When I was a little child," she said, "I was afraid of the dark."

"I don't believe that, hardly. But at any rate, you beat it."

"I went up to the top room in the tank house and locked the door just at dusk and threw the key out the window. And there I stayed till the morning. It was very hard. But before daylight came, I was no longer afraid of the dark."

"How old were you when you did that, Mother?"

"I was seven, I think, or six."

He sighed and shook his head at her. "I have to go now," he said nervously.

"I won't try to persuade you, Christopher. I won't tell you what it means to me, or how big things are made to look small by facing them. I'll say good bye to you, if I have to."

He took her in his arms and kissed her forehead.

"I'll tell you this . . . that every day I'll pray for more strength, and, when I find strength, I'm going to come back to Royal Valley and find Harry Main . . ." His voice trailed away. For she was nodding and trying pitifully to smile as though she believed the lie. He could not endure the strain for another moment and, whirling away from her, he caught up his pack and rifle and ran through the door.

Her voice stopped him.

"What are your plans?"

He turned, glad that he had the darkness of the night to cover his face.

"Christopher, only tell me where you're going, so that I'll know how to pray for you, and where to turn my face toward you!"

"I'm going up to the woods beyond Emmett's. You remember that little cabin where we camped one summer six years ago?"

"I'll think of you there, dear!"

"Aw, Mother, forgive me if you can!"

And he turned and ran blindly through the night.

CHAPTER
EIGHT

Bitter Thoughts

The greater excitement began very early in the morning when Peter went into Christopher's room and found matters in disorder there, and Christopher gone. He went hastily down. Everywhere he hunted for Christopher, and everywhere Christopher was not to be seen. And then it was found that the strong, flea-bitten roan was missing also. That explained matters clearly enough.

Christopher had fled! So Peter went bounding into the house and, as a matter of course, went straight to the head of the family . . . his eldest brother, Samson. To that dark and somber man he told the terrible news, and Samson listened with a look of agony in his eye.

"It's the waiting," said Samson. "There was never a son of our father that could be a coward. But it was the waiting that killed him! But, Peter . . . what will happen to Mother when she finds out?"

"She mustn't find out. It would be the death of her."

"How can we keep it from her? Won't she miss Chris in five minutes? Doesn't she really love him more than she loves all the rest of us put together?"

They stared at each other, unable to find a solution to this dreadful problem. And, in due course, the rest of the brothers were gathered in a solemn conclave, where each had a different opinion.

Duncan was for rushing off single-handed, meeting with the famous Harry Main, and destroying him in order that the shame of Christopher Royal should not be noised abroad.

"You'd never have a chance against Main," said Samson bitterly. "None of us would. And Chris would have simply died if he'd met him, because the fellow is a devil. The only language he understands, really, is the chattering of a fanned Colt. But what's there in death compared with the shame? No, I won't let you throw yourself away, Duncan. But what's to be done with Mother?"

"Go straight to her, Samson, and tell her the truth. That's the only way."

"Go straight to her? I'd a lot rather go tell her that Chris is dead!"

"It's your business to talk to her. You're the oldest. And, besides, do you think we could pull the wool over her eyes for ten minutes? She sees through me as though I were made of plate glass, and I think that I'm as politic as the rest of you."

That advice of Peter's was considered, though bitter, a wise pill to swallow, and therefore Samson Royal went straight to his mother and found her already down in the garden, working with her own trowel with her usual energy. He helped her to her feet.

"Mother," he said, forgetting the speech which he had tried to prepare on the way, "Mother, I'm sorry to say that Christopher seems to have left . . ."

She waved the trowel at him. "Of course, he has," said Mrs. Royal.

Samson stared. "Of course?" he echoed, completely at sea.

"Dear Sammie," said his mother, "can't you understand that Christopher won't fight with Harry Main right here in my home? But he's gone off to meet him!"

"Gone to meet him!" exclaimed Samson. "Without saying good bye to any of us?"

"Of course! Of course! Samson, you can see that he wouldn't want to trouble the rest of you and say good bye in a melancholy way when he goes out to die?"

"But it doesn't seem like Christopher's way of doing things," said Samson.

"Do you really believe that you understand him?"

Samson frowned in thought. "No," he said slowly at last, "I suppose that I forgot that he's his mother's son, after all."

He went back to tell the new idea to his brothers. They accepted this interpretation without any hesitation, for they were accustomed to taking the word of Mrs. Royal as the truth. And they went out to their work without further question.

The morning mail brought further news to Mrs. Royal. It was a brief note from Harry Main, addressed to Christopher, and she opened it without hesitation.

Dear Royal, ran the note, **I'm going to be at Yates's place this evening. Will that do for you? I'll expect to hear from you there.**

While she sat in a gloomy quandary over this note, there was a call from Georgia Lassiter on the telephone.

"Missus Royal, we've heard very, very odd news . . . that Christopher has left the valley just as Harry Main came into it!"

Ah, how cold was the voice of Georgia! What wonder? For she had been raised in a family which was full of legends of war, and three quarters of her uncles and cousins had died fighting for the lost cause of the Confederacy.

"He's simply made a meeting place with Harry Main outside the valley," said Mrs. Royal. "You couldn't expect him to want to shed blood on my doorstep, Georgia dear."

There was a little silence, and then a voice broken with mingled grief and joy came ringing back: "Ah, why didn't I think of that? But I've been wondering and terribly worried. Because I was afraid . . . afraid . . . oh, well, that's all gone! I'll never doubt again."

Mrs. Royal, left to herself, turned the problem for the thousandth time in her mind. Something led her up the stairs, and into the attic to those old boxes where the worn clothes of the family had been stored for years — not that there was ever much chance that they would be needed, but because Mrs. Royal was a woman of system and thrift. And, moreover, whenever she thought of giving the clothes away, something always held her back.

She opened the box where Christopher's things had been deposited. It seemed to her, as she lifted them out and looked them over, that it was not a mere collection of clothes, smelling of moth balls, but Christopher himself, resurrected and lying there, preserved in her memory. She could remember with an odd and unhappy distinctness how he looked in this blue sailor suit, that last day that his father saw him on this earth. What were the thoughts of that stern spirit now, as he looked down from the kingdom above and peered into the heart of the craven? Here was the first pair of long trousers that had made Christopher so inordinately proud. She could remember with what care he had always hitched them up at the knees before he sat down.

None of her other sons had been able to appreciate the graces of society as Christopher had done. Not one of them had ever been so close to her. There had always been a feminine delicacy in the instincts of this lad that enabled him to look into her mind and know what she felt before she could express herself in words. And, when she looked forward to old age, it was always with the thought of Christopher as a son and as a friend to lean upon. The rest of the world was a dim thing in prospect, but Christopher's gentle and wise heart was a vision of sunshine.

Now he was gone. He was already worse than dead! She wished with a stern bitterness that she could have closed the book of her thoughts when he was in his

second-and-twentieth year, say, the most admired and
loved man that had ever ridden a horse down Royal
Valley. Then there would have been in her heart, to the
end of her days, a fixed worship of this gentle boy, a
fixed belief in the great man that he might have
become. But now he was gone, and her heart was filled
with grief.

She closed the box and hurried from the dimness of
the attic, with the ghosts of her sad thoughts about her.
In the brighter sunshine of her own room, new courage
and a new idea came to her. Death itself, for
Christopher, seemed to her no tragedy now. It was only
the desire to let him die bravely, or at least where no
third person might see his cowardice.

She caught up a pen and paper and wrote hurriedly
upon it:

Dear Main:
**I am waiting for you at the little cabin in
the hollow above Emmett's. Come when you
can.**

Christopher Royal

Then she doubted. For it might very well be that
Main would question the genuineness of this
handwriting.

She hunted through her desk until she found a letter
from Christopher. Then, with a resolute hand, she
rewrote her note, making the letters as bold and firm
and sweeping as the hand of Christopher himself. She
addressed the note in the same manner.

Then she called Wong, the cook. He was the only person in the household so stupid that he would not think this a most suspicious affair. To him she entrusted the note with a word to drive down the valley as fast as he could and leave the letter at Yates's saloon.

Presently she heard the wheels of the buggy grinding down the gravel of the driveway. She knew that Wong was gone and that she had set in motion the wheels of death that must overtake her son before another twenty-four hours had spun away. In the meantime she was to wait, striving to close her eyes against the passing of time, and praying every moment, with all her heart, that Christopher would find in his soul enough courage to let him meet death as a man should meet it.

She went down to her garden. There she could leave behind her most surely the thoughts of her boy.

"Where is Lurcher?" she asked of Granger, the gardener. "He's always basking there on the terrace at this time of the morning."

"Lurcher's gone," said the gardener. "I called him for his breakfast, and he didn't come in. I whistled and hollered for him. You know that he never leaves the ranch. And so I'm afraid that something must of happened to him here."

But Mrs. Royal's breath caught as she heard. For could it be that the strange dog had indeed left the place and followed her boy, with an animal's strange instinct for an approaching death?

CHAPTER
NINE

The Phantom

When Christopher stumbled away from the house toward the corrals, you may be sure that half his mind was behind him in the house with his mother. But instinctively he found the saddle shed, his saddle, bridle and rope, and dragged them out into the corral. He had hardly emerged before a dozen sleek-coated horses started to their feet in a corner of the enclosure, ready to bolt from threatened danger, but they were already too late to flee. He could pick out the roan by the size and the ugliness of his head, and the snaky loop of rope darted through the air and settled true to its aim. The rest of the saddle band fled, and he went on methodically with the saddling of the roan, glad that this work had not caused enough disturbance to waken the cowpunchers in the bunk house.

When the horse was saddled at last, he swung into the saddle, and the big gelding, having his head, thrust it well out and down and proceeded to unlimber himself with a little artistic pitching. Christopher let him have his way, because he rather enjoyed anything in the way of excitement that would take his mind from his wretched self.

That struggle did not last long. The bone-breaking grip of his knees and the iron of his hand upon the reins soon assured the roan that fighting was no use. He stopped, and shook his head, as though partly bewildered. At that moment he received a cruel prick with the spurs, and his head was quickly straightened at the fence.

Ears flattened, eyes trailing fire, mouth agape under the pull of the bits, he bolted straight at the loftiest part of the fence, and Christopher let him go. As he rode, he wondered grimly to himself what other man in Royal Valley would have put an untried mount at such an obstacle? Aye, but courage across fences was not what was needed in his life. Courage to face a fighting man was the thing!

The fence rose sheer before him, then the roan pitched into the air. His two trailing hind hoofs clicked sharply against the upper bar, and then they were away across the field beyond.

He gave the big horse his head for two miles up the valley and by the time they had come to Fisher's Well, where the road forked toward Emmett's on the right and toward Cluster Cañon on the left, the roan had had enough of such high life. He came back to a moderate canter and then to a soft, sweeping trot that brushed the miles away behind him with a wolfish ease.

There was a miserable satisfaction in the heart of big Christopher as he considered the action and the breathing of his mount. A few days on the road and the roan would be in such condition that Harry Main, desperate rider and expert trailer as he was famed to be, would have much to do to keep up with such a pace as the fugitive could set.

But then, even Harry Main could not fathom, surely, the problem that now lay before him. And unless Christopher had a mind reader working against him, he was confident that he could lie in secure hiding among the tall, dark woods above Emmett's.

After that, he would wait a number of days until it was certain that Harry Main was away from the trail, and then he would ride down to a new country, and far off where the name of Royal had never been heard and his race of tall brothers had never been seen.

He headed the roan onto the right-hand road and turned to look back down the valley, perhaps for his last look at it. He could see the lofty roof of the Royal house looming above the distant trees, and nearer at hand a shadow slipped from one bush to another, across the road.

"Coyote," murmured Christopher, and turned his face forward again.

When he was climbing the divide, leading toward the upper ranges of the hills, he glanced back down the winding trail again. There was not much light. There were clouds enough to kill the stars, and behind the high-blown mist the moon sailed in a pale-gray canoe. But still there was enough light to show him once more a shadow, skulking from bush to bush behind him.

He drew rein at that and instinctively reached for his rifle — for since when had coyotes begun to trail lone riders? The creature behind him was not half large enough for a wolf!

After a moment, hearing nothing but the hiss of the wind through the willow by the creek, and seeing nothing but the hurried bobbing of the heads of the trees, he turned his face forward along the trail again.

Yet it worried him. For, though wolves and bears were apt to trail men, all other animals were either unable to keep up with the pace of a horse or else were too thoroughly afraid of the lords of creation to come near for any length of time. And so this small thing remained a mystery to him that troubled his mind as he toiled up the slopes, with the good horse bowing his head to the work.

He reached Emmett's in the gray of the coming dawn, and passed it, keeping well within the forest, so that only now and then could he see the lights of the little village, twinkling dim and cold through the mist which lay pooled in the hollow. Beyond Emmett's he rode up to the dell where that deserted cabin stood in which they had passed the vacation those years before. He could see to the right the hilltop from which he had sighted the big grizzly in the valley beyond — that grizzly which he had trailed for three days and nights before he caught up with it and finished its marauding life with a well-placed bullet.

Now it was his turn to be hunted! He dismounted, and, throwing the reins, he entered the cabin. It was far gone with moldering time now. Those years before it had been small and simple enough, but now it was a complete wreck, and a board of the flooring crunched away to rotten pulp under the weight of his stride as he entered. It was so damp, so dark, so utterly dismal, that he was half inclined to spend the night beneath the dank and dripping trees rather than in this place, and yet, when he thought of the matter, he could see that the more hopelessly ruined the shack was, the more perfect would be his security in it.

So he entered with a shudder and, lighting a match, looked around him. He noted the table, leaning to the floor in a corner of the room, and the fallen branch of a great tree, blown down in a storm that had crunched its way through the rotten roof and showed its ragged butt as though even now ready to fall farther.

Yes, the cabin was a complete wreck. But now he felt that he was satisfied. It was safe — safe from all men, and, therefore, it was dearer to him than any palace of a king.

As he crossed the old, brush-grown clearing again, the wind slashed and tugged at his slicker, and the rain cuffed his face with cold fingers, but in the dripping forest he busied himself cutting a number of tender fir branches, till he had gathered a great armful.

These he carried back to the cabin, beat the water out of them thoroughly, and then built them into the foundation of a bed in the cabin. He laid down his meager blanket roll over them, and then he looked about to take care of the horse.

By this time the roan had cooled off so much that there was no danger of chilling him by removing the saddle, and now he remembered the little natural meadow higher up on the creek, surrounded by trees so tall and thick that it was amply fenced in against all manner of bitter weather.

To this place he led the gelding. The grass was tall and matted with the remains of old crops around its roots. The dense trees shut out the cutting edges of the wind, and yonder was the leaning rock, which stood out so far from the side of the mountain that it made a natural shelter against the rain, unless it was blowing from the east.

What better place could a hardy cow horse have asked — one that had fought its way through half a dozen of the range winters? He hobbled the roan here, and left it contentedly cropping the grass beneath the shelter of the hanging rock.

Then he turned back toward the cabin, and, passing through the trees, he was sure that in the freshening daylight a small animal darted from one tree to another. He could not be certain that he had actually seen any shape, however, and, since the light had not strengthened to such a point that he could effectually study a trail, he marched on to the cabin, kicked off his boots, and lay down with a grunt upon the damp bed.

He was very tired. Body and soul had been worn by the trials through which he had been passing and by the long ride he had made. And so sleep dropped in a sudden wave over him and had almost swallowed his senses when he awakened again with a start and sat up, a cold sweat on his forehead, for it seemed to him that something had been watching him from the entrance to the cabin.

Yet it could not be! He gritted his teeth as he clutched his rifle and started to his feet. If there were the dread of man in him, at least there was no dread of any other beast, and he would be able to prove that he dared as much in the hunt as any human in the world.

So he leaped to the door, but, when he glanced toward the clearing through the growing glow of the dawn light, it seemed to him that he saw a subtly moving form melt like a shadow among shadows into the margin of the wood. He jerked the rifle to his shoulder and fired point-blank. The range was very short; his hand was never steadier; and he was confident that he must have nailed the fugitive with the bullet.

He was so very confident, indeed, that he did not even go out to look for the dead, but turned back to the cabin and to his bed, where he stretched himself and allowed himself to drop securely toward slumber until . . . He sat up again, this time with a racing heart, and, as he sat up, he made sure from the corner of his eye that a fugitive form was leaping through the doorway into the day outside.

He had only a glimpse, but his hand moved lightning fast to snatch a revolver and fire. There was no sound to answer the shot. He rushed to the door, and once more all that he saw was the dark and ominous face of the forest, rising tall and deathly silent before him.

He sprinted around the shack, thinking that the creature must have dodged out of sight by that route, but still there was no sign of it high or low. As he leaned his broad shoulders against the wall of the shack, the dreadful thought came to Christopher that it was no animal of flesh and blood at all, but a phantom sent to cross his way with a foreboding of doom.

CHAPTER
TEN

An Ancient Creed

He had no need of sleep after that. There was no trace of the white mist that had obscured the hollows and tangled among the forest trees as he was climbing the trail. All was bright sunshine — far brighter than the lowlands could ever know.

So he began to cut for sign through the woods. But though he thought that he found traces, here and there, so thick was the carpeting of pine needles that lay everywhere beneath the trees that he could not make sure of anything that he saw by way of foot impression upon the soil.

Where the pine needles did not lie, grew rank, tall grass, with the matted dead remains of other seasons entangled about the roots to such a degree that the tread of a horse upon it could hardly have been distinguished from the step of a bear, for it curled upward again the moment the pressure of the step was removed.

Then, as he came to a pause, he heard the sudden howl of a wolf not a hundred yards away — a cry that went thronging through the trees and seemed to well up to his ears from every side. He made no effort to trace the beast by the cry, for the grim surety came to him that tracing would do no good. Twice he had tried the nature of this phantom with good powder and lead, and twice the thing had escaped from him unscathed.

Perhaps it would have seemed a small affair to some, but to Christopher, whose nerves were already on edge and whose whole spiritual stamina had been broken down by shame and grief and self-disgust, this was enough to carry away the last of his resolution and to make him determined to leave the cabin behind Emmett's as soon as possible, hunting out another hiding place deeper in the mountains — some place, for instance, where the cheerless woods would not be standing so perilously close to him.

He went to the roan at once, saddled it, rolled his blankets, and started forging through the pass that opened above him. It was a cheerful cañon, after the depression of the hollow, and he enjoyed the keen morning sun which smote between his shoulder blades. It was just such a day as leads to the dispelling of all foolish illusions.

So he followed the dim trail along the edge of a creek, until the way turned into a shallow ford. He was in no hurry, and, therefore, he dismounted and examined the bottom of the ford, to make sure that it was safe for the roan. The rocks at the bottom seemed firm and secure enough, and he led the gelding across. On the farther side he paused to mount once more, and, doing so, he scanned the valley up which he had just been riding.

It was very open and clear. There was hardly a stone big enough for a prairie dog to have hidden behind, and there was not the slightest sign of the ghost wolf that had haunted him before. He nodded to himself with satisfaction and had turned to put his foot in the stirrup when he found himself looking straight into a pair of eyes — human eyes that watched him from close by.

It was an Indian, so old that his wasted body could have illustrated the legend of Tithoonus, and clad in such tatters that his half-naked body and his clothes, and even the homely fishing rod which he held, melted into the patchwork of the valley side with its bronzed rocks and spotted shrubs. And yet Christopher was a little startled that he could have been so close without noticing the presence of the other. That was before he studied the eyes of this stranger and saw that they were vacant with age. There was no more life in this withered creature than in a dying tree, say, or some blind growth that floats in the depths of the sea, untouched by the sun.

Said Christopher: "Do you have luck here, my father? Do the fish take the bait?"

The ancient Indian looked at him without interest, and then, lifting his head, he glanced at the pale blue of the mountain sky. When he spoke, it was with a voice wonderfully deep and hoarse and with a humming indistinctness of sound, so that it passed away into the noise of the brook and was almost lost there.

"The Great Spirit sends the fish and the fisher," he said. "Sometimes the fish are taken, and sometimes the fisher!"

Christopher, staring at him, was sure that he was in contact with something other than an ordinary Indian. Here was a man of such age that he must have ridden his ponies and taken scalps long before the repeating rifle had been dreamed of. Even the revolver was still an unheralded invention in the days of the youth of this chief. How much had been seen by the old man? Half the continent had first been explored, and then fought for, and conquered, and peopled during the span of his existence.

"However," said Christopher, falling in with the old fellow's own phraseology, "the Great Spirit has favored men a little more than He has favored fish, you must admit."

"How?" asked the Indian gravely.

"He has given us brains."

"To walk on the dry land, but the fish lives in water. Can we follow him there?"

"He has only a thin stream or a little muddy pool for his life."

"His rivers lead down to the ocean, my son."

Christopher stared. It was very odd to find so much mental agility in so dead a body as that which sat before him.

"However," said Christopher, "He has given us a soul, you know."

"Look!" said the chief, and he scooped up some sand in his claw-like hand. "How many grains of sand are here? But, if all of them were the souls of men, only one of them all would come to the life of the Sky People and stand before the face of the Great Spirit, and ride His horses there and take scalps, and live in happiness."

"Only one?" asked Christopher, enchanted by this voice from the past and this prophet of a dead creed. "But what of all the rest?"

"Some," said the chief, "will die having done no great deed. For many men grow old, and they have done nothing greater than to skin a buffalo or to make an arrow." He let most of the sand sift away from his bony fingers. "And there a few who have fought like men and been strong and true, but in the last moment they turned coward before their enemies, and the enemies have taken them and split their heads with axes, taken off their scalps and left their souls to blow up and down the earth forever like that leaf, never resting."

Christopher turned and regarded the little spinning, twisting, drifting leaf with curiosity. The thought sent a thrill of coldness through him. "But suppose," he said, "that these men have fought bravely and been overcome in battle by numbers but not with fear?"

"That cannot be," said the chief. "For the brave men cannot die in battle. It is only chance that kills them . . . and that is the Great Spirit, leaning from the sky, to take them because he has watched them too long and wished to have them close to Him!"

"Then only cowards die?" asked Christopher, smiling a little.

"Only the cowards," nodded the Indian. "All these people have souls so that they may suffer. They see death always before them. It is curled up like a

70

rattlesnake among the rocks. It stands in the darkness of the teepee and watches them like a hawk. It whistles for them in the wind. It beats on them in the hail and rain. It strikes for them in thunderstrokes. So that the cowards are always dying."

"But some men are brave until they come to their death battle!"

"Yes," nodded the chief, "some are brave in little dangers, but their souls turn to water when they see great odds before them. But it is always the thing we fear that kills us, otherwise nothing can take us from the earth except the hand of the Great Spirit!"

"Come, come," said Christopher, "you will not treat all of your friends and family so harshly, because I can guess that a great many of them died in battle."

"Ah," said the Indian gravely. "All of my people and the families of my brothers have died in battle. They were all cowards."

"Are you still sure of that?"

"Oh, yes."

"Then I must say that the Great Spirit is a spendthrift, to throw away so many good people and let their souls blow up and down the world."

"I shall tell you about the Great Spirit," said the old man, perfectly calm and speaking from a great height of dignity. "He is like you and me. We have known many people. We have seen ten thousand faces, but we have only one friend. And so it is with the Great Spirit. He has seen ten million souls turn to powder and blow away in the wind, and only one is left, but that one is a bright soul and worth all the rest, and so the Great Spirit, when He has made sure that the one soul really shines, snatches it greedily up to Him in the sky, and there they live happily together."

As he spoke, he had shaken out the rest of the sand grains, and now he held up between his thumb and his forefinger only a single little fragment of quartz, transparent with a gleaming thread of gold in it, so that it poured forth a stream of sparkles in the keen morning light.

Christopher could not help being moved by such imagery. He said: "But consider yourself, father. Certainly no enemy has ever taken your scalp . . ."

The other nodded at once, unoffended. "And yet the Great Spirit has allowed me to grow old and thin as a blade of dried grass? That is true. But it is because He could not be sure. Sometimes I seemed to shine, and then sometimes I seemed very dark and dull. He watched me in battle, and He saw me ride through the ranks of the Sioux as though they were the standing brush in the field. He saw me make their heads fall, as a little boy with a stick makes the heads of the tall cornflowers bend. He saw me take many scalps and count many coups, and often His heart grew hot with joy, and He stretched his hand down from heaven so close that I could feel his fingers in the wind, tugging at my hair. But always He drew his hands back again and waited, and watched, for He could not be sure."

"But," murmured Christopher, "how could He have doubted?"

72

"With men, He knew I was brave. But . . . listen!"

He held up a cautionary finger, and up the valley floated the echoing, dismal call of a wolf.

CHAPTER
ELEVEN

Watched

Christopher, remembering the phantom in the hollow, shuddered a little. He could not help it.

"It is always there," said the old man, leaning his head to listen as though to hear a terribly familiar music. "It is always somewhere between me and the edge of the sky. Sometimes, it is so far away that I do not hear it. Sometimes, it holds its voice and crawls up to watch me, but it is always there."

He nodded his head with a religious conviction.

"But what is it, father?" asked Christopher, beginning to feel his flesh creep.

"It is the werewolf," said the old Indian, "that has kept me away from the Great Spirit for all these years."

"A werewolf!" exclaimed Christopher.

"There are two kinds of werewolves," said the chief, holding up two fingers of his hand. "The first are the ones which have been men and become wolves. They are only terrible for a short time, and then they become stupid. Then there are others. They are the wolves that cannot become men until they have killed the warrior who has been marked out for them." He closed his eyes and then added: "When I was a little boy, I frightened the horse of Black Antelope, the medicine man, and he got a fall when the horse bucked. I was very happy. I danced and yelled with pleasure to see him in the dirt. But then I heard him shouting out of the dust cloud, 'The werewolf is waiting to take you! May he take you soon!'

"I saw that he had known this for a long time, but the knowledge had been forced from his lips by his passion. Then I could remember, young as I was, that often I had seen wolves, skulking near me. Fear jumped in my throat. You are a young man and a big man. Have you ever been afraid?" He leaned forward a little and a cruel flame appeared in his eyes as he scanned the face of Christopher. Then he leaned back, nodding. "You will understand," he said, "what I am saying."

A little chill passed through Christopher as he saw that his secret was plain before this terrible old wizard of the mountains.

"When I knew that it was a werewolf that was waiting for me," said the Indian, "I did not fear men. If the Great Spirit had meant a werewolf to inherit my soul, then I could not die until that one wolf reached me, if it were able. Therefore, I laughed at men. In battle I knew that their bullets could not touch me. I went into the fights, singing my songs, and the Sioux became women before me. They turned their backs upon me, and I shot my arrows between their shoulder blades. I became a great man in my tribe. But I never hunted at night, and after dark I stayed in my teepee, until one cold winter night a wolf put its head through the flap of my teepee and snarled at me.

75

"The next day, I saddled my best pony and fled to the south and left my squaws and my children behind me, for I felt that the time had almost come, and that the wolf was about to take me. He was a brown wolf, young and strong. If I had stayed, the wolf would not have dared to face me. I should have rushed out into the night and fought with it, though I carried nothing but a knife. But I was afraid, and the moment that fear lays a whip on our backs, we cannot stop running. So I have been fleeing all the days of my life, and the wolf follows me. I saw him only so long ago as the waning of the old moon when it was like the paring of a fingernail in the sky. He is a gray wolf now. His back is arched, and his belly is tucked up with age. One of his fangs is broken. With the other he still hopes to cut my throat. But some day I shall hear him, leave my fire, go out in the darkness, and call to him, with my knife in my hand. I shall fight him and kill him and, when he is dead, the Great Spirit who has waited and watched so long for me will snatch me up in His fingers and make me happy forever."

The Indian ended his tale in a raised voice with a glitter in his eyes, but at that moment the wolf call boomed with a melancholy note up the pass, and the eyes of the chief were instantly struck blank. The fishing rod trembled in his hand.

When Christopher had given the old fellow half the tobacco in his pouch, he rode up the trail again, but he was a very thoughtful man. Of course, the whole matter was plain to him, and he could see how the momentary malice of the old medicine man, Black Antelope, had poisoned all the following years of this man's life. Yet he could not smile at the superstition. He had lost the callused hardness of self-assurance, and into his opened soul strange thoughts dropped, like those falling stars which show the blackness of the heavens.

When he reached the ridge of the divide, he looked across a far prospect with the mountain crests tossed up as rough and crowded as storm waves on a sea. After all, why should he flee into this unknown region? For, if there were indeed anything supernatural following him, it was better to face it in a place he knew.

Suddenly he turned and rode down the trail up which he had just passed. Not that I would have you think that he took as true all that the Indian had told him, or any of it. But, no matter how sophisticated we may become, superstitions will leave a trace and a taint within our souls. So it was with Christopher, and he was like the man who sees the moon over his left shoulder, and scorns the superstition of bad luck, but cannot keep a chill from passing down his blood.

Whatever it was that had haunted him, he was sure that it had been a living creature of flesh and blood. He was sure, and yet a coldness was spreading through body and soul. And it happened that just now, halting the roan for breath, he looked back and saw, or thought he saw, a shadow behind the shadow of a bush. He took quick aim, fired, and then spurred the roan furiously back to the spot.

There was nothing there. He dismounted and examined the ground. It was a soft sand which would have registered the impression even of a falling leaf, and yet there was not a trace upon it. He stood up and mounted again with a prickling sense of dread coursing up and down his back.

Yet there had been, he felt, an infinite amount of truth in what the old Indian had told him. The fears that we flee from are those which will eventually master us. Those that we face shrink away from us in turn and become as nothing.

So he went straight back to the deserted and moldering cabin in the hollow, which he had left so gladly that morning. You will say that he should have carried his philosophy a stage further and gone back to his home to outface his first impelling terror — the dread of Harry Main and his guns. But to tell the truth, his mind did not dwell upon Harry Main. This other uncanny fear had overmastered him, and its problem, to be scorned and mocked by his consciousness, continually lurked in the back of his brain.

When he got to the cabin, it was mid-afternoon. A rabbit had lifted its head above a rock a quarter of a mile above the edge of the pines of the hollow, and he tried his Colt with a snap shot. When he rode to the rock, he found the rabbit's body secure enough, the brains dashed out by the bullet. No, his hand had not lost its cunning or its surety.

He cleaned the rabbit on the spot and carried it on toward the cabin for his dinner. But, as he went, the darkness of his brain increased. He had fired at the rabbit with no more skill and surety than at the ghost thing that had been hunting him in a wolfish shape, and yet the other had twice escaped.

The moment he entered the dark circle of the pines, he regretted his return to the spot, for the stretching shadows that covered him darkened his spirit more than his eyes. He cooked the rabbit and ate it, but it was with a forced appetite, and he went about his preparations for the night mechanically. His heart was not in them. He had to urge himself forward continually with the remembered words of the old chief.

He decided, as the evening began, that he would try his nerves in the forest itself while the darkness gathered, and so he sat down beneath the trees and lighted his pipe. It suddenly occurred to him that the glowing light in the bowl of the pipe would be like a guiding lantern to direct any danger toward him and to blind his eyes against all drifting shadows — such as the form of an old gray wolf, its back arched with age, its belly gaunt, with one broken fang and the other capable of splitting open the throat of a man.

Now he wished mightily that he had continued on his way through the unknown mountains to the north and the east, but he would not saddle the roan for a night journey. It was not because he pitied the weariness of the horse, but because he dreaded the trip through the solemn woods worse than death.

He left the trees at last and went into the cabin. He found that he was crossing the clearing with a slinking gait and with his head down and, though he forced himself to walk erect, his heart he could not lift.

So he came to the cabin and laid down his blanket roll there. Outside the wind was rising and, across the moon, volleys of high-blown clouds swept and crossed the threshold of the cabin with waves of light and shadow.

The whole world had become an eerie place, indeed, and a setting in which all that was wild and strange might happen. And then he thought of the old Indian, and his lifetime passed in the midst of just such dread as this reënforced by a superstition that turned fear into a thing as concrete as a pointed gun.

What unbelievable force of nerve and courage had maintained the old man so long — living as he did, in the lonely middle of the mountains, waiting for death in a strange form? He pulled the pile of branches that supported his bedding to a corner of the cabin from which he could watch the door. There was a window also from which he could be spied upon, but a ragged fragment of a board was nailed across it — and no wolf could jump through.

He smiled at his own conceit, but you may be sure there was no mirth in his smile.

CHAPTER
TWELVE

Only a Man

It seems most strange that Christopher Royal should have been brought to such a nervous state because a lurking shadow had crossed his path a few times. But, undoubtedly, he was unstrung chiefly by his interview with the old Indian whom he had met that day fishing at the side of the brook.

However that may be, he had almost reached the point of hysteria, listening to imaginary sounds and watching the alternate dimming and brightening of the moonlight on the floor. And then came a thing that blinded him with fear.

Beyond the door, in the clearing, he heard the unmistakable though soft crackle of a twig beneath an approaching, stealthy foot! All of this time he had been telling himself with a breathless insistence that there was nothing at all in his dread beyond a sort of fear of the dark, and that, when the morning came, he would simply mount the roan and ride away from this wretched nightmare in spite of the advice of the crazed Indian. Now came the positive proof that there *was* a living creature in the clearing — a creature that guessed his presence in the cabin, for, otherwise, why should the

cabin have been stalked with such care? Too paralyzed
even to think of clutching the Colt at his hip,
Christopher stood up against the wall opposite the door
just in time to see a shadow cross the dim moonlight
that passed the threshold of his door. It was not like the
shadow of a wolf. Christopher suddenly glanced up and
found himself peering into the face of Harry Main!

He had never seen that famous man in the flesh
before, but he could have recognized him even by
dimmer light than this as the brother of Cliff Main,
whom he had killed by luck rather than by valor. In the
hand of Harry Main the revolver was quickly steadied
on its target.

"It's all right, kid," said Harry Main. "I'm here to
finish you off, but there ain't any need for me to rush
around about it. I understand everything. You lost your
nerve, waiting for me, and you come up here in a blue
funk. I understand all of that, and I'm gunna wait till
you've had a chance to get hold of yourself before I
tackle you with a gun. You can depend on that, because
I keep my promises."

He dropped his revolver back into the holster. An
instant later he was startled with a thrill of cold fear, for
he had seen Christopher standing against the wall, a
very picture of abject, helpless, frozen terror only a
moment before, and now he heard Christopher break
out into a wild and ringing laughter while he cried:
"Are you the wolf? You?"

"Am I the wolf? I?" asked Harry Main, retreating
toward the doorway behind him. "What in the name of
heaven do you mean? Are you crazy, Royal?"

Perhaps no man in the world ever looked closer to insanity than did Christopher at that moment. For his life, which had come to a stop, was beginning again, and, as it began, a flare of warmth and fiery self-confidence flamed in his eyes, dilated his nostrils, and made his breast heave.

Under the dreadful shadow of an unearthly fear, he had quite forgotten that it was the original dread of Harry Main that had forced him from his home and into the mountains. He had quite forgotten that, and there remained before him only the overpowering horror of a supernatural enemy.

To such an extent was this true that, as he had been standing against the wall, he had been saying to himself, quoting the Indian: *A werewolf is one of two kinds — either a man turning into a wolf, or a wolf, turning into a man.*

To be sure, if one looked closely at the handsome dark features of Harry Main, one could not help finding something decidedly wolfish in his appearance. There was a smallness and a brightness in the eyes, which were moreover set abnormally close together, that gave his face a touch of animal cunning. The bulge of his jaw muscles added a rather brutal strength to the lower part of his face. He looked as brown, too, as a creature capable of living without any covering other than its own pelt.

But Christopher was not ready at that moment to mark small differences and peculiarities. What mattered to him was that he had been more than half expecting the dreadful apparition of a wolf or a wolf-man in the doorway. And instead, here was a man — a mere being of flesh and blood like himself. That was why Christopher laughed — laughed at the sight of that famous and dreadful Harry Main! He laughed out of pure relief and excess of thankfulness and joy that, after all, he was to be tested by something less than supernatural power.

Now, when this flood of relief had coursed through the veins of Christopher and when the laughter had burst from his lips, he could not help crying out: "By eternal heaven, it's only Harry Main!"

Harry Main had been fairly certain that this fellow was insane the moment before. But he rather doubted it now after facing Christopher for a moment, and he began to wish that he had kept his Colt in his hand.

"Only Harry Main!" A very singular remark, surely, concerning the most terrible of all those practiced gunfighters who rode the mountain desert. It literally took the blood from the heart of the man of might and threw it all into his face. "And what more do you want to have on your hands than Harry Main?" he exclaimed.

"What more? Why," cried Christopher, "if there were half a dozen of you, I should still laugh at you, Main! I should still laugh at you!"

Harry Main listened and positively gaped with childish wonder, and with horror also, for he could not feel that this was stage playing. There was a ring of such tremendous sincerity and honesty about the words of Christopher that a more skeptical man than Harry Main would have been convinced.

84

Main said: "I'm about to finish you off, Royal. I dunno that it's any pleasure to me to have to kill you, but you took that out of my hands and left me no choice in it. You murdered poor Cliff . . ."

"That was a perfectly fair fight," declared Christopher.

"Fair?" cried Main, his hot temper rising. "Why everybody knows that Cliff was only a kid!"

"He was two years older than I," answered Christopher.

The heat of Harry Main increased. For, having found no ready answer, he was naturally all the more enraged, and he exclaimed: "You ain't gunna be allowed to sneak out of that blood this way, Chris Royal!"

"Sneak out? Sneak out?" said Christopher. "Why, man, I'll tell you an honest fact . . . I was never so glad of anything as I am of the sight of you tonight!"

"The hell you are!" growled the gunfighter, and he stared more closely at Christopher Royal.

But it was true. Yes, it was very true. He would have been the worst sort of a blind man not to see that Christopher meant all that he said and had not the slightest fear of his famous antagonist.

"Oh, yes," said Christopher, "but since you seem a decent fellow, Harry, I rather hate to have to send you after your brother."

"D'you hate to do that?" snarled Main. "Why, I'm ready to tear your heart out, if you got the guts to stand up to me!"

Another cross passed like a shadow over the face of Christopher. And then he shrugged his shoulders, as though to get rid of the idea.

"Well?" asked Main sharply.

"I'm thinking of the long stretch after I've dropped you, Harry, as drop you I surely shall. And, besides, I'm wondering if we wouldn't both be happier if we had sunlight instead of moonshine for our work."

"Moonlight is good enough," declared Main.

Christopher nodded. "You're getting nervous, I see," he said very kindly. "And if that's the case, why, we'll have it out now, man, of course. I suppose that you might become rather a nervous wreck if you had to wait until the morning."

"To the devil with your coolness!" cried Harry Main. "Me turn into a nervous wreck? I ain't got a nerve in my body, and, when it comes the time for the guns to work, I'm gunna show you I mean what I say."

"You shoot very well, I hear," said Christopher.

"That's best told," said Harry Main darkly, "by them that ain't no longer got a voice in this here world."

"By the dead, you mean?" interpreted Christopher, nodding. "You've killed a great many people. I've heard that you've killed all of fourteen men, Main?"

"Up to tonight, and not counting the greasers, yes. And you'll be the fifteenth white man."

"I shall?"

Christopher looked at Harry Main and then smiled brightly and carelessly, as though to announce that he did not care to argue such an absurd suggestion. And a little mist of perspiration — a cold sweat — came out upon the forehead of Harry Main.

"All right," said Christopher, "if you're not afraid to wait until the morning . . ."

86

"Do you think that you can bluff me out? I'll have your nerves all frazzled out if you wait that long in the same house with me."

"Will you?" murmured Christopher, stretching his arms out luxuriously. "Well, you watch me."

And he threw himself down on the bed, took a turn in the blanket, and was almost instantly asleep, leaving Harry Main standing by the door, with the killing power still gathered in his face and a strangely empty and foolish feeling in his heart.

CHAPTER THIRTEEN

Ready

It must be admitted that it was a most peculiar situation for Harry Main. He had most certainly prophesied to himself that Christopher Royal, in spite of the shooting of Cliff, had turned yellow when he started up toward the higher mountains and, with that sense of surety supporting him, Harry Main had proceeded with a sort of contemptuous carelessness on the trail of revenge. He had never started out on a manhunt without feeling that he was superior in his skill with guns to any other man on the range.

And now this surety had been snatched out of his hands. He sat down and watched the pale, slow hand of the moonlight stretch across the floor and find the hand and then the face of Christopher. He stood up, leaned over the sleeper, and saw that he was smiling as in the midst of a happy dream.

No wonder that Main scratched his unshaven chin in great anger and perturbation. Such coolness was absolutely inexplicable to him, because it never occurred to him that Christopher had been existing in this cabin under the shadow of a fear so much more awful than that of any human being that it made even the hostile presence of Harry Main not a terror but an actual comfort. And having no key to the situation, Harry Main began to feel that, so far from having reached a craven fugitive, he had come up with the bravest man he had ever known.

But to have fallen asleep in the presence of the gunfighter — the great and celebrated Harry Main — that surely was a thing not to be believed. And sleeping — yes, and snoring — that lad most certainly was. Why, then, had Christopher left the valley? Simply because he wished to take the ugliness of battle away from the vicinity of his home? It had seemed a most hollow sham and pretext to Harry Main, at the first, but now he began to believe that there must be something to it.

He began to regard Christopher Royal more closely, and there was much about him that deserved the narrowest scrutiny. He watched the heaving of the high-arched chest while the young fellow slept, and he regarded the wide and smooth slope of the shoulders, and the strength of the jaw, and, above all, the long-fingered hands. Men said that there was both infinite might and great speed in those hands, and Harry Main, who was an expert in such affairs, could well believe it. The weight of a Colt, for instance, would be no greater than that of a feather to the power of this man, and the round wrist and the tapering fingers promised the most flashing and dazzling speed of execution.

Now it seemed to Harry Main, at about this time, that the hours of the night were marching along with a very painfully slow step, and that the morning lingered with disgusting persistence beneath the edge of the eastern sky.

He himself tried to lie down and to rest, but, when he had stretched himself out in a resolute composure and closed his eyes, it always seemed to Harry Main that his terrible young companion was slowly opening his eyes, then peering sidewise, and then sitting up and reaching for a gun . . . At that point of his imaginings Harry Main would be snatched out of semi-slumber and sit up with a jerk, only to find Christopher Royal sleeping most peacefully.

Two or three times this was repeated, and at last Main abandoned all attempts at resting. He stood by the door, or he walked up and down outside it, watching a pale mist that had boiled across the face of the moon and that was now gathering under the heads of the great forest trees. Frequently, however, he had to drag himself away from his thoughts and peer through the open door at young Christopher.

Rage began to grow up in the breast of Harry Main. He felt that by a low trickery Christopher Royal was enjoying a heartening and strengthening rest, whereas he, Harry Main, who had entered that house with the drop on the man he wanted and who had surrendered that advantage willingly because he did not choose to murder but preferred to fight — he, Harry Main, walked up and down through the night fog and wondered what the devil had ever entangled poor Cliff with this cold-nerved devil of a boy!

Why not end the matter, now that there was no eye to watch? Main strode through the door with the Colt ready in his hand. But, when he leaned over the sleeper, his finger withdrew from the trigger. Once before, and long ago, just such a crime as this had attracted Harry Main, and on that occasion he had not resisted temptation. But he had long since vowed that he would never have another such stain upon his conscience.

So he went back to the door, stealthily, without making a sound, as he thought. Then, turning around, he found the eyes of the supposed sleeper fixed steadily upon him. It was far from a pleasant experience for Main.

Christopher sat up and yawned in his face.

"It was better not to do that," he nodded. "I see that you're all shot to pieces, Main. And look here . . . if you want to postpone this business until the nerves have had a chance to settle down again, of course I'm agreeable to that. I don't want to hurry you ahead, you understand."

"Hurry me ahead? Hurry me ahead?" snarled Main. "Why, if the daylight would only come, I'd polish you off in half a second."

"Polish me off?" smiled Christopher, standing up and stretching forth his arms. "Well, man, the day has begun."

"What!"

"It's a thick mist. We often have 'em in this hollow. And that's what blankets the sun away. But . . . look here. It's seven o'clock. And let me know, old fellow, if you want to fight now, or after breakfast?"

There was such a world of good humor in his voice that Harry Main felt his heart shrink into a cold, small knot.

"Now," said Main steadily. "You can bring in the gun work now, and I'll be contented. But damn me if I'll wait for another five minutes to play the nurse to you!"

"Nurse?" laughed Christopher Royal. "Well, well, the odd thing about it all, from my viewpoint, is that when I left the valley I was actually afraid of you, old fellow. Frightened to death of you. And now, as a matter of fact, I'm almost sorry that I shall have to turn loose a gun upon you."

Harry Main lowered his head a little for the purpose of scowling out beneath his gathered brows at the other, when he suddenly realized that no facial expressions were apt to daunt the very composed self-sufficiency of this young man. He could not help saying suddenly: "Royal, when you left the valley, it wasn't to meet me up here. I dunno why you sent me the letter. But I know that you never intended to meet me here."

"What letter?" asked Christopher.

"What letter? Why, the one where you told me that you'd be waiting for me in this cabin . . . the one that the Chink brought down to Yates's place for me."

It took the breath of Christopher to hear this. Certainly he had dispatched no such letter, and there was no one in the world who knew where he intended to hide himself with the exception of his mother. But could she have done such a thing, and betrayed him to his enemy? Then, in a blinding flash, he understood everything, and the prayer which she must have breathed to have her son dead rather than shamed — her blind hope, too, that when the crisis came he might find a mysterious strength to meet the emergency. And he had done so. For, whether he could master Harry Main or not he could not tell, but master himself he certainly had.

So he looked up again to Main and said gently: "You've guessed the facts. I was afraid of you when I left."

"Then what happened?"

"Something that you wouldn't understand. There's no use in trying to talk about it or to explain."

"I'd like to judge that for myself."

"I'll tell you this," said Christopher suddenly. "After what has happened to me up here, I feel as though there's no real harm that can be done by a bullet."

"All right," said Harry Main. "I guess that's beyond me."

"And there," said Christopher, "is a bit of blue sky for you. It's broad enough day, and I suppose that we have to go through with this thing."

"We do," said the gunfighter solemnly.

"Notwithstanding that I wasn't at fault with your brother?"

"You?"

"I give you my word of honor, Main, that I tried to back out of the fight. I didn't want his blood on my hands. I didn't want to fight with anybody, as a matter of fact."

Harry Main listened with a thoughtful frown, and again he felt the transparent honesty of this youth and felt a shudder go through him. "That ain't what matters," he said at last. "The only fact that counts is that you stood up to poor Cliff and killed him, and now everybody expects me to stand up to you and kill you . . . or to do my best. And that's what I'm here for."

"I understand," nodded Christopher. "Your reputation for being invincible is worth more to you than your life. You've got to risk that to protect your good fame. Well . . . there's nothing that I can say to that."

"No," declared Harry Main, "there ain't anything you can say. But are you ready?"

"Ready," said Christopher, and they walked out of the little cabin side by side.

"It ain't much better than moonshine, though," said Main, regarding the fog which hung in dense clouds through the trees. "We'll have to stand close to each other with our guns, old-timer."

"Yes, that seems logical."

"But, by heaven, kid, you're the coolest hand that I ever had to shoot at. We'll take ten paces."

"All right. Which way?"

"Stand here. I'll measure off the distance."

He stalked ten strides away, halted, and spun about toward Christopher.

"Are you ready, Royal?"

"Ready!"

CHAPTER
FOURTEEN

Beyond Fear

No matter what doubts had been passing through the mind of Harry Main during the long hours of the night, they deemed to disappear, now that he faced his foe in the open, and it seemed to Christopher that the very body of the other man swelled with passion. A gathering battle fury glittered in the eyes of the gunfighter. He was like a bull terrier that seems to have a ten-fold power poured into it by the mere chance to bare his teeth at an enemy.

As for Christopher, he felt no passion, and certainly least of all did he feel fear. The fury that was rising in the other would have appalled him beyond words only the day before, as he well knew. But now he was possessed of a perfect calm, a cool indifference, and, though he stood on the ground at point-blank range from this proved man slayer, he had the attitude of one who looks on a strange scene from a great distance. Instead of fear, out of that calmness a great sense of superior might flowed through him. He looked at the terrible Harry Main and looked down on him. He remembered what the Indian had said, and of how as a young brave he had careened through the ranks of the enemy, laughing at their bullets, because he was conscious of a stranger and more deadly fate than mere bullets or arrows could deal out to him.

So it was with Christopher Royal. As he stared at Harry Main, he could not help wondering where that other and haunting shadow might be, and was it not ever present, watching the man who had been marked down for it? And the instant that Harry Main was gone, would not that devilish film of a creature be at his heels once more?

"Harry," he called.

"Go for your gun!" said the other, trembling with a dreadful eagerness. "Go for your gun, kid. I give you the first chance!"

It was like a wrestler offering his hand openly to a weaker foe, but Christopher merely smiled.

"Go for your gun!" yelled the gunfighter again.

"I want to ask you for the last time," said Christopher, "to think the thing over, will you? I don't fear you, Main. But there's no reason I should try to kill you, and there's no reason why you should kill me. Do you think that you will ever be taunted for not having butchered me? No, people know you too well, and your record is too long."

"My record is a fighting man's record," said the killer, growing momentarily more savage. "I'm no damn chattering jay . . . like you. I've give you warning, Royal!"

"I've heard your warning, and I take it," said Christopher, "but I won't go for my gun first."

"What?"

"I mean what I say. Make the first move, if you will. I'll never shoot except in self-defense, man!"

"By heaven!" cried the other, "your blood is on your own head, for being a fool. I offer you the free chance. There ain't nobody here to report it on you."

"Except one's conscience," said Christopher, "and that's enough!"

A wolf howled up the valley, and a sudden shudder went through the body of Christopher. It seemed that the other noted it, for he said instantly: "That varmint is going to yell again in a minute. He's got something cornered! He'll yell again, and, when he yells, that'll be the signal for us, Royal. You agree?"

"Yes," said Christopher, feeling that there was a sort of hidden fate in this arrangement, "I agree to that. He'll howl a death yell for one of us!"

"Exactly. Afterwards, kid, I'll treat you fine. I'll see that you don't lie here and rot in the middle of the woods. I'll cart your body down into the valley where somebody can find you on the road and let your folks know."

"Thank you," said Christopher.

He looked a trifle away. He raised his head boldly and looked up to the smoke-white mist, now riven away in the heart of the sky so that dim, delightful blue shone through.

"Are you prayin', kid?" asked the gunfighter savagely.

"No, no," said Christopher. "I'm only pitying you, Main."

He said it so impulsively and so gently that Harry Main started convulsively. He had been in a hundred battles but never before had he seen a man in the presence of death conduct himself in such a manner as this. He was amazed, and the awe took possession of the very nerves of his fingers and made them half numb. He rubbed the knuckles of his right hand swiftly into the palm of his left — swiftly, for at any moment the fatal cry of the wolf might ring up the hollow.

"And if the bad luck should come to you, Harry," said Christopher Royal, "where shall I take you, and where shall I send your last message?"

"Cut out all this fool's talk!" snarled the other. "I don't want to hear no more of it!"

"What, man? Is there no one to whom you want to send your last thoughts? Is there no kindness for any one?"

"I've seen the world for what it is," said the other grimly, "half sneaking, and half lying, and all hypocritical. There ain't nobody that likes nobody else, except for what they can get out of him. Folks have knowed me, and they've used me. I've knowed them, and I've used them. And when the finish comes, I thank heaven that there ain't nobody that can say that he's trimmed me worse than I've trimmed him. Because where the score was ag'in' me, I've used a gun and settled it that way."

"Heaven forgive your unhappy soul," said Christopher.

"You talk partly like a fool, and partly like a sky pilot!" sneered Harry Main, gripping at the butt of his revolver. "I'm going to wipe out that smile of yours with a Forty-Five slug of lead in half a minute."

Christopher looked up once more to the blue heart of the heavens, where the fog was still rapidly thinning, and through that remaining film of cloud he could see the splendors of the sun flooding across the upper sky. At that moment, while his glance was still high, the booming note of the wolf's cry pounded up the valley, mixed with its own flying echoes.

Harry Main, the instant that he heard, bounded to the side and tore out his Colt as he sprang. It was an old trick of his in which he trusted implicitly, for it had won many a battle for him. But Christopher, seeing the move, had no doubts. His own weapon glided smoothly into his touch. At the hip he spun it up. From the hip he fired, and he saw Harry Main fire his own weapon into the ground, and then lunge downward, very much as though he had intentionally fired downward at an invisible enemy and then fallen down to grapple with it hand to hand.

Christopher did not need to go forward to investigate. He knew just where his own bullet had struck home, and he raised his head in an odd quiet of the soul and saw that the last wisps of the upper mist had been cleared away, and, in a deep well of blue, shot through with golden sun, the heavens opened above him as though for the free reception of a winged spirit.

Then he went to poor Harry Main and turned the body on its back. He had been shot straight through the heart. The top buttonhole of the open coat had been the target of Christopher, and right through that slim target the bullet had torn its way.

He closed the eyes of Harry Main. While he was on his knees, performing that last rite, a chilly sense of being watched from behind made him leap to his feet. He looked behind him into the underbrush beneath the woods, for from that direction he knew the eyes had been upon him. The thing was back once more to hound him!

There had been no joy in him for the victory. There had been no exultation. It was merely the assurance that came at the heels of his conscious superiority. There had been no chance for poor Main from the first instant that they faced one another in the cabin.

But Harry Main was forgotten. All that was remembered was the dreadful unseen thing that moved so noiselessly around him. What was it?

When he had gained control of himself once more, he went to the roan and found him down-headed, dull-eyed, with his lower lip hanging and a tremor in his legs. He had a wisp of green grass hanging from his lips, and, when he was led to the water, he refused to drink.

Christopher, with a terrible sinking of the heart, felt that he understood what had happened. The gelding, too, had seen more than the eye of a brute could understand and had felt more than an animal heart could stand.

He rubbed the strong animal down and swung into the saddle. And the gelding, taking more heart with his first steps along the trail, was soon going ahead at a good gait and lifting his head more as he warmed up.

Straight down the hollow rode Christopher, for the first thing to do was to take the word of what had just taken place to the people below. He must send for the dead body, and then he must carry word of what he had done to his mother. And how could he face her, or she him, since he knew that she had sent Harry Main to face him in this hiding place?

However, all of that was very far away and of little importance, and what really mattered was simply that he get out of these tall, dark woods as fast as he could. He rode with a terrible conviction that he would never pass through those woods alive. Now he was in the grip of whatever power it was that hounded him. The old Indian, it was true, had kept the foe at bay for three-quarters of a long lifetime, but that old Indian had a power of will such as Christopher felt that he could never aspire toward.

His head was never still as he went through the shadows. But he could see nothing except soft shiftings of shadows, which well might be the quiet passing of some pursuer. On the other hand, it might be the mere effect of the shifting lights that passed down through the wind-stirred trees. As for hearing anything, every slight murmur was lost in the continual patter of dropping water, for the fog had left the branches and the twigs covered with dim, silver drops.

So he crossed the little dark-hearted brook, and, turning the next winding of the narrow forest trail, he came on a sight that stopped his heart. In the middle of the way, flat on his back, his arms thrown crosswise, and his dead eyes fixed sightlessly upon the trees above him, lay the Indian.

CHAPTER
FIFTEEN

Back to the Valley

Christopher dismounted instantly and ran to the spot. As he leaned over the dead man, he groaned with veritable horror. The throat of the Indian had been torn across — and not by any knife. It had been ripped open — just as by the fang of a wolf!

So the long trail of the old hero had come to an end. And how long before Christopher's end should come, also? He felt that his knees were turned to lead. He staggered back to the roan and was coming toward him with outstretched hands when something in his way of approach startled that most patient of horses. He tossed his head and with a sudden, frightened snort he fled on down the trail.

Christopher, left alone, called after him until the wailing notes of his own voice frightened him. Then he went on in the same direction, but every step he took was one of agony. He gave up all control and dashed madly forward, blind with terror. And then, behind him, he was sure that he heard the breathing of a pursuer. So he whirled with a gasp of terror and flung his back against a tree. Just behind him the fleeting shadow darted out of view behind a tree. His pounding heart turned to ice!

He felt, now, that his death was to follow that of the Indian. Destiny was thick around him. To make all sure, presently he heard a faint whine, and it drew before his imagination the dreadful picture of an old wolf, gray with years, his back arched and his belly gaunt, and his grinning mouth showing only a single fang for murder.

Then it seemed to him that he saw something drift noiselessly into the midst of a small bush. Yet he was almost sure that the glitter of eyes shone out at him. Instinctively, without aiming, he jerked up the muzzle of his gun and fired.

There was a yelp of fear and pain and then out of the covert, straight toward him, wriggling on his belly with fear and with pain, came the familiar form of Lurcher!

Christopher, watching him and sick with wonder and relief and pity, suddenly understood all that had happened. Lurcher, the silent hunter who never left the Royal ranch, had indeed left it this time, because in his dog's heart he had known that some great trial lay before his master. He had trailed the big rider, but from a guilty distance, and, when he tried to come closer at last, he had been received with a bullet that must have missed him narrowly. Again as he strove to crawl in out of the cold of the night to his master — to his master and away from the wolfish voices in the woods — poor Lurcher had been fired at point-blank. It was most miraculous that he had not been killed.

This was the hunting ghost, then, which had filled Christopher Royal with such supernatural dread that even terrible Harry Main had meant nothing to him. He dropped on his knees and Lurcher, moaning with joy and terror and pain combined, stood up and staggered into his master's arms.

Tears poured into the eyes of Christopher. He dashed them away. But still his lips were trembling with pity as he worked over the hurt dog. Off went his coat. His shirt was ripped to shreds. He cleansed the wound of the bullet which had passed through the breast, close to one shoulder, and out the side of the hound through a gaping wound. Then he stopped the flow of the wound with dust — and with his prayers. He felt that this poor trembling, heartbroken, spiritless creature had been the strange instrument through which his own soul had been saved from much, much worse than death, and he worked for Lurcher with a passionate intensity.

He saw the great eyes grow dim. He took his pocket flask of whiskey and forced a bit down the throat of the weakening dog. And then — the bleeding stopped as if by a miracle. A sheer miracle, indeed, Christopher always considered it. After that, he made the bandage, tenderly but firmly; and last of all he took his coat, and, using it as a litter, he carried Lurcher out of the woods.

He had thought that he was deep in the heart of the forest, but now he found that the crisis had come upon him when he was on the verge of the trees. Clean, sweet sunshine beat upon him as he issued from the damp and the shadows, and he saw the familiar beauty of Royal Valley spread out beneath him. Just below there was the Kendrick house with a banner of smoke hanging white above it, and he thought that he had never before seen a picture of such beautiful quiet as this which was before him. Indeed, it appeared to Christopher as though he had never beheld it before — or as though he had always been living in a dream until this time.

Lurcher was rapidly dying in his arms. Twice he stopped, as he was hurrying down the hill, and laid the hound upon the ground for the sake of letting him recuperate. Twice, under his hand and his voice, the dog opened his eyes and smiled vaguely at him, as only the eyes of a dog can do. And then he hurried on once more, never daring to break into a run for fear lest the jarring would prove instantly fatal to Lurcher. He reached the front gate of the Kendrick yard and kicked it open with such a crash that pretty Mary Kendrick came running out onto the verandah.

She screamed loudly at the sight of him. "Oh, Chris, Chris!" she cried. "Harry Main has killed you, and you've come here to die!"

"Don't talk foolishness," he said. "I'm not hurt. It's only blood from this dog . . . the finest dog in the world. Where's there a bed for him?"

"Bed? Chris! For a dog!"

"Yes, yes, yes! I mean what I say. Where's there a bed for him? I'll pay for it! He's got to lie soft and be contented."

In the little side room off the verandah there was a fine old couch where Lurcher was laid down to bleed and die.

"Now get Doctor Hutchison on the telephone and tell him to come over here as fast as he can gallop his horse, Mary!"

"But Chris! The dog is shot right through the body! He can't live! And do you know that Harry Main is looking for you and threatening . . ."

"Harry Main will never threaten anyone again. Get the doctor, I say! And tell him that there's a thousand-dollar case here for him . . . a thousand dollars if he saves the life of a dog!"

She gave one more frightened glance at him to make sure that he was not mad, but her brains were still addled when she reached the telephone. Presently she was calling across the wire: "Missus Hutchison! Missus Hutchison! This is Mary Kendrick. Christopher Royal isn't dead. He's here. But maybe he's dying. I don't know. Harry Main shot his dog. Then Christopher fought with him with his bare hands and killed him. Isn't it terrible? I think I'm going to faint. Christopher is quite mad. And he says that he'll pay your husband a thousand dollars for saving the life of the dog . . ."

At this point in the recital there was an interruption made by Mrs. Hutchison's smashing the receiver into the hook. There is a time for politeness. It is not, however, when there is an opportunity to win a thousand dollars.

She bounded to the back porch. Her voice, wire drawn and piercing as a knife, stabbed the air. "Hank! Ha-a-a-n-nk! Hurry! Hurry! Hurry!"

And Hank hurried. When he got to the Kendrick place, his horse was staggering and Hutchison himself was pale with expectancy and terrible hope. He had never seen a thousand dollars gathered together in all his life. Here was his great chance. The word of a Royal was a great deal better than a gold bond for any amount within thinking distance.

So old Dr. Hutchison reached the house of the Kendricks and rushed into it, not even as much as waiting to rap at the front door. He found himself in a house of terrible turmoil and confusion, in which the domestics and the family hurried here and there on urgent errands. Then he was shown into a small room where Christopher Royal, his big body half-naked to the waist and his clothes streaked and spotted with crimson, was on his knees beside a couch, and lying partly on the couch and partly on the arms of his master was an old hound, whose glazing eyes were fixed upon the eyes of Christopher as though in them he saw his only stars of hope.

The long arm of Christopher reached out and jerked the doctor also upon his knees. "Forget it's a dog, Hank," he said. "Think it is a human being. And I can tell you that he has meant more than any human being in my life. No matter what you can do for him, you get five hundred. And if you save him . . . a thousand! You hear?"

"My heaven, yes," said the doctor. "Don't I, though?"

And that was the beginning of the strangest scene that had ever been witnessed in Royal Valley, for day and night the two men would not leave the side of the dying dog. Christopher because, whenever he moved, there was a moan from Lurcher; and the doctor because his skilled attention was bringing Lurcher alive through each succeeding hour when it seemed as though death must take him at the next moment.

The doctor had a growing reward dangling before his eyes, and, when Christopher saw that the old skilled veterinary was actually accomplishing some results, his delight knew no bounds, and he could not contain himself. On successive days he raised the proffered sum to fifteen hundred and then to two thousand dollars.

And so it was that Royal Valley came to hear of the "Two-Thousand-Dollar Dog."

CHAPTER
SIXTEEN

A Queer Dog!

All of this time, it must be remembered, Royal Valley had other things to consider. When the party went up into the hollow, according to the directions of Christopher, to find the body of the famous Harry Main by the cabin near Emmett's, they also found on the way that there was a dead Indian, lying along the trail in the forest.

They buried him at the side of the trail and put up a little mound of stones to mark the spot. Then they went on and forgot all that they had seen of him when they saw Main, indeed, lying with a bullet through his heart. They carried Harry Main down into the valley and laid him out in state in the church, where he was viewed by literally thousands.

Cliff Main had lain there before, and now the more famous and more deadly brother lay there also. Men came who had felt his bullets in their body. And others came who had heard the hiss of them going by. And still others there were who had merely been witnesses.

All of these followed the body to the grave, almost with the air of mourners, and afterward they rehearsed again the wild and grand feats that they had seen this man perform. By hundreds and hundreds those who had never been sufficiently blessed to see the great Main in action drank in these words of the wise.

Royal Valley was particularly glad to hear all that magnified the greatness of Harry Main, just as the Jews of another day were glad to magnify the greatness of Goliath, they having their own David. That David was acting very oddly now but, given such a bit of freakishness as this frantic struggle to save the life of a mere cur, was forgiven.

"You can't expect a gent like Christopher Royal to act like common folks. Everything about him is big . . . and different!" they said affectionately.

He had explicitly denied the story that described him as rushing bare-handed upon terrible Harry Main and killing him by sheer might of hand and frightful heroism in the face of odds. For that matter, there was the unbruised body of Harry Main, with the bullet through his heart, to deny the tale most effectually. But that was not enough. For men will believe what they want to believe, and the most catching story is always the most lasting one. Christopher was made into a prodigious hero, and all the while he was by the bed of a sick dog too busy to pay attention to his fame.

Mrs. Royal started the instant that she heard where he was, but she was passed on the road by Georgia Lassiter on a flying horse and with a pale, lovely face. Poor Georgia! She got to the Kendricks' house and entered only to find her lover too deeply engrossed in his labors as a nurse to pay the slightest attention to her. She turned crimson — and then she fell to work to help.

After her came Mrs. Royal, to whom her son merely extended a stained hand and said: "I understand everything. And it's all right, Lurcher and you saved me."

Mrs. Royal did not quite understand. But she was a patient woman, and she could wait for explanations. Just what Lurcher had done she could not dream.

And how could any mother be expected to understand how a common, spiritless hound could have been magnified into a danger so terrible that the mere encounter with a celebrated gunman was as nothing to her son?

On the fifth day the crisis came. The doctor, rising to shaking knees, motioned Christopher away from the bed. Unshaven, hollow and black about the eyes, with sunken cheeks and parched lips, they stared down at the sleeping dog and saw Lurcher quiver and jerk and whine in his sleep.

"He's gunna win through," said the doctor. "He's sleeping sound and fine now. He'll be a better dog when he wakes up. But always lame in that off shoulder. Mind you, he's sure to be lame in that shoulder."

"Confound it, man," said Christopher Royal, "you've done the greatest thing in the world. I'll never forget it!"

They rested their arms on one another's shoulders and wavered a little with weariness and gladness as they looked down upon their accomplished work.

112

Then Christopher could sleep in turn, and, when he awakened, he found Georgia sitting on the floor beside him. For he would lie on the floor in the same room with the dog.

"Hush," she was saying. "Hush." As he stared up into her face, she added: "There are no such things as werewolves, dear Chris."

"No such things," he breathed, and, gripping her hand, he fell asleep again.

You may say, if you will, that this is only a history of how a dog found a man, but as a matter of fact it is a narrative of how a man found himself. The Royal blood had been reclaimed for Christopher, and it was never to be lost again.

Only once did he try to tell the story of the facts to Georgia. He failed dismally, because, after he had finished, she merely looked with a smile at him and said: "Oh, of course, Chris, you want to tell me that you're not a hero at all. But that's always the way with the really brave men. They always think that the things they do are accidents. And, of course, what you say about yourself is right, and what everyone else in the valley says about you is all wrong. You silly dear."

I think that even Georgia, though she was as large-hearted as the day, grew a little jealous of Lurcher before the end, but the old hound had secured a lasting place in the household and could not be removed to his death's day.

It was a common sight, in Royal Town, to see an old, gray-tinged, lean-ribbed hound trailing along behind the tall, graceful figure that Christopher Royal remained throughout his life.

"A queer dog for such a handsome man to own," strangers would say.

And the answer was as ready as "a borrower's cap." "Looks like a common dog, don't it? But everybody in these parts can tell you that two thousand dollars was spent on the same hound, sir."

Such a remark was sure to silence all objections because, as the saying has it, "You have to pay for class."

Christopher had paid. And not in cash only. For to the end of his life, while all the rest of his hair was black, there was a decided sprinkling of gray about the temples, and one deep crease drawn down the very center of his forehead.

The werewolf had put its mark upon him.

THE FINDING OF JEREMY

Frederick Faust often admitted that one of the primary sources for his story ideas came from folk tales. It is definitely evident in the short novel he titled "The Finding of Jeremy." It was first published as "His Back Against the Wall" under the byline John Frederick in Street & Smith's *Western Story Magazine* (3/12/21), and it was brought to the screen as HIS BACK AGAINST THE WALL (Goldwyn, 1922), a silent film, starring Raymond Hatton and Virginia Valli. There is a significant similarity between the central event at the beginning of this short novel and that to be found in one of the folk tales collected by the brothers Grimm, "*Das tapfere Schneiderlein*" ("The Brave Little Tailor"). In the folk tale the brave little tailor instigates a battle between two ogres and then, once they kill each other, takes credit as the victor.

CHAPTER
ONE

The Rebuff

A fly had been dropped in the ointment of perfect happiness for Jeremy Dice. Many elements had gone into the making of his joy this evening. In the first place, he had upon his arm at Kadetzsky's ball the prettiest girl at the dance, Dorothy Petwell. In the second place, he had distinguished himself by the introduction of a *pas de deux* entirely new in popular dancing — a pair of dragging steps with a jar at the end of them that had enraptured every girl to whom he had shown it and had made other young gentlemen grind their teeth in anguish. In the third and most important place, he could say with perfect assurance that tonight he was the best-dressed man on the floor. Kadetzsky's ball was the only occasion during the year when they aspired to full dress. During the rest of the twelve months the young swells of the society labored and saved and racked their brains for the means to produce a dress suit that would include at least one novelty. Young Saylor had easily borne away the palm last year; it had been Harrison Bean the year before; but tonight Jeremy Dice was the victor. He appeared in a delicately fitted suit whose tails arched out and floated behind him like chanticleer's two most gorgeous feathers. His necktie was white, edged marvelously with thin black. Above all, his waistcoat was white, crowded with black stripes so small and neatly patterned that at a distance the garment gave the effect of a distinguished gray. It was, indeed, a stunning costume, and Jeremy, as usual, wore it to the very best advantage. Yet, while this triumphal evening wore on, as stated before, a fly was dropped in the ointment. It was a remark made by Dorothy Petwell.

"Some day after we're married, Jeremy dear, we'll go out West, won't we?"

Jeremy looked down at her in amazement. Even in the midst of his astonishment he found himself admiring her hair. For Dorothy Petwell worked in a Fifth Avenue hairdresser's establishment, and she set the fashion of hair modes at least three weeks ahead of the other girls who danced at Kadetzsky's.

"West?" gasped Jeremy. "West? Why West?"

"I'll tell you why. I get, oh, the most wonderful letters from my cousin, Jim, out in Wyoming. He says it's a . . . a . . . 'man-sized country' . . . that's what he calls it. 'The country makes the man' . . . that's what he writes to me."

"Hah!" said Jeremy. "I call that bunk." He arched his not overlarge chest. He was distinctly not Grecian, but, being a tailor, he made the most of his possibilities.

"Being a tailor is well enough," went on Dorothy, "but . . ."

He was astonished by her seriousness.

"But you could be something more," she said, looking earnestly at Jeremy Dice. "You're a natural leader of men, Jeremy. You ought to be out where there are real men to lead. Riding horses, you know. Throwing ropes and things on cattle. Why, they take great big bulls by the horns and wrestle with them and throw them, Jeremy, dear. Think of doing that. You could, if you tried."

"Hmm," Jeremy said.

A fragmentary picture of himself, facing a bull, flashed into his mind. He gracefully waved aside the compliment with a lean, firm hand. The girl followed the gesture with her eyes. Usually the hands of Jeremy Dice fascinated her.

"Good hands for cards," somebody had once said. Work with the needle and scissors had made them exquisitely swift of movement. There was something of cat-like speed and sureness in every movement that Jeremy made with his hands. One was aware of much nervous force piled up in him, and Jeremy's hands connected with that nerve power.

But tonight those hands did not satisfy Dorothy Petwell. They seemed too much like her own hands. She had in mind the brown, huge fist of cousin Jim. She sighed.

"I think it's pretty good right here in little old New York," said Jeremy Dice. "You'll get over these romantic ideas, Dottie. Believe me, the West ain't all that it's said to be. Too much work . . . too little coin. That's what it means. Besides, here I am working my way up in the business. The boss says I'll be picking off a junior

119

partnership one of these days. What d'you know about that?"

He had saved this choice bit of news. And Dorothy Petwell gasped.

"But," she said a moment later, "a tailor isn't . . ."

"Isn't what?" he asked, angry and aggressive.

"Doesn't ride horses," she replied foolishly.

He looked down at her again in pity. She knew that she had been absurd, and she dared not meet his eye.

"Of course, he doesn't," and Jeremy Dice chuckled. "D'you expect me to sit a saddle and thread a needle?"

At this she did look up. He was surprised to see a shadow behind her eyes rather than in them. If he had been any other than Jeremy Dice, leader of fashion at Kadetzsky's ball and rising tailor, he would have imagined that she was judging him, weighing him, and finding him light, indeed. Although Jeremy felt that this was impossible, something in the attitude of Dorothy Petwell piqued him. He deliberately slighted her for the next few dances and turned his attention to other girls, who received him brightly. For was he not the finest dancer, the aptest and most gracefully dressed man on the floor? An air of distinction surrounded Jeremy that included the girls to whom he favored recognition. At length he returned to Dorothy because he had found that she still watched him in a thoughtful manner, not at all envious of his new companions.

She greeted his return without undue joy. Then, alarmed, he began to court her deftly, softening his voice to talk of her own affairs. She persisted in being absent-minded. She was not hard, she was worse — she was thinking of other things.

So a shade began to fall over the triumph of Jeremy Dice. Not that he began to criticize himself. He attributed it all to the pig-headedness that he felt to be a characteristic of all girls. He grew so concerned that finally he allowed Dottie to take him into the reception room. It was there that the terrible blow fell. He should have known. He should have remembered that the boss had said he was going with his daughter to this affair. He should have remembered all this, but it was brought thunderingly home into his mind by a great voice that called from the side of the reception room: "Dice! Hey, Dice!"

He turned. He was aware of the big, bloated form of the boss, his face more red-purple than ever, perspiration streaming down his face and over his tight collar. It was, indeed, Stanislas Gorgenheim himself. And a cold, sick wave sped through the veins of the tailor.

He bowed and started on, smiling, but the big voice pursued him.

"Hey, Dice. Don't run off. It's you that I want to talk to. Come back here, Dice!"

"Do you let any man talk to you like that?" Dorothy whispered at his shoulder in a singularly small voice.

"It's the big boss, Dottie. I got to talk to him. He . . . he doesn't mean anything by it. It's just his way. Wait a minute. I'll be right back."

"No, I'll go along."

Very slowly he returned. He came in range of the sound of Gorgenheim's puffing.

"Good evening, Mister Gorgenheim," said Jeremy pleasantly. He had disarmed the boss more than once by his address, but this time fate ruled otherwise.

"So," the fat man said. "You got it, eh?"

His thick finger pointed, swept over Jeremy from the heel to the shoulders. And Jeremy understood that all was known. The sense of disaster paralyzed him. Then: "Hush, Mister Gorgenheim. Let me explain . . ."

"It is not the hushing," retorted the boss in a loud voice.

Everyone in the room was listening. The walls seemed to Jeremy to be covered with bright, wide eyes.

"It is not the hushing," repeated the big man. "It is the suit. Where did you get it, maybe, Dice? Maybe you paid me? No? Maybe you bought it, no? Where did you get it, eh?"

"Mister Gorgenheim . . ."

"Jeremy Dice, you have the suit stole!"

"Mister Gorgenheim, I only borrowed it . . ."

"Borrowed! I am a child, maybe, no? Hushings, is it? No, it is takings. Go back and put that suit where you got it in the shop, Dice! Go quick!"

Jeremy could not speak. A deep-hearted prayer that the floor might open and swallow him was not granted. He turned away, and about him he saw the faint, small, condemning smiles from the women. The men were chuckling openly and whispering about it. Oh, there would be nothing else talked about for a month at Kadetzsky's. He was ruined.

"I suppose you want to go home?" Dorothy asked after he rejoined her and they reached the hall. He looked down stupidly at her.

"Well, you'll go along, won't you, Dottie?"

"I'll stay. Joe will take me home, I guess."

Out of the depths of his shame he fired a little. "I suppose you're turning me down, Dottie, just because I wore a suit that didn't belong to me?"

She did not speak.

"Ain't you a little ashamed, Dottie?"

"Listen, Jeremy," said the girl very calmly, "it isn't the stuff about the clothes. But . . . I've just seen a good many things. First of all, I see that you're just a tailor."

It was brutal, but they were alone. Dottie Petwell had only a moment.

"Go on," said the tailor stolidly.

"Now you do look mad. You look like a big wildcat. But I'm not a man. You can't fight me. Why didn't you look like that when you faced that fat, horrible Gorgenheim? You stood before him like a whipped puppy, and you made me sick, Jeremy. I . . ."

"You want me to go West, eh?"

"I never want to see you again . . . until you're different."

"Listen," said the tailor, "I don't think you ever *will* see me again . . . you or any of the rest." And he fled.

CHAPTER
TWO

Going West

Jeremy's mind was a blank. Somehow he reached his room. He stood vainly, trying to understand. He had worn a suit out of the shop, something he had done before many times. Because of that crime he had broken with his girl, had incurred the wrath of his employer, and had snapped a cord binding him to his past. He saw little except the contemptuous face of Dorothy Petwell.

"What does she want me to be?" he cried softly.

He thrust his fingers through his hair and rumpled it, tore his collar open at the throat, and leaned to peer into his mirror. The lean, savage face that he saw there frightened him. He sat down and began to collect his wits.

"Something has happened," he kept saying aloud. "I . . . I'd like to break something."

Only a tailor — the phrase kept coming back at him like a persistent echo. He felt that he would be able to hear it in every still moment during the rest of his life. *Go West!* He was a little over thirty years old, had a good job with steady advancement behind him and

124

before him. Suddenly all these bright prospects became nothing. *Only a tailor* damned them.

Unquestionably there was a good deal of the child and the dreamer in Jeremy Dice, or he would never have sustained the impulse long enough to act on it. But, when a child grows sullen, it is apt to throw itself off a cliff or chase its own family with a knife. Jeremy was wrapped in sullen hatred of the world. A sullen man — or child — hates the world because he feels that the world despises him.

At any rate, before dawn of the next morning Jeremy Dice was far westward, shivering in the black night in a lumber yard beside the railroad. A round-faced man, ragged, stood shivering beside him.

"Which way, cull?"

"West."

"You and me. There's the Four-Twenty. Come on."

And half a minute later he was riding the rods.

It was the most terrible day of his life. A score of times his mind jumped — as from the unconscious to the conscious. The cinders cutting into his face, the rush of freezing air, the roar of the train, the vast chuckling of the wheels on the rails — he would become aware of these in that jump of the mind. How did he happen to be here? What was he doing, imperiling his life to get to a place where he did not want to be?

Yet, he kept at it. Behind his mind there was the childish, sullen determination to show them. He would go West. In a way, after starting, he was ashamed to turn back. Eventually he would return to Dorothy

Petwell. "I've been to your old West. Nothing there but desert. Now I'm back. Take me or leave me, New York for mine."

He was riding shamelessly on top of the freight on this evening. It had been deathly hot all day in the box car, with siftings of acrid dust through the cracks. It got into his nose and made him sneeze. It got into his eyes, and the tears ran down his cheeks. He had blessed the oncoming of night and the dicker with the friendly brakeman that had enabled him to climb onto the top of the car. The scent of alkali was still in the air, keen, subtle, drying the throat, yet it was heaven compared with the heat of the car during the day. On either side, before or behind, he could see nothing except limitless flat. Unquestionably this was the crossing of the desert to which everyone had been referring. Sometimes, glancing over the obscure flat, he wondered if human beings actually lived out here so far from Broadway.

Mostly he kept his chin up and his eyes on the sky. The stars were marvelously close and bright. It occurred to Jeremy Dice that he was really seeing them for the first time. To be sure, he had noticed them now and then on the boat for Coney Island when he rode on the top deck. But usually his sky was blocked at night by the upper reaches of skyscrapers, and he had never looked higher than the electric signs on Broadway. But here it was different. His eye leaped a dizzy distance past the lower, brighter stars into infinitely far-off regions where they clustered like a faintly luminous dust.

"Oh, Lord," and Jeremy Dice sighed, "this is a queer old world."

He looked up to the brakeman.

"I'm all right," he said.

"Good," said the brakeman. "I like to see 'em comfortable. But what about me?"

"It's all right. I fixed it with Jem."

"Jem ain't me. Jem stopped end of the last division. You're starting all over, bo."

Jeremy shrugged his shoulders. "How much?"

"Oh, I'm reasonable. One buck will fix me fine."

Dice reached into his pocket. His hand leaped out again as though it had been burned. It slipped swiftly through his clothes, pocket after pocket.

"I . . . I've been rolled," he cried. "They've picked me!"

"That old stuff?" retorted the brakeman. "Say, bo, I ain't a new one. Come on! Fork over the stuff. I'll take it in nickels, that's how reasonable I am."

"I tell you I'm busted!"

The brakeman sighed. "All right. I don't argue. We're stopping about two miles up. Off you go."

"Off in the desert?"

"Then come through, you fool."

"I swear I haven't got a cent. Jem must have rolled me. Then that's why he grinned when he passed me."

"If Jem has it, that don't do me no good. Rules are rules. Pay or get off, bo!"

And he waited.

Despair seized on Jeremy Dice. Only a moment before he had looked over that dusky flat and wondered if human beings actually lived there. And now? The train was slowing, the brakes screaming far up the line, and there was a procession of swift jars as the cars halted. The rattling came to Jeremy.

"Now," said the brakeman.

Jeremy did not speak.

"A tight one, eh?" said the brakeman. "Well, maybe it comes to you hard, but rules are rules. You sit here and think it over a minute. I'll be back."

But, when the train started, gathered momentum, still the brakeman did not return. The freight was laboring slowly up the grade when the man first reappeared.

"All right," he said, extending his hand. "I'm glad to see you've come to time."

"Friend," said Jeremy solemnly, "I wasn't fooling. I have no money."

"Why, you poor fool, are you trying to put one over on me?"

A spark of wrath glowed in Jeremy's bosom, but he extinguished it swiftly.

"Friend," he began, with a quaver in his voice, and reached up his hand.

Had the motion been a shade slower, or had it not been night, all might have been well. But the brakeman's suspicions were aroused. When that hand swept up at him, he flinched, saw a vivid picture of a death struggle with the hobo on the top of the train, and put a quick period to that picture by smashing his heavy lantern into Jeremy's face. The moment he struck, he regretted the blow and stooped with a cry to catch the falling man. Jeremy was stunned. He had slumped over as limp as a rag, and the train, swaying at the same instant, caused his shirt sleeve to tear through the fingers of the brakeman. He catapulted from the top of the car.

The brakeman stood shivering. For a moment he was about to give the signal to stop the train, but he thought better of it.

"One fool more or less," he muttered, "what difference does it make?"

Considering the distance he fell and the speed, the chances were large that there would be one the less. But one thing favored Jeremy in his fall, and that was the blow of the brakeman's. It had deprived him of his senses, and he fell limply. If he had braced himself with knotted muscles, he would have broken his neck without fail. As it was, he struck the slope of the grade and whirled to the bottom.

CHAPTER
THREE

Two Bandits

He wakened a full hour later with a feeling that someone was beating him at the base of the brain. Gradually, his senses clearing, he found that this sensation was simply the pulsing of his blood. When he sat up, the blood rushed back from his head to his heart, and he nearly swooned. Slowly his head freed itself of the mist. Once it had, he set about learning the extent of his injuries with gingerly touches of his fingertips. High up on his forehead, and running through his hair, was a deep cut that must have gone to the bone, but it had ceased bleeding. The back of his head was not lacerated, but there were two great bumps that ached at the lightest touch of his fingers. He tried his legs, his arms. They were oddly numb, but no bones were broken. Across the shoulders also he was sadly bruised, and the skin had been raked along one shin so that, when he stood up, the trousers came painfully away from the raw flesh.

The moment he was on his feet, however, he forgot his sense of bodily injuries. There was a greater calamity than any fall. He was alone on the desert, and the only thing that could lead him back to men was the railroad. He looked gloomily down the iron rails, glimmering dully in the starlight and drawing quickly out of sight in the dark. He might walk those rails until he died of thirst before he reached a settlement of any kind, he decided. On the day before they had whirled by many a dreary stretch when he thought they would never come to a station. Stories that tramps had told him flocked back in his mind, of men who had been thrown from trains on the great mountain desert and who had perished there miserably.

"Buzzards is what bury you," someone had said, "and they sure pick the bones clean."

Hopelessly he looked around him with a feeling that he must begin to do something. All was flat on that awful horizon, all except to the left, where low hills, apparently, swelled against the night sky. For some reason he breathed more easily when he saw them. He did not connect hills with the desert. Men perhaps might live yonder. He turned toward them and began to limp in that direction. Presently his muscles loosened. His head still ached, but the pain was subsiding, and action began to bring back hope.

"Everything looks hard until you finish it," decided the tailor and stepped out more briskly.

What a lot he would have to tell to Dottie Petwell when he met her again. He would double, treble the number of the brakemen. In a fearful night combat with three men he had been slugged on the head and thrown from the top of a speeding train! The thought of Dottie's popping eyes comforted him hugely. He was even smiling when the ground began to angle up, and a

131

few minutes later he was among the hills. The darkness had made them seem ten times farther away than they were in reality.

But his spirits began to flag again. They were gloomy, low-huddling mounds of sand rather than real hills. Nothing could surely grow in such soil as this. It puffed up into dust under foot and rose in acrid scent of alkali to his nostrils. Finally he gave up for the moment and sank down to rest and think, if that were possible. But, when he glanced up, the wide sky looked down brightly, mercilessly upon him. The stars were like so many human eyes, seeing his misery and ignoring it. They accentuated his hopelessness. How many other men had they seen sink into the sand to become buzzard bait? A vague wrath rose in him, a hatred and rebellion against the world. And then — when he glanced sidewise — he saw a flat-topped hill with straight sides. Straight sides in this sandy soil? Springing to his feet, he ran to one side. He saw the flat side dissolve and spread into a regular triangle at the top, the immemorial form of a roof. The house of some man!

He shouted huskily and broke into a shambling run, regardless of the choking dust, regardless of his weariness. The house grew out upon him. It was a black-windowed shack. But, of course, everyone would be asleep at this time of night. He had no idea how late it might be. He reached the front of the little shack and shouted again.

There was not a reply. In a fury that he should be allowed to stand there, perishing of thirst, he beat at the door with his fist. It gave way at the first stroke and fell into the interior with a crash. At that he sprang back, alarmed. But there was no clamor of an enraged inhabitant. Suddenly the truth came sickeningly home to him that it must be a deserted cabin. He stepped to the door again and lighted a match. By the flickering light he saw the truth. The bunk in one corner sagged halfway to the floor. The sheet-iron stove was a stumbling ruin. Two chairs were in tolerable repair. That was all. Across one end of the room was a platform built close to the ceiling, and over the edge of the platform projected the ends of some straw — a rickety ladder led up to this haymow. On the whole there could not have been a more disheartening ruin.

After a moment of reflection he knew that no one would have built a house without accessible water near at hand. To hunt for it at night was absurd. Besides, he needed rest more than he even needed water. As the match burned out in his fingers, he dropped it to the floor, ground it under his heel, and then stretched himself on the boards. It needed only a moment to convince him that it would be impossible to rest in this manner. The hard floor made his head throb, and his bruised shoulders ached. Then he thought of the straw.

The ladder creaked and complained under his weight. One rung broke under his foot and let him down to the next one with a breathtaking jar. But he got safely to the platform and, lighting a match, saw a sufficient quantity of old straw lying there. It was a dark, shiny yellow with great age, but it was more

133

inviting to Jeremy Dice than any mattress he had ever seen. He bunched it conveniently and then stretched himself gingerly upon that improvised bed. It was, however, more inviting in appearance than in fact. For not even the loose straw was more than momentarily comforting to his shoulders and sides. Twice he came within a verge of sleep in spite of the pain, and twice a peculiarly hard twinge wakened him again.

He was beginning to twist and turn, consumed with nervousness, when he heard the sounds from the outside, first the snort of a horse and a grunt as it stepped into some unsuspected depression in the sand, and then a deep murmur of men's voices. Of all the sounds that Jeremy had ever heard, there was none more welcome than that humming of voices. He sat up, grinning expectantly in the dark, and gathered his breath to shout. And then a distinct voice broke in on him, close to the house.

"Here we are. Whoa, Belle, you old rattletrap. I know this ain't home as well as you do. Did you ever see such a hoss, Arizona?"

"She saved your skin tonight, Lew. They ain't any doubt of that . . . and I don't blame the fool hoss for wanting to get to her home."

Something for which he never after was able to account checked the shout that had been forming behind the lips of Jeremy Dice. He even moved back from the edge of the platform.

"Hello, the door's gone down since I was here."

"How long ago?"

"Last month. I'd just shook off the sheriff the day before, and I hit the shack plumb spent. Them boards was like down to me."

At this Jeremy edged far back. *Sheriff!* A tingling chill went up his back.

"Strike a light, will you, Lew? Can't see why you always carry that lantern in your pack."

"If you don't see any use for it, why d'you want me to light it?"

"Well, we're fools if we do light it. Maybe they might follow after and see the light."

"They ain't going to follow, I tell you. But we'll sit in the dark."

"How can we count coin in the dark? Besides, I guess you're right. They won't follow. Could you make out the one you dropped?"

"Harry Welling, I think."

The other whistled. "Him!"

"What about it?"

"He was a handy gent with a gun himself."

"They don't none come too hard for me, pardner. You stay with me long enough, and you'll find out."

"Meaning you're a pretty hard one yourself, eh?" said his companion dryly.

"Hard enough, son. Hard enough, and you can lay to that any time when you're lying awake, wondering about me."

The speaker scratched a match, raised the glass of a very small lantern, and in a moment a soft but steady light filled the shack. The tailor flattened himself on the platform. Suppose they should see him? Suppose this rotten platform should give way? Suppose he should make some unavoidable move as a nerve twitched? It would be sudden and terrible death, for he was unarmed. But what would arms have availed him against these practiced fighters? It was easy to discover what they were — two bandits, fleeing from the scene of a crime with at least one dead man left behind them and pausing here to divide the profits.

"There you are," went on the voice of the one who had lighted the lantern. There was a click as he placed it on the floor, and the light diminished around the tailor.

"Sit down, Lew. Sit down and be comfortable."

"Fine chance for me to be comfortable. Saddle-sore, Arizona."

"Lew Shaler saddle-sore? You got soft in jail, Lew."

"Go easy on that."

"Get some straw from up there. That'll give you a padded seat."

"You got some sense, Arizona!"

The tailor heard a heavy foot stride across the cabin.

CHAPTER
FOUR

Dividing the Spoil

His heart fluttered and stopped, and the paralyzing cold ran up his back again and centered at the base of his head. But with the cold sensation there grew a grave determination to fight to the end rather than submit to the two and be shot like a cur. Cautiously he gathered his knees under him. A hand fell on the ladder and stirred it.

"They's a rung broke out of the ladder, Arizona. Maybe the rest would give way under me. You're a pile lighter than I am. You go up, will you?"

"I ain't so much lighter. I'm pretty nigh man-sized, Lew. You can lay to that."

There was a growl in response. "Some day you'll grow up and stop being so damned proud. Every time I ask you to do a thing, you act as though I was insulting you."

"I need all my time, doing things for myself."

"But ain't I older than you? Ain't the older man got the right to lead in things and do a little directing? What sort of a bringing-up did you ever get, Arizona Pete? That's what I'd like to know!"

"A gent like you, talking about bringing up," retorted Arizona Pete. "Say," he broke off, "what's that?"

"What?"

"I thought that platform shook just then."

The tailor, relieved, had flattened himself again on the boards.

"It's the wind, Arizona. Think they's something up there on the platform?" He chuckled.

"Don't laugh like a fool before you find out whether or not I'm wrong."

"How you going to find out if you don't climb that there rotten ladder?"

"Touch a match to the shack when we leave. The old joint ain't any good. Besides, if they was to be any rat around here, that would burn it out."

"You got a pretty good head for a kid, Arizona."

"Not such a kid, either. But I got a little imagination."

"Don't be always firing up when I look crosswise at you. Well, get out the stuff and we'll start work."

"There it is."

There was a heavy impact on the floor and mixed with the sound of the fall was a melodious jingling. A feverish curiosity began to work in Jeremy Dice. It was like the impulse that urges a man to throw himself from a great height. Or rather, it was more like the impulse that makes the boy select for his pillaging the orchard he knows beforehand is the most securely guarded with guns full of pepper and salt.

Inch by inch he drew forward on the platform, his hair prickling, but a sort of cold joy growing in him.

Once he stopped, wondering at himself in horror. But again the very danger tempted him on, and he continued that cat-like, soft approach. A psychologist might have said: "*This* is a new man." But Jeremy Dice was not a psychologist. He only knew that the danger was filling him with a fierce pleasure. In reality, he would not have changed places now with any man in the world. He selected a place where the straw bunched high at the very edge of the platform, and, when he reached it, he cautiously moved the straw so that he secured a peephole through which he could stare down at the pair.

They were even more formidable in appearance than in voice. Each was dressed in overalls, riding boots, a vest, and had a handkerchief of vast proportions knotted around his throat. Each wore a big-brimmed sombrero. Each would have been a commanding figure even among big men. But here the points of similarity ceased and the points of divergence commenced. The younger of the two, Arizona Pete, was a tall and athletic fellow. Even as he sat cross-legged on the floor, his back was erect and his head nobly poised. Like his companion, his face was veiled in a beard of several days' growth, but, in spite of the unshaven skin, he was not bad looking, except that the eyes were animal-bright and restless. His companion was more squat and bulky with shapeless strength. By some inches he was appreciably taller. His squat-featured face and the length of his arms suggested a gorilla to the tailor. And he, too, had those animal-bright eyes.

"And now," Lew Shaler was saying, "how d'you figure the stuff had ought to be split?"

"What do you mean by that?" the other fired at once. Throughout he seemed to fear that his companion in crime would take an advantage if an opening occurred.

"I guess I talk tolerably plain. How do you expect to split the stuff?"

"The easiest way. Fifty-fifty."

The gorilla-faced man gaped. "Come easy, Arizona. I'm talking serious."

"And so am I."

The older man shook his head. "Arizona," he said, softening his voice to a whine, "is that the way to talk to a gent that found you down and out and showed you the way to some easy money?"

"You showed me the way to some crooked coin," said Arizona steadily enough, "and I done my share to get it."

"*You* done your share? Do you mean that?"

"Didn't I do all I was asked to?"

"There you are," declared Lew Shaler sadly to an invisible audience. "There's gratitude for you. Arizona, I'm surprised."

"Sorry. But that's where I stand."

"No, you don't, Arizona. I'll tell you why you think you're going to stand on that. You figure that old Lew Shaler is trying to do you, eh?"

"Maybe I do. Why?"

"Why? Because it cuts me up a pile to have you suspect me of that, son. Look here, did you ever hear one of the boys say that Lew Shaler wasn't square?"

140

"I dunno. What you driving at?"

"I'll tell you what I'm driving at. I'm driving at what's to come. This here coin . . . it ain't nothing to me. But I see big hauls ahead of us. I see chances where we can make ten times as much as this. Could you get it without Lew Shaler? No, between you and me, you couldn't. The reason ain't that you haven't got brains. Because you have. But you don't know the ropes. Would you know how to boil down the soup? No, you wouldn't. Would you know how to doctor a safe? No, you wouldn't. Could you even use a can opener? No, you couldn't. But old Lew Shaler, that sees you got brains, is the boy that's going to teach you. Now, I ask you, with me teaching you all those things, is it square for you to want to get as much as me out of it? Ain't it true that when a boy starts out learning a trade, he works for a while for almost nothing? I'll tell you what. I've had bright lads step up to me and say . . . 'Lew,' they says, 'lemme come along and you show me what you know, and I don't ask you for a cent.' That's what they says. But I wouldn't listen to 'em. No, sir, I says, wait till you find a gent with brains, Lew. Then get him and cotton to him, and you'll both get rich. And that's why I picked you up, Arizona, because you ain't like the rest. You got lots of nerve. You got a good eye. You know a gun as good as the next one. And you're quick to learn."

He finished this lecture and eulogy with a smile, and Arizona Pete perceptibly weakened under the attack.

"I ain't denying that you know the business," he averred. "And I don't want to be no hog. All I want is to get my fair share. And I ain't going to be beat by no man. What you say about keeping on together, that looks pretty good to me. But only if I get my fair share. I ain't going to be nobody's underdog."

"Which I ain't asking you to be nobody's slave," broke in the yegg hurriedly. "Me ask a gent like to play slavey?" He laughed. "Arizona, I value you too high for that. I'd be ashamed to tell you how high I value you because maybe I'm wrong about you. No, sir. All I ask is what's my due. Now, look back over what we done. I ask you, who planned the job?"

"You done that, right enough."

"And when things looked shaky, who threw the old plan away and dug up a lot better one out of his head?"

"You done it, Lew, and I ain't denying that it was a damned clever piece of work. I admire you for it. It was fast thinking."

"Then you come down to the safe. Who done all the fixing?"

"You done that, but I was keeping guard."

"And mighty good guard you kept. Which the way you fooled that old gent that come along asking questions with me inside fixing the safe . . . why, I near busted out laughing. You're smart, Arizona, that's what I call you . . . smart!"

"Hmm," growled Arizona and flushed with pleasure. "I ain't anybody's fool."

"You ain't, son. But let's go on. When we made our getaway, and when they was closing in on us from the right, who was it stopped 'em by drilling one of 'em clean?"

"You done that."

"Yes, sir, and it was a hard thing to do. You come out of this with clean hands, son, but I got the guilt of murder on my head."

Arizona snorted. "Lew Shaler, when you take on like that, you make me laugh. If you ever give a thought for all the men you've killed, you'd never think of nothing else. Why, it wasn't no more'n knocking over a rabbit for you to shoot young Welling."

"Wasn't it? A lot you know about it, Arizona. You that never touched a gent in your life."

"I don't like the way you say that."

The tone of Lew Shaler changed with startling suddenness. "Son, I'm tired arguing. I'll tell you what you get. You get one-third. I get two-thirds. Start counting." He kicked in between them two blackened canvas bags.

Arizona Pete sat with his elbows resting on his knees and returned no answer except for a smile that began slowly and never reached his eyes.

It was a sinister expression, and the tailor shivered behind his pile of straw. He was wondering: *Jeremy Dice, would your blood turn into water if a man ever looked at you like that?*

CHAPTER
FIVE

After the fight

Lew Shaler remained unperturbed. He returned glare for glare, meantime saying rapidly: "Arizona, think quick and think twice. Don't make a fool out'n yourself."

"Speaking personal," returned Arizona, "I dunno why I should let an old goat like you bluff me out. Besides, I could use that whole sack of coin pretty handy."

"Is that final?"

"I reckon it is."

"You poor fool kid."

Even while the pitying expression was drawling out of the wide mouth of Lew Shaler, his right hand twitched back with unbelievable speed toward the heavy gun in his holster. The left hand of Arizona shot out. The maneuver was repeated in reverse on the opposite side, and the two men started to their feet, each with drawn gun, each with his wrist locked by the grasp of the other. There was no speech now. They glared at each other beast-like. Suddenly the tailor found that he had lost all fear. He was tingling as he tingled when he watched a prize fighter. This was the same, except that there were guns instead of gloved fists.

For a moment the gladiators were standing without motion. But the keen eye of the tailor discovered that each was straining, silently, terribly. Then, as an imperceptible advantage apparently fell to the part of the older man, Arizona Pete whined with dismay and rage and flung himself to one side. At the same instant both revolvers were discharged.

A bullet splintered the boards beside the tailor's head, but he rose to his knees unaware of the danger. They were still spinning; again both revolvers were discharged. Again both men escaped harm, for neither of them could twitch in the muzzle of his gun enough to bring the body of his enemy into line for a shot.

It was Arizona Pete who saw that the struggle along this line was futile to continue. He dropped his revolver to the floor and, unburdened by it, succeeded in wrenching his hand clear. A moment later he had whipped a murderous knife from his belt and drove it at the throat of Lew Shaler.

Lew had instantly imitated the maneuver of his enemy in dropping the gun, and now, tearing his right hand clear, he shot it across and seized the darting hand of Arizona. There was a twist, a yell of pain from Arizona, and the knife also dropped, tinkling, to the floor. At the same moment both men wrenched themselves away, and, the instant there was clearance, Lew Shaler tore open his shirt.

What the significance of that move might be, the tailor could not tell, but Arizona Pete, with a shriek of horror, leaped in and drove his fist into the face of the bulkier man. The impact flung him back against the wall with a crash that sprang the rotten boards. He bounded away from them as if they were springs, and, as Arizona strove to scoop up a revolver from the floor, the huge fist of Lew Shaler landed fairly on his cheek bone and split away skin and flesh. Arizona was whirled like a top by the blow. He straightened from the whirl with a howl of pain, and, hitting inside the flailing arms of Shaler, his fists cracked twice on the flesh with a sound like a clapping of hands, and two dark red trickles went down the face of the older man. Evidently he saw that to engage in this fighting at long range was a hopeless thing for him. Abandoning all effort to strike with his fists, he extended his huge arms and lurched at his slenderer opponent.

Arizona saw the coming danger. He danced away to one side, swerved, and again planted both fists in the face of the older man without receiving a return blow. He began to laugh, taunting Lew Shaler. But the big man whirled and charged again, like a bull, the shack trembling at his footfalls. This time his lowered head drove through the straight-shooting fists of Arizona. He came close. His long arms were wound about the body of Arizona, and the two crashed together on the floor with Lew Shaler on top. A strong heave from Arizona spun them over. Here and there they rolled, a confused mass of striking legs and winding arms. At first the advantage was with Shaler's greater weight and strength, but Arizona had on his side the merciless advantage of youth. His wind held better; his muscles were better equipped to withstand a prolonged struggle. Eventually the tumbling ceased with Shaler flat on his back. Arizona's left forearm was under the wide shoulder of his opponent, and the gripping hand was buried in Shaler's thick neck in a stranglehold, while his right knee was ground into the hollow of Shaler's left arm.

Only the right arm of the older man remained free. He balled the fist and, clubbing it, struck desperately into the face of Arizona Pete. Twice and again those short, deadly blows thudded into the face of Arizona, splitting the flesh above his eyes, opening again the old gash on his cheek bone. But he retained his grip in spite of the punishment he received, and Shaler began to relent. His blows were more hurried, less powerful. They beat a weakening tattoo in Pete's face, but his own face was blackening. His eyes bulged, the veins stood out on his forehead, and he struggled for breath.

Jeremy Dice heard the grim mutter of Arizona Pete: "It's science that counts . . . science that kills you, Shaler . . . damn you."

His grip closed harder than before. A peculiar gasping, whining sound broke from Shaler's throat, and for a second he ceased struggling. In that second, however, a new thought must have come to him. He drove his right arm desperately between his own body and that of his foe. The hand tore at his shirt as it had done once before, and Arizona Pete shouted in dismay. Yet he would not relax his death grip. He merely flattened his body as far as he could against the body of Shaler, but the fear of death had nerved the older man

147

with superhuman strength. His hand struggled, jerked out and back, and then there was the explosion of a gun.

Arizona Pete leaped up like a wolf, with a yell, and staggered back. Shaler, turning on his side, fired once more. Arizona swayed and pitched on his face.

With his gun poised, ready for another shot at the first movement, Shaler sat slowly up. Arizona did not stir. Except that his right hand, having fallen by chance on the butt of one of the fallen revolvers, he began to draw it slowly toward his side. This Shaler did not see. He was sitting up, rubbing his throat, and gasping in breaths of the vivifying air, while the purple of his face slowly changed to a brilliant red. And so, as he turned his head from side to side, gasping, his eyes encountered the eyes of Jeremy Dice, who was on his knees on the platform.

For a moment his eyes bulged as though he had seen a ghost. Then, with a grin of indescribable malice, his hand closed on his gun. There was no time for the firing of that shot. Arizona Pete had twitched over on his side and fired once, and the larger man sagged to the floor, dead. And Arizona — a sight that Jeremy Dice would never forget should he live to be a hundred — dragged himself up to his feet by the wall of the shack. He turned, his mouth sagging, his eyes dull, made one step forward — and fell, dead, over the body of Lew Shaler.

For a time it seemed to Jeremy Dice that the two mighty men were still struggling before his eyes. It seemed incredible that those two great hulks were now

148

an inert mass, one on the other, no more dangerous than dead cattle. He began to feel his own heart return to a normal pulse. The pain of the wound on his forehead, long forgotten, stung him again. By the dull light of the lantern on the wall he climbed down the ladder and stood, trembling, on the floor. He turned quickly toward the dead men. While his back was turned, it had seemed to him that huge Lew Shaler had thrust aside the body of Arizona Pete and had sat up, grinning with malice as he had done before, his revolver in his hand. But the dead lay where they had fallen, their limbs oddly twisted. The great right arm of Lew Shaler was outstretched on the floor, but the empty, upturned palm would never hold a weapon again. A queer sense of horror and of awe came over Jeremy Dice as he bent over the dead.

Straining his back with the heavy burden, he lifted and dragged Arizona Pete from his victim. He laid the two side by side, composed the distorted faces, closed the eyes, still terrible and brighter in death than common eyes in life. From their necks he removed the bandannas and spread these over their faces. Those formidable hands he folded upon their breasts, and then stepped back, the revolver of Lew Shaler in his hand, to look over his work. He was deeply relieved for some reason. He felt that the horror had been lessened, almost removed. In his heart a certain sympathy and respect for these men began to rise. Their deaths had been terrible, but had they not been almost glorious?

He looked to the revolver in his hand now. It was not the first time he had handled a pistol. In the shooting galleries he had spent many an hour shooting at the spinning little clay ducks, but his own proficiency only made him marvel the more at the consummate ease with which these fellows had wielded the heavy Forty-Fives, shooting as if by instinct rather than by aim. He turned the gun in his hand, pressed the trigger slightly, and instantly there was a dull explosion — the trigger was set with the lightness of a hair's weight, it seemed. From now on he handled it more cautiously. It had been suspended under the shirt of Lew Shaler. He made a loose fastening for it inside his trousers. It sagged them a little, but the big weapon was concealed with hardly a bulge in the cloth. He tried it. It came out smoothly, easily, and could be restored with a gesture.

From this point his courage began to grow surprisingly. He saw a folded paper bulging in the pocket of Lew Shaler. Removing it, he found it to be a placard printed on thick, white paper. A large photograph topped the sheet — the unmistakable wide features of Shaler himself. Under it was printed in large letters: **$2,500 Reward.** Under this was a description of the man in detail. In one corner there was a red stain, and he stowed the notice in his pocket. It would be a convincing testimony for Dottie Petwell.

CHAPTER
SIX

Discovery

Dice turned back naturally to the money bags, and for the first time he saw that this coin that had caused the double killing was now in his power because his mind had been working behind a haze of deep excitement. The excitement continued, but now it was a new fear. Suppose that posse of which the two had spoken should be indeed on the trail? Suppose they should see the glimmering of this lantern on the wall? Suppose they should come upon him while he was counting the money?

This threw him into a panic. He caught up one of the bags of money and ran to the door. Outside all was dark, quiet. The stars burned with as pure and cold a light as ever. The bandits' two horses stood nose to nose, their heads fallen, their ears sagged back with weariness, and each was pointing the toe of one hind foot. Perfect pictures of rest. But they gave to Jeremy Dice a feeling of security. When he wished, he could tie the money behind one of those saddles, give the horse his own head, and be led back to some settlement in the desert.

As for a posse approaching, there was not a stir across the hills — only the rush of the wind, that was now increasing. It seemed utterly impossible that men would pursue two desperate fugitives, Jeremy argued within his own mind. Had he been among the pursuers, he would certainly have dissuaded them from any forward movement.

He turned back more calmly to take stock of the loot. He untied the bags and spilled the money out on the floor. It suddenly filled the room with a yellow glow — or it seemed to do so to the dazed eyes of Jeremy. To him, money meant faded, worn, rustling slips of paper. Gold was not money. It was treasure. And here was gold. It set his heart beating with a feverish restlessness. Gold. Already it had caused two murders. He glanced uneasily toward the dead, as though he expected them to sit up of one accord, grinning at him, as though they had been playing a game with him all this time.

But the dead remained dead, and the gold washed in two bright tides to his very feet. He thrust his hands into the mass of it. The cold, smooth coins slipped through his fingers and fell back, chiming and rustling among their fellows. He tossed a double handful up. Falling, some of the coins raced to obscure corners of the room and clicked against the walls. It had been a gleaming shower. Jeremy Dice would have been astonished could he have seen how his own face had grown pale, the quiver of his nostrils, and the set of his jaw. It was a long, lean, fighting jaw, like that of a bull terrier. Somewhere in the past men of action must have figured in his ancestry.

He began to count the loot. Tens and twenties — they were comfortable, broad coins. They checked up in swift handfuls, very heavy — twenty to a stack. And quickly he was setting out little piles all around him.

Now and then his mind flashed three thousand miles away. He had set up an establishment of his own. He had hired Sanson, the best of Gorgenheim's cutters. He had gone around and called on Gorgenheim's best customers and drawn them to his own shop. He had called on his former boss and snapped his lean fingers under that red nose. For how could he ever fear any living being after he had witnessed the battle of Arizona Pete and Lew Shaler? He saw himself calling on Dottie Petwell. He felt, now, that he had never really loved her. Indeed in his small life he had never known a single real emotion. One glimpse of the struggling bodies of Arizona and Lew Shaler had taught him what passion could be. Not that this came clearly home to the slender-fingered tailor. By no means. It was only a vague feeling. At the end of his reflections he was deciding that he would marry Dottie Petwell not for love but simply because she was the best-dressed girl of their set in Manhattan. She was the idol of Kadetzsky's. But his picture of Manhattan itself had grown small as though with distance, as though all those skyscrapers were tiny toys. Beside the struggling forms of Lew Shaler and Arizona Pete the picture of Manhattan was a flimsy thing. They could have crushed it under heel.

It may be seen that Jeremy Dice was plunging far into fantasy. Out of this fairy world he was brought with a start by the neighing of one of the horses

153

outside. And then, far off, an answering whinny. Jeremy Dice sprang to his feet and swept up one of the sacks full of gold, knotted the string about its gorged throat with trembling fingers, and leaped to the door. He glanced back. There lay wealth, rolling on the floor, calling to him. With a groan, he ran back. While he was bending, the neigh came again, close to the house and once more the answering whinny — but this time closer — terribly close. It seemed to thunder in the very ear of Jeremy Dice. All at once a paralytic cold came over him.

"I am lost," said Jeremy aloud and dropped the sack of gold on the floor. *Oh, to have had one minute's start, and one of those horses racing under him.*

There was a muffled rushing of horses' hoofs, swishing through the loose sand. A growl of voices, then a shout answered. Then, half explosively, half in a murmur: "It's his hoss. It's Shaler's hoss! Spread, boys. Rankin, back me up. Bob, get in behind me. They're here."

A great trembling spread through the body of Jeremy Dice, so that to control himself he folded his arms high on his chest and leaned against the side of the room. His lips were shuddering in a sort of palsy; he compressed them. His knees knocked one against the other. He dropped one foot over the other. And that was the picture seen by Sheriff Lawrence, pushing through the door, crouched, a revolver in each hand. That was how Jeremy Dice was introduced to the men of the mountain desert.

The sheriff and the two men crowding behind him saw a lean, meager figure of a man of about middle height, leaning against the rotten, battered wall of the shack. His face was a ghastly sight. High on his forehead, and exactly in the center, was a narrow, deep gash, running up into the hair. The hair itself stood wildly on end. One side of his face was darkly streaked. His clothes were also stained and begrimed. Yet this grisly face appeared to smile. The lips were compressed, and the faint, sardonic lines were forming at the corners of his mouth. His coat and trousers were rent to almost veritable rags, deep gashes in the cloth as though strong hands had torn them. His legs were idly crossed; his arms were folded carelessly across his breast. He seemed to mock them, and withal — perhaps because of those wounds and that struggle-stamped body — there was peculiar dignity about the slender man.

Upon him the sheriff stared with startled eyes. "Who?" he stammered. Again: "Who are you?" But the stranger disdained speech. As a matter of fact, his tongue clove to the roof of his mouth, impelled there by the yawning mouths of those two revolvers.

"Hands up!" gasped the sheriff.

Jeremy Dice did not move. He was, indeed, incapable of motion. How close he came to death then — for the nerves of the sheriff were at the snapping point, and his forefingers were curling hard and harder around the triggers of his guns — Jeremy was never to know. He compressed his lips a little more — to the sheriff it

155

seemed that his grin broadened. A man who smiled in the face of two steady guns!

And then, something drew the sheriff's glance to one side — his gaze remained where it had fallen. Two giant figures, stiff and stark, with the red bandannas across their faces. Sheriff Lawrence went slowly in. Other faces packed through the door behind him. The sheriff put up his guns slowly. The others obeyed in dead silence.

Still that silence continued while the sheriff stalked across the room, raised the bandannas one by one, and then stepped back. He took off his hat. He stared at the slender figure of Jeremy Dice. The others imitated their leader. They went and peeked hastily, awe-stricken, under the bandannas. They took off their hats. They stared at Jeremy Dice.

It suddenly burst upon the terror-frozen mind of the tailor that these strong men were not circling around him in hostility. Indeed, their faces were the faces of children, viewing a master. He remembered the faces of a crowd that had stood aside to see a champion pugilist swagger down the sidewalk. The expressions had been one and the same.

The broad-shouldered sheriff stepped forward to the door. He called: "Halloo! Boys! Come in. It's over."

There was another rush of horses, the sound of creaking stirrup leather, and the grunt of horses as men dismounted. New faces packed into the door. The sheriff was standing close, and now he turned and stretched a solemn arm toward Jeremy Dice, the tailor from Manhattan.

156

"Boys," he said hoarsely, "he done it. You can see the marks on him. He done it. He killed 'em both!"

The others gaped. Jeremy began to recover his composure.

"Stranger," said the sheriff, still solemnly, "I dunno your name, but I'm standing here ready to tell the world that you're about nine-tenths man. My name's Lawrence."

"And I," said the tailor in his small, gentle voice, "am Jeremy Dice. I'm glad to know you."

CHAPTER
SEVEN

The Famous
Fabrication

The other introductions followed with a rush. Jeremy Dice felt his lean hand crushed in successive grips, heard deep, rough voices growl their greetings, felt sharp eyes pry at his own from beneath brows drawn down by years of squinting over sun-white sands. He was frightened by the adulation that had been drawn down upon his head. But it was not his fault. They had interpreted the scene as they found it, and what wonder?

But wouldn't they know? That was the great question. Would they not contrast his slender hands with those broken bulks that lay side by side in the corner? Would they not see the ludicrous impossibility of the New York tailor overwhelming two such giants, two such hardened, proved fighters? He almost feared that this was a scene of mockery. But, no, their earnestness appeared manifest on the surface.

The very hugeness of the contrast was in their eyes the proof positive. Here were some twenty veterans of horse, desert, and gun fights who had pursued a foe worthy of their steel and now had come upon those foes vanquished by a single hand. If Jeremy had been six feet, the thing would have seemed incredible. But he was not tall. He was slender — his very lack of muscle convinced them. Lew Shaler and Arizona Pete could only have been overcome by a mysterious power, and Jeremy Dice was a soul-filling mystery.

Back of the mind of every man was a single thought. That thought was the picture of the almost mythical *gentle* badman. For there have been terrible men on the mountain desert, men of bulk, brawn, and vicious deeds. But more terrible still have been some few mild-eyed men, small, without nerves, courageous as sword blades, nervous and lightning swift of hand. Their names can be checked off on the tips of the fingers of one hand. Some were manhunters on the side of the law. Some were outlaws. All were surpassingly terrible. Their names had passed into legend, magnifying their prowess. And each of the twenty in the posse, looking upon the wan face of Jeremy Dice, seeing his narrow shoulders, feeling the cold touch of his hand, had said to himself: *This is one of those destroyers that Dad told me about. He's a ringer for Billy the Kid!*

Once they had reached this conclusion, they hugged it to their breasts. They were proud of it. It was natural for a story that they would tell their children. If Jeremy Dice had attempted to explain, they would have laughed him down. Those stern, simple, credulous minds had instantly endowed him with all the characteristics of a hero.

Of course, Jeremy could not know all that was going on inside their minds. But he did see that they had given their imagination wings.

The sheriff had taken up the guns of the outlaws. He examined the chambers. He turned to Jeremy Dice.

"Mind if I look over your gat, partner?"

"No."

He drew out the weapon of Lew Shaler. He passed it to the sheriff, and the sheriff opened the chamber. He turned to his posse.

"Boys, Lew and Arizona just about emptied their guns ... Dice, here, fired three shots ... and they's three bullets in Lew and Pete."

He paused, impressed, and the crowd shook its assembled head.

"D'you mind telling us how you done it?" asked the sheriff, with a plea in his throat.

A wave of honesty, the desire for confession, welled up in Jeremy Dice. "Sheriff Lawrence," he said in an uncertain voice, looking down at the floor, "the fact is that I didn't do anything. I had just happened along, when ..."

The sheriff cut him short by shaking his head and turning to the others. With them he exchanged a wise smile. The man-killer was, indeed, like one of those legendary figures whom they all had in mind. He was not only terrible beyond credence in action, but he was also modest. Lawrence turned again on Jeremy.

"Dice," he said, extending an argumentative forefinger, "maybe it's something that you want to cover up. Maybe you got a little past of your own. I dunno. I'm just supposing." He winked suggestively at Jeremy Dice. "Suppose, maybe, that they's places where some other sheriff would be glad to get his hands on you . . . if he could safely. Just suppose that. But it don't make no difference here. I tell you, no matter what you've done other places, you're among friends here. You've bumped off two murdering, robbing hounds, and we're all behind you, eh, boys?"

There was a hoarse murmur of assent.

"So, Dice, suppose I start the story for you. We know that you found out Arizona and Lew Shaler was planning this little safecracking game. You laid low, said nothing, and waited till they got started off with the loot. Then you cut in on 'em, after they'd shaken off the rest of us. You slipped up on 'em when they was sitting in this shack, counting the loot . . . I see the coin partly stacked up there and partly lying loose. You found 'em sitting here. Maybe they'd taken off their guns . . . it's hard sitting down on the floor when you got a gun strapped to your hip. You found them guns close to the door. You stepped in and cottoned onto 'em. Then you stuck up the pair of 'em. We know it must've run like that. All we want is the details of how it was finished."

He paused, waited. Jeremy Dice stood with his head bowed. The picture the sheriff had painted had swelled on his mind. He saw himself slip softly through that door, snatch up the guns that lay on the floor, and then hold up the two bandits with his own weapon.

Jeremy raised his head. He smiled faintly. "Maybe it would sound queer," he murmured.

There was no answer. Belief, credence was stamped broadly on every face.

"You're right, Sheriff. When I came in, I saw the guns on the floor. I raked them to one side with my heel and pointed my gun at the two of them. I backed them into that corner against the wall with their hands over their heads."

He was seeing the imaginary picture. He was lost in his own narrative. His face worked, flushed, his lean fingers moved, and the crowd watched him in breathless suspense.

"I intended to shoot them both. But I changed my mind. It seemed a little hard to kill them both in cold blood. So I put away my gun and started to talk to them. They took their hands down."

"Good heavens!" exclaimed the sheriff. "You let 'em take their hands down?"

"Why not? I thought I could get out my gun before they could hurt me."

The sheriff gasped and exchanged glances with the crowd. Miracles were thickening around them.

"But Lew Shaler watched his chance. When I had turned away a little, he picked up that chair" — Jeremy Dice pointed to one of the chairs, reduced to a hulk by the impact of those struggling bodies — "and threw it at me. I reached for my gun . . . but . . . it stuck in my clothes, you see?"

"Yes, yes. Go on, Dice."

That difficult point was passed, thank heavens. "The chair struck me on the head."

"We can see the cut. Knocked you out?"

"It knocked me against the wall."

"Ah."

How hungrily they followed the details.

"And they ran for their guns, but I jumped in at them."

"And stopped 'em?"

"I didn't have time to get to my gun. I had to stop them with my fists!"

"Them cuts on their faces ... and look at his knuckles, boys. Raw to the bone where he hit 'em." The sheriff interpolated this information and interpretation in a swift aside. "Go on, Dice."

"A man his size stopping 'em both," ejaculated somebody.

"I knocked them both back and went in after Lew Shaler, hitting for the face."

"He was cut to ribbons, all right," muttered a swift commentator.

"But he wouldn't go down," sighed Jeremy Dice.

There was a mutter of excitement from the crowd. They were weighing the slender form of Jeremy Dice with their eyes. They were seeing that pale face on fire, that wiry body putting panther power behind every blow.

"And Arizona got past me to his gun. I saw him stoop at the same time that I knocked Lew against the wall . . . it stunned him a little. I whirled in behind him and sort of half pushed and half carried him toward Pete. Lew was stunned, but not down, you see. Pete was blazing away, trying to get me without killing Lew. I held Lew off with one hand, got at my gun, and, reaching around, I shot Arizona. He was so close that the muzzle touched him."

"I saw the burn on his vest," ejaculated the sheriff. "Go on, pardner. Good heavens, boys, it don't seem no ways possible!"

"Shut up, Sheriff, you keep interrupting Dice."

Jeremy had thrown himself into the imaginary scene. "The gunshot seemed to bring Shaler back to his senses. As Pete dropped, Lew caught my gun arm at the wrist . . . I thought the bones were going to break. I had to let the gun fall. I clinched with Shaler. We went down. Struggled around. Finally I caught Lew on his back, my left arm under his shoulder, and my left hand in his throat. He began to choke."

He started, for there was again that gasping sound from the crowd.

"He was nearly gone when I saw Arizona coming to life and getting to his knees. He looked a horrible sight, I assure you, Sheriff. He staggered over and got to Shaler's gun. Then I jumped off Shaler and ran for my own gat. Arizona was shooting, but his aim was wild . . . he was dying on his feet, you see. When I turned, Lew Shaler was coming at me with his big arms out. I shot him, and he went down." Jeremy paused. "That was all there was to it."

But how was he to account for the interim in which his wounds ceased bleeding? He was staggered by the necessity of that explanation. Then his mind cleared.

"After that, Sheriff, something queer happened. You see, I'd been battered about a little . . ."

The sheriff ran his eyes over the tattered body of Jeremy Dice. "I'll tell a man you were, pardner."

"And . . . when I saw they were both down and dead, my head swam. I went down on the floor and lay there. After a while I heard a horse neigh. I'd just got to my feet when you came in."

And that was the origin of the most famous tale of a gun fight that ever went the rounds of the mountain desert. Twenty bold men stood drinking in the incredible words and believing them all. Twenty honest men heard the prodigious lie without a questioning thought. The sheriff strode forward and stretched out his hand.

"Dice," he said, "I want to shake hands again. I didn't see how you done it. Now it's clear as day, but my head's still spinning with it. And . . . it was a mighty lucky thing that you didn't collapse while Shaler was still alive . . . that devil, Lew Shaler."

A voice broke in, reverent, curious. "The thing that beats me is how you come here without a hoss? Leastways, I didn't see none."

Again Jeremy Dice was staggered. Perspiration poured out on his forehead.

"Sheriff," he said, smiling wanly, "I've got to confess that I'm no good with a horse. No nerve when I get in the saddle. You see, I was thrown some time back, and since then I've always kept away from a saddle when I could."

They were gaping upon him, but, oddly enough, they were all smiling and nodding. All great men had their weaknesses, and the weakness of this man-killer —

165

ludicrous and wonderful to tell — was horses. Horses! Not a man there but had been born, almost, in the saddle. Each, staring at Jeremy Dice, marveled that a thing so simple should be the weakness of his daring superiority but in that one point. Because he felt this touch of superiority, each man instantly believed all the rest that had been predicated about Jeremy Dice.

"So I didn't come here with a horse," he said slowly, watching them. "I knew where they intended to stop. So I got the train and dropped off when it came even with the hills. Then I came over here and waited."

It was done. It was believed. Preparations to depart began.

CHAPTER
EIGHT

West of the Rockies

If you wish to humanize a wise man, show him doing one foolish thing — saving orange peels, perhaps, as the great Johnson is shown to have done by the still greater Boswell. If you wish to humanize a cunning man, show him guilty of one great and simple error. If a brave man is to be humanized, show him afraid of one thing that no one else dreads.

Therefore, never was there a more auspicious tale than that of Jeremy Dice concerning his fear of horses. In the first place, it was instantly illustrated. For no sooner had the most gentle horse in the outfit been selected and brought to him than the bold men of the desert had to swallow their laughter as they watched the cautious manner in which Jeremy Dice, the terrible, climbed into the saddle. Indeed, it was a painful thing to have to choke back laughter for fear of being filled full of lead.

That restraint grew. It was observed that when the horse trotted, Jeremy bounced ridiculously in the saddle, and his elbows flopped. This was almost too much even for men who were held in check by fear of death.

Presently the restraint was removed because Jeremy, looking across to the working face of one of his companions, flushed and laughed feebly. It was the signal. A yell of joyous mirth rang instantly through the night. The sheriff was the first to begin and the last to leave off. Everyone was delighted. If a man would submit to being laughed at, it showed that he was a good fellow. Here was a desperado fresh from a double killing, yet he meekly laughed at his own weaknesses and permitted others to laugh as well. This was almost unprecedented — but, for that matter, everything that Jeremy did was unprecedented. The men of the posse fell back in pairs and commented on the foolish appearance of the great man in the saddle. It was noted that he grunted when the horse galloped, that he groaned when the horse trotted, and even clutched the saddle when he walked. They would have scorned any other man in the world, so childish and helpless in the saddle. But for Jeremy Dice this weakness was the key that unlocked their hearts. They swore to each other that he was a rare one, a good fellow, all right in every essential respect. They vowed to drink in his honor long and deep. They did more. They held down the gait of their horses to a snail's pace for the sake of Jeremy Dice.

The sheriff, pressing in at Jeremy's side, pointed out the gentleness of the horse he rode. He assured him that all was well, treated him, in short, as if he were an infant first seeing the ocean but all with reverence — as a royal child, say, might be treated by old courtiers. Jeremy took advice humbly, received and obeyed instructions to squeeze the saddle with his knees and turn his toes in, things that wonderfully eased the ride for him. It pleased the sheriff infinitely to give these instructions. He had played a secondary rôle on this night. Indeed, if the shameful truth were to be known, he had been casting back in his mind to see if he could not remember a man answering the description of Jeremy under the ban of the law. But he could not remember. Now that he found this great man so mild, so willing to take advice and follow instructions, his mind was opened, and his heart was softened. He began to wish nothing but good luck to his companion. He issued his orders to Jeremy on the horse in a loud and authoritative manner, so that the rest of the posse could see that he was not overawed by his distinguished guest.

So the eight miles to the flourishing town of Chatterton were at length covered. The dawn had come, and then the early day, and then the red sun went up over the hills. It had showed Jeremy Dice sinking in the saddle with weariness, thirst, hunger, to say nothing of the intolerable chafing of the saddle. He even reeled when they swerved to one side, and the posse bolted at a gallop straight for the village.

To tell the truth, he might have fallen from the saddle, but the sheriff was there to support him. He checked the leaders who had set the pace with a shout.

"You damned leather-headed chumps!" shouted Sheriff Lawrence. "Ain't you got no sense? Why, even a hoss could see that Dice is sick. And wouldn't you gents be sick if one of you had a set-to with bare hands ag'in' one such as Lew Shaler? To say nothing of two like him?"

He showed his teeth with gathering rage as the others brought their horses back to a shamed trot, and then to a walk.

"Ain't he near had his head split open? Ain't he looked at death pretty damn' familiar about a dozen times tonight? Ain't he one mass of bruises and cuts? And just because he sets his teeth over it and don't whine none, you gents think he's as chipper as you maybe . . . you that ain't done nothing but sit in your saddles and talk a pile tonight. I never seen such men. I'm ashamed to lead out a posse of gents like you."

But here Jeremy Dice, cutting in on the tirade, protested: "Be easy with 'em, Sheriff. They're all friends of mine."

That small sentence locked him into the inner heart of every one of those hard riders. The procession went on more slowly, but now one rider cut away from the rest and shot off as fast as spurs would urge his willing mustang. He melted swiftly into a mist of dust.

Presently the others wound through the hills and came in sight of Chatterton. It was typical of the desert — but it was all new to Jeremy Dice. The one winding street, the crooked little alleys that ran off from it, like creeks feeding into the main stream. The unpainted shacks. The few stores with imposing signs in red and black paint, the blowing dust in the street, the uncurtained windows. The horses downheaded at the rack in front of the saloon.

170

This Jeremy Dice saw through a mist, for now the long fatigue was telling heavily on him, and the pain of his head was a torture. They had offered to tie up his wound for him before starting from the old shack, but he had refused, feeling it was more the part expected of him. And the sheriff had agreed. It would be better to wait until they got to town, and the wound could be properly cleansed. Now the eyes of Jeremy Dice cleared.

Life came to those apparently deserted shacks. Faces came at the windows, and then men, women, and children poured out into the street. Everyone was pointing at Jeremy Dice. The posse fell back a respectful distance so that everyone could see. Their messenger had scattered the cream of the news beforehand, but now the posse was cornered one by one and forced to tell more in detail while the hero went down the street, slowly, the sheriff at his side supporting the uncertain figure. They saw the wan, stained face, the tattered clothes. This was the way a man might well look who had conquered Lew Shaler and Arizona Pete — single-handed, barehanded! Yes, he had faced them both, for a time, without a weapon in his hands.

Shouts went up. There were yells for Jeremy Dice, but he did not turn his fallen head. In truth, Jeremy was well nigh fainting with exhaustion and pain. Dimly he saw a man rush down the street, gesticulating.

"Keep your hands off him, Brownell," the sheriff warned. "Yep. He nailed 'em both, and he got all your money back. I got it in the saddlebags, and I'll count it over with you to see all's straight. You're lucky, Brownell, that's all I got to say to you." Later on he said in Jeremy's ear: "You certainly got yourself a home with him. And he's rich, Dice, rich as a mine."

The words came to Jeremy as a voice in a dream. They reached a halting place at last.

"Here's the hotel. Lemme help you down. Why, you don't weigh nothing, pardner. This way. Lemme take care of you. Have a drink first? All the boys are aching to have a drink with you. Ought to do you good."

He was too weak to protest. Presently the long bar was before him. A noisy crowd thronged on every side.

"Keep your hands off him. We got a case for the doctor, that's what we got. Where's Doc Jordan?"

"He's been sent for."

"We'll pull you through, Dice. You can lay to that. We'll pull you through, or I'm a liar. All right, boys. Are you ready? A long cheer for the gent that bumped 'em off. Let her go!"

What a crashing cheer went into the brain of Jeremy Dice and shuddered home to his heart. His lean hand closed around the glass. He attempted to raise it. Then blackness assailed his brain. As he staggered and the many arms received him, he attempted the confession. "Boys, I'm . . . no . . . good." That was all. He fainted dead away.

Eventually the confusion died away, and they put him in the best bed in the hotel with the doctor at his side.

"If you don't do a neat job, Jordan, you're through in this town," the sheriff said solemnly.

"Nothing to worry about," the medical man assured him. "Dice is badly shaken up. That cut in the forehead will need three stitches, and it'll leave a scar. Besides, there are a number of contusions, none very serious but . . ."

"Leave out the big words, Doc, and show us the big work."

The sheriff stood over them, grunting in sympathy when the needles pierced the flesh.

"A highly nervous organization, I should say," pronounced the doctor when the bandages were finally arranged. "You say he handled two big men? Shaler and Arizona? Surprising, of course, but not altogether inexplicable. I have known cases of small-muscled men doing remarkable things in a burst of nervous frenzy. A species of insanity, I suppose. However, this boy will get well in a few days. Let him have rest."

"He'll have the best rest that Chatterton can give him," said the sheriff heartily.

The whole town agreed with him. When the sheriff came downstairs later to the crowd that waited for word from him about the patient, he said: "Do you know what he said when he keeled over in the saloon, boys? Poor devil had done enough to kill most of us, but, when he dropped, he seemed sort of ashamed of himself. He said to me: 'Boys, I'm . . . no . . . good.'"

In this manner Jeremy Dice finally won for himself the hearts of Chatterton's strongest men. West of the Rockies there is one virtue praised above all others, and that is modesty.

CHAPTER
NINE

The Heroic Coward

It had been a collapse caused by physical exhaustion. As a matter of fact, Jeremy could have risen from bed the next day very little the worse for wear, but the doctor forbade this. For the good of his reputation it was necessary that he make out the case to be as serious as possible. The whole town of Chatterton and the entire range around it were intensely interested, and the stronger he made his patient's condition out to be, the better it would be for him. Besides, Brownell, the banker, had agreed generously to pay the expenses.

So it was announced that the patient was in a critical nervous condition. The doctor uttered his theory. According to the medical man some people are capable of storing away nerve energy just as storage batteries conserve electricity. At the critical moment this nerve energy is called forth. It comes in one terrific burst. In the instant of action the man does prodigious things. Afterward there is a relapse. All that nerve energy has been exhausted, and it may be some time before he is capable of doing anything again.

It was above all necessary that Jeremy Dice should be kept in bed for several days. Even after that he would need close care, easy exercise, attention. Chatterton declared to a man that these things should be done. Chatterton was delighted with this singular case. Everything about Jeremy Dice was new and different from other men, and the good people hoarded each peculiarity. Such things make good tales in the future.

So Jeremy wakened in a darkened room. He wakened with a consuming sense of guilt, flowing in upon him. *When will they find me out?*

It was necessary that he should escape from the town as soon as possible. They would pay him the reward money, of course, and with that in his pocket he would fade swiftly from the picture and hie him elsewhere — back to Manhattan. Worst of all, there would be no tale to tell Dottie Petwell, for she was very apt to write West and make inquiries, and then the terrible and shameful truth would be known — he was only a tailor.

It had never seemed to Jeremy before a shameful thing to be a tailor. He had been proud of his deft workmanship. He had gloried in the clothes he produced. But now it appeared that there were larger and better things for a man to do. Such as facing two desperadoes single-handed. He shuddered at the memory of that prodigious lie. Still, at the time it had seemed unavoidable. Indeed, he was torn by two impulses. The first was to flee before his shame was known. The second was to stay and prove to Chatterton that it was right in its opinion of him. But he knew that, if he remained there and the test came, the bitter fact of his cowardice would come to light.

At present all he could do was lie and wait. He stirred, raised his head, and looked about him. At once a girl rose from a corner of the room and came to him. She was not a beautiful girl according to standards set by Dottie Petwell. For instance, half of her ears were shamefully exposed. And her hair itself was a glowing red — there seemed almost to be a fire in it — and, as she passed the window and the sunlight struck her, her whole face was illumined. She came into the shadow again, and he could see her better.

She was a brown beauty if ever there was one. Her skin had been tanned in successive coats, but it was not a disagreeable color. It was new to Jeremy Dice, but he enjoyed its novelty. Neither was the tinge of color under her olive cheeks artificial. Even the faint mottling of freckles across her nose and under her eyes was not a disfiguring feature. That nose tipped up just a bit, but the mouth and chin were beautiful, particularly from the angle at which he saw them. Moreover, she had a pair of straight-looking blue eyes. He had never seen eyes that could hold one so steadily. Jeremy wanted to look away and steady himself — but he could not stir his glance.

"Lie back again," said the girl.

"Oh, I'm all right," said Jeremy jauntily. And he heaved himself up on one elbow, preparatory to hitching higher on the pillows. At that, a firm strong hand caught his shoulder and thrust him gently but inevitably back and down.

"Those are the orders of the doctor," said the girl, "and I'm going to see that they're followed."

176

There was such sternness in her voice that Jeremy surrendered at once. He lay, staring up, feeling very unheroic — quite lost, in fact.

She seemed to feel that she should explain: "I asked for this place. So I have to make good."

"And . . . who are you?"

"My name is Mary Welling. I'm the sister of the man Lew Shaler . . . murdered."

She looked past Jeremy up to a picture on the wall. When she glanced down again, there was no emotion in her face.

"I'm sorry," said Jeremy Dice faintly.

"I'm here because you did what the sheriff couldn't do," said the girl steadily. "And I want you to know that there's nothing my family wouldn't do to help you back on your feet . . . and afterward. We aren't a very clubby lot . . . we Wellings. But when a person does a friendly thing for us, we never forget it . . . none of us. So, you write that down in red, Jeremy Dice."

It would have been a rather mannish speech if it had not been for the voice of the speaker.

"Matter of fact . . . ," began Jeremy.

"Stop talking. I'm to talk to you, read to you, do anything you want. But you are not to talk. That's the orders." She added: "What shall I read?"

He closed his eyes. He could not speak for a moment, for the sense of his sin had rushed in on him as it had never done before. It was like soot in his throat, choking him. He had been shamed before, but now he felt like a thief in the night who had sneaked through the door and stolen like a dog into this girl's esteem. It occurred to him, with wonder, that he would not have been ashamed had he stolen in this manner into the admiration of Dottie Petwell. But this girl was different — her eyes were so straight. What would be needed to wrench him from his pedestal and hurl him to the depths of her contempt? The knowledge that he had told a lie — *the* lie. He dared not carry the thought further.

"You're in pain?" asked the voice of the girl. "It's your head, I guess?"

Confession tumbled up against the teeth of Jeremy Dice, but, when he opened his eyes and saw her face, the words died. How could he kill that look and write it over with scorn?

"There's no pain," he said huskily.

"I guess that isn't the truth. Well . . . I don't suppose a man likes to have his troubles talked about. What do you want me to read?"

"Anything."

"All right."

Presently a book was opened. She had begun. The words had no meaning to Jeremy Dice. He listened to the voice, and his own thoughts went on, minute after minute, carrying him through the pit of shame.

"You haven't heard a word I've been saying," she said presently.

"Shall I tell you why?"

"If you can say it in ten words."

"I can . . . almost. It's about a thing I've done."

"Hush," said the girl. She raised a finger that stopped him, and then came and stood beside him.

178

"I know how it is, Jeremy Dice. When a man is sick and hurt, he feels like talking. Then he says a lot of foolish things. I don't want to hear about your past. The sheriff has told me some things."

"What?"

"Well, that you've probably had a good many fights with other men . . . that your record may even be pretty black. But I don't care about that. None of us cares about that. We like you for what you are. We value you for what you've done. Maybe you've been pretty bad. But we know you did one fine square thing. And . . . and you killed the man who murdered our Harry."

What could he say? It seemed that fate had nailed him to the cross of his own lie. She would not let him speak. Afterward she read again, and Jeremy Dice allowed himself to sink into a pleasant dream, listening to her voice.

CHAPTER
TEN

Cheers — and then some

The days rolled by smoothly. Now and then a deputation came into the room. It was forbidden to disturb the distinguished patient often. Therefore, when the doors were opened, the good people came in groups. Sometimes it was a number of housewives. They brought him jellies. They tugged great-eyed children forward for a glance at him. Sometimes it was a number of young girls, very self-conscious, full of blushes, with their looks directed always at Mary Welling and never at the man they wished to see. Sometimes the influential citizens of the town strolled in, tiptoed softly about, murmured to Mary Welling, saw that Chatterton's patient was doing well and was properly cared for, and went out again with a grin and grunt for Jeremy Dice. Sometimes a few of the young cowpunchers came. They brought the fumes of cigarette smoke with them in a cloud. They were bright-eyed young men always, with lean, brown faces, and capable-looking hands. They always did exactly the same thing — waved their hands with apparent carelessness and said: "How are you, pardner? Here's wishing you all the luck!"

One and all of these groups were banished in the same manner by an austere wave of the hand of Mary Welling.

"The way I run people out, I'm getting myself hated," she confided to Jeremy.

They were on the friendliest footing possible. He had even told her that he thought his being kept in bed was all the bunk. She asked him sternly if he thought he knew more than the doctor. Her father had gotten up too soon after a fever once, and the result had been a relapse that brought him to death's door. She told Jeremy Dice this with a solemn shake of the head. But when he smiled at her, she laughed.

"I'll tell you what," she burst out on that occasion. "I like you, Jeremy. You aren't like the other boys. Take any man I know under forty, and he's too serious. Thinks too much about himself. But . . . you're different."

It sent a tingle through the blood of Jeremy to hear that. He was not used to such speeches from girls. He and Dottie Petwell had been almost engaged, but she had never actually confessed a weakness for him in words. She would have felt it to be immodest and unmaidenly. Her confessions had consisted of side glances, pressures of the hand, smiles that might mean almost anything. If she had heard this speech of Mary Welling's, she would have smiled behind her hand in a certain way that Jeremy Dice knew. It drilled him to picture it. She would have said: "Awful bad breeding, ain't it, Jeremy?"

Yet, somehow, he was not really shocked. He wanted Mary to say it over again with the same glitter of her eyes and ring in her voice. Yet, after all, she said it in praise of nothing. She praised him because he did not boast of a thing he had never done.

Once, wakening on a mid-afternoon suddenly, he called to her with a sharpness that brought her running to him.

"Mary," he said to her with infinite solemnity, "some day I'm going to be the things you think I am now. I'm going to try to be, I mean."

At this she frowned. "What do you mean by that?" She started, and without waiting for his answer, she said sternly: "Jeremy Dice, are you being silly, the way the rest of them are?"

He tried to deny it, but a guilty red stole across his face, and the girl turned her back on him and walked to the window. He felt that he had offended her greatly, and that he had been ridiculous. When he heard her humming a soft old tune to herself a moment later, he was relieved. He could not have offended her seriously, he decided, if she forgot it so soon afterward.

Until he died, Jeremy Dice would remember that tune. It was "Robin Adair."

On that same day Sheriff Lawrence and Mr. Brownell came in. They had a heavy suitcase between them. At least it was a burden that they handled as gingerly as if it had been a great weight. There was a flush on each face, and they looked about the room with the foolish smiles of those who know that they are about to perform a good action. The sheriff cleared his throat to make an oration.

"Jeremy Dice," he said, "it was sometime ago that you stood in a shack, confronting two outlaws who . . ."

In spite of himself Jeremy Dice could not help glancing sheepishly across the room to Mary Welling. To his astonishment he saw that she was standing with her head high, a flush in her cheeks, a transfiguring smile on her lips. Her face was the face of one who hears a glorious tale or sees a fair country.

He looked back at the sheriff, bewildered. The sheriff was reaching the heart of the harangue, finishing it off in rounded periods that made the banker nod his pleasure. It appeared that the whole countryside had been harried for a long time by the celebrated Lew Shaler. From cattle rustling to claim jumping, from safe breaking to robbery on the high road, there was nothing in the catalogue of crime to which the versatile Lew Shaler had not, at one time or another, turned his hand.

The result had been that the worthy citizens of Chatterton and the vicinity had groaned under this illegal oppression. At huge expense many times a year they had organized expeditions to comb the hills and the desert for the outlaw, but always he had eluded them. At still further expense they had even brought in and maintained celebrated manhunters who had vainly attempted to catch the marauder.

All, all had failed. The depredations continued on a larger scale. And then, after his most daring crime, carrying thousands of dollars out of the bank of the respected Mr. Brownell, this consummate ruffian and his companion in crime had encountered a single man, not a large man, said the sheriff with a rather too-pointed eloquence that made Jeremy Dice again guiltily seek the face of the girl, but a man who had a large heart and fighting spirit. That man had ended two careers of crime. The community was grateful. The range was grateful. The state was grateful. And finally, Mr. Brownell was grateful.

The state had given its reward — twenty-five hundred dollars. The ranchers and townsfolk had raised this price to the extent of five thousand dollars more. And last of all the generous Mr. Brownell willingly gave out of his pocket the sum of twenty-five hundred more, making up the munificent total of ten thousand dollars that they now had in the form of ninety pounds of gold coin of the country.

So saying, the sheriff raised the suitcase and, depositing it on the chair beside the bed, stepped back with a glance at the banker as of one who knows that he has risen to a great occasion.

But what the tailor was seeing was the picture of the two giants struggling breast to breast. He looked away from that memory. No matter what their crimes, they had been valiant men. Perhaps in an earlier time they might have done great things in a different vein. And he, Jeremy Dice, was to be paid for killing them. He turned his head and looked at the girl to see if she were not laughing. But her chin was still raised, and a singular happiness was in her eyes.

184

Jeremy Dice sank back on the bed and closed his eyes.

"Take the money away," he said faintly.

"What?" cried three voices in chorus.

"It's blood money," said Jeremy Dice. "Take it away!"

The sheriff was stunned. Mr. Brownell was incredulous but not unpleased. Twenty-five hundred dollars was quite a blow even to his prosperity.

"Can you beat that?" said the sheriff, feeling more for his wasted speech than for the ten thousand dollars.

"My friend," began the banker in protest, but Mary Welling cut him short.

"He means it," she said to him softly, almost fiercely. "No, we can't understand. But that's his way. He's . . . different. Now, go away, please."

They obeyed, lugging the suitcase with them. After all, if they had not had a chance of giving that money away and of hearing the gratitude of the hero, they had gained something fully as valuable — a story that would stand many retellings. They hurried down to the eager little crowd in the street.

Mary Welling, however, had gone from the door and hurried again to the window. Jeremy Dice followed her retreating form with an abashed glance. He had hoped that she would be glad when he did this thing. Now she turned her back on him. Truly, she was other than Dottie Petwell and the girls he had known. There were recesses of her mind, he thought, into which he would never penetrate, should he live to a ripe old age. He turned these things over for a few seconds.

185

Then he called to her, but she did not turn. It seemed certain that she was very angry. "I was only wondering," he said apologetically, "if you'd maybe read to me for a little while."

She turned and came slowly toward the bed. He could not be certain, at first, because she was in the shadow, but, when she came close to the bed, he saw that there were, indeed, tears in her eyes.

"Oh," said Mary Welling, "you're a man."

She saw a queer look of pain come in his face.

"Hush," he said hurriedly. "Don't talk like that. You make me feel . . . like a sneak thief, Mary."

She glanced at him in wonder, but then resigned herself. After all, she would never be able to understand him, so she sat down and took up her book, fumbling the pages blindly until her eyes should be clear once more.

"What's all that infernal noise in the street?" cried Jeremy Dice petulantly.

At that she raised her hand. "Listen," she said, looking past him with the same starry eyes.

He bent his ear — made out a name — his own name. They were cheering him in the street.

CHAPTER
ELEVEN

The Severe Test

In spite of himself the doctor could not keep Jeremy Dice in bed forever. He was eventually permitted to sit up, then to walk a little in the room, and finally the day was named when he could leave the hotel and go his way.

On the morning of that day a middle-aged man of distinguished narrow beard and neatly trimmed mustache came to the "hero." In his language, in his manner, there was the same scrupulous care that showed in his clothes. One might have put him down for a club man who had acquired his brown on a golf links. He introduced himself as Henry Welling.

Afterward Jeremy wondered how this suave gentleman had been able to come so quickly to the point without seeming abrupt. Within a moment he had lodged with Jeremy Dice an invitation to come out to his ranch, near Chatterton, and stay there until he was thoroughly back on his feet. Stay indefinitely, if he would.

"You want to take me into your home?" said the tailor, wondering. "But you don't know me really."

"We've heard a great deal about you from Mary . . . we feel that we know you very well."

Jeremy Dice shivered at the idea of remaining any longer in the region of this town. A score of things might happen. Suppose, for instance, yonder brakeman should happen into the town and recall that Jeremy Dice was the hobo he had thrown off the train not so long ago. Or, in any of a dozen manners that Jeremy Dice could imagine, his past might overtake him — and then would come the crash. Or suppose that some venturesome youth should wish to measure himself against the vaunted prowess of Dice? The very thought turned Jeremy cold.

"I can't come," he said. "The truth is that if you knew . . ."

There seemed an organized conspiracy to keep him from telling the truth. He really wanted to unbosom himself to this grave-faced gentleman, but Henry Welling raised a prohibitive hand. "We aren't frightened by your past," he assured. "You see, I understand that, when a man reaches a certain stage of proficiency with weapons, it means that he has had actual combats. Your story, Dice, may be a story of violence, trouble, and battles. Very well, we take that for granted. But, when in spite of a turbulent life, a man remains a gentleman . . ."

Jeremy did not hear the rest of the sentence. The word "gentleman" to him was always set off in the brackets of expensive clothes, club life, butlers, and a taint of scandal perhaps in the high life. That he, a tailor, should aspire to such a position! He blinked the

188

thought away and looked sharply at the rancher. No, he was not being mocked.

"The truth is," the other was saying, "Missus Welling misses our boy." He stopped a moment, frowning to control his emotion. "She would be very happy to have you for a while, at least. So should we all." He raised his head. "Mary, say a word to urge him."

Jeremy looked at her in a species of terror. He felt that if she asked him he would go in spite of himself and risk all the dangers of the situation and all the shame that was sure to come upon him in the end. She looked seriously back at him.

"If you don't come, Jeremy, what in the world can I do with my time?"

Jeremy Dice sighed. "I'll be glad to come," he murmured, "for a day or so."

Three hours later the buckboard had whisked them out to the ranch behind the tails of a free-swinging pair of bays. For the last half hour Henry Welling had been driving through his own property. It seemed a world by itself to Jeremy Dice. An endless succession of low-rolling, brown-burned hills. Here and there was a drift of cattle. He wondered how they lived on that short, dead grass, but apparently the desert had made Welling rich. They came to the ranch house, one of those square buildings that are far larger and more spacious than they seem on the outside. Two tall stories but it was so wide that the house seemed squat. The drive wound through cottonwoods toward it, and an extensive grove tumbled back on all sides from the hill on which the ranch house stood.

There was a profusion of servants. Two to take the horses, another to open the door. Jeremy felt as if he were stepping into some feudal domain. Mrs. Welling met them in the hall, and she took Jeremy's hands in both her own. She was a quiet, gracious woman. White hair and a pathetically wrinkled forehead could not entirely obscure the beauty that had once been hers. Jeremy could see a lovely girlhood behind the years — far more beautiful than Mary, indeed.

They gave him a big, high-ceilinged room in the second story. It had a little alcove lined with books at one end. In an opposite alcove there was a great fireplace, and in the space between the big double bed was almost lost. Mrs. Welling had shown him into the room and left him hurriedly, as though she dared not stay there long. He wondered at this until he had looked about him more thoroughly. The place seemed a complete apartment in itself — the adjoining bathroom, the big, roomy closets, a family could have lived there. It was furnished in a peculiarly intimate manner also, as if they had long expected him. There were mounted heads on the walls — deer and two massive bear skulls with the monstrous claws dangling underneath. The grinning teeth made Jeremy uneasy. He found in one closet complete fishing equipment — nets, rods, and all. And clothes for wading were there also. In another closet there was a whole armory of shotguns, rifles of every caliber from a brace of Twenty-Twos up, and revolvers particularly. All had been well used. He knew enough about weapons to tell that. As he stepped back and closed the door, the truth

190

occurred to him at the same time. This was the room of the dead boy!

He gasped at the thought, but he knew that it was the fact. Those light rifles were the first he had ever owned, and the whole procession of his firearms was represented there in the closet in neat order. And this room was the boy's domain — those hunting books and novels in the library, the furs on the floor, the mounted heads. What a fool he had been not to guess it at once. They had taken him, Jeremy Dice, the consummate liar, the little tailor from the East, to fill the place of the dead son. For the void must be an intolerable and aching one in that house. He could see at a glance that the will of the dead youth had been law in this house — that the life of the establishment had revolved around the son and heir. He, the pseudo-avenger of the boy, was brought here to fill that niche for a while, at least until the pain of the loss grew less with time.

It overwhelmed Jeremy Dice. He sat down and rested his face between his hands for he felt that he was Tom Thumb in the seven-league boots. He had stepped into the shoes of a bigger man, a man capable of exchanging shots with Lew Shaler himself. He was a miserable hanger-on from the stage, a wretched scene-shifter called by chance to take the rôle of the great star. The large room dwarfed him, embarrassed him, filled him with a sense of loss. The moment he realized the truth he made up his mind to slip away as soon as possible.

But it was easier to resolve than to execute. Whether it was Mary Welling taking him out and teaching him to ride with infinite pains and much laughter, or her father

191

gravely talking over with him the affairs of the ranch and telling tales of men and events, or Mrs. Welling with her sad, quiet smile that welcomed him when he returned from an outing, he was absorbed into the life of this family. How could he leave?

He had to stay a longer while. As soon as he discovered this, he set himself rigorously to prepare in time of peace for war. In other words, he shut himself up in his room every day for some hours and practiced with that revolver of Lew Shaler's that the outlaw had worn next to his heart. He never fired it, of course, but he practiced hour after hour, whipping the revolver from the holster that he now wore strapped against his thigh. He practiced until his head spun and until his arm ached from shoulder to wrist from handling the heavy weapon. It was not that he ever expected to rival with his skill the speed and sureness of men who were practically born gun in hand, but he wished to equip himself so that, in case of a crisis coming on him, he could at least strike a blow in self-defense. So he labored arduously. He had done fine work with the eyes all his life and swift work with his fingers, and he learned, with astonishing speed, how to whip the gun out on the tips of his fingers and then whirl and point from the hip at something in the room — a corner of the mirror or the knob of a door. At length, the sinews of his forearm grew hardened to the tugging of the weapon, and his fingers were accustomed to its weight.

His sessions were discovered. For though he told the family that he was in the room reading, Mary Welling one day took him aside, very grave of face.

"Jeremy," she said, "what is it? Are you planning to go back to the old life?"

Then she told him how they had heard, downstairs, the padding of his feet as he leaped and whirled. How he had been seen through the window from the top of the barn, working with the revolver.

"It's just habit," he explained to her. "I keep in training. Because someday I may have to fight again." It was the first lie he had ever directly told Mary, and the weight of it hung in his mind for a long time.

"Oh," said the girl, and her eyes misted, "if you keep it up, sooner or later you'll go back to the old ways, Jeremy. If a man keeps ready for trouble, he'll find it sooner or later."

But in spite of that, he would not give up his work. He dared not. Also a certain confidence was growing in him and a feeling that, when the time came, he would be able perhaps to give a good account of himself. Then the test came.

They were sitting in the big living room — Mary was at the piano — when they heard a clatter of hurrying feet and excited voices. One of the cowpunchers broke into the room. There were others behind him with scared faces in the doorway. Henry Welling rose to meet the intruders.

"It's Tampico Joe and Garrison!" cried the first man. "Tampico came back from town all lit up and carrying a bottle of the red-eye with him. He got ugly . . . started to jump Garry. Some of us got at him and threw him into the back room and locked the door, but now he's smashing the door down and swears he'll murder Garrison!"

"Get Garrison out of the way."

"We've tried to. But Garry won't budge. He's ready for trouble himself. He says it's an old grudge between him and Joe, and that now's a good time to settle it. And it's murder. Garry ain't any match for Tampico. And, when Joe breaks down that door, he'll come out shooting!"

"Very well," said the rancher, "I'll go out and quiet him."

He started for the door, but Mary Welling caught him and stopped him.

"No, no!" she cried. "Dad, what could you do? Tampico is a madman when he's drunk. He'd as soon shoot you as shoot a dog."

Suddenly all eyes turned. A breath of waiting fell on the room.

Waiting for what? Jeremy Dice looked behind him. There was nothing but the wall. Then he understood. They were looking at him — at the great gunfighter. They were waiting for him to offer his services — the man who had beaten Shaler and Arizona Pete single-handed. The blood deserted Jeremy's brain. He felt the scar on his forehead tingling. What could he do? He became conscious only of the eyes of Mary, in all that room. She was staring at him in a sort of horrified wonder, questioning. He moistened his white lips.

Stay where you are, thought Jeremy Dice. *I'll go.*

Still they stared, waiting. Then he realized that the words had only formed in his mind and had not been uttered.

"I'll tend to this," said Jeremy Dice aloud and turned to the door.

CHAPTER
TWELVE

Tampico Joe, Badman

The girl intercepted him. "You won't kill him, Jeremy?" she was pleading. "You won't have to do that?"

He smiled bitterly. Kill him? Kill Tampico Joe? He had heard that hardy cowpuncher often referred to as the roughest man who ever swung a rope in the service of the rancher — too expert and ready with his gun and only retained because of his uncanny ability in taming half-wild horses. Jeremy Dice, the tailor, kill Tampico Joe? He made no answer but stepped past her into the hall. She followed. The cowpunchers fell back before the great Jeremy Dice and gave him ample room to lead the way. And Jeremy hurried on. As well get it over. If he paused, he knew that he would never be able to go on again. For there was a curious coldness in his legs and his arms, and that chill was striking in and coming close to his heart. If it ever reached that spot, he knew that he would become openly a shamefaced coward.

Even as it was, he knew that his arms and hands were useless, paralyzed. He could not have dragged the heavy revolver from its holster where it now pulled down brutally from his belt. It would have slipped through his nerveless fingers. Why go on, then, and face inevitable death? Because shame whipped him forward. He could have shrieked with hysterical laughter to think that he, Jeremy Dice, was stalking at the head of these practiced fighters, these cowpunchers of Henry Welling's. That they were holding back, trusting to him in everything, was ludicrous beyond speech. Why not turn and face them and cry desperately: "I'm a sham, a farce! I never killed Lew Shaler or Arizona Pete. I'm a cheat . . . but for heaven's sake don't make me go to my death!"

The words were even trembling on his lips. He faltered, almost turned to the men, and then he thought of the face of Mary Welling. Back there in the living room she had doubted him for the split part of a second. He had seen that doubt, and it filled him now with a sort of horror. She was trying to make up for her moment of failing faith. He heard her assuring the cowpunchers that Jeremy Dice would straighten things out. They must keep back and give him room. That was all that was necessary. He would drop Tampico Joe with a neatly placed bullet through the fleshy part of the arm or through the leg, a wound from which the drunkard would recover in a few days, all the better for the lesson he had been taught. He might even shoot the gun from the hand of Tampico Joe. Yes, that was probably what this super-gunman would do.

She's saying that about me . . . a tailor . . . and a coward, Jeremy Dice groaned to himself.

No fear of the cowpunchers flocking about Jeremy and making his work harder. They fell far back and gave him ample room. As the procession hurried out of the house and reached the path to the bunkhouse where the men slept, there was the noise of Tampico Joe, battering at the door and shouting curses at Garrison and the rest of the world — threats of vengeance and bloodshed on all the cowpunchers who had locked him up. He was no dog. He was a man, and he'd show 'em what Tampico Joe could do.

Jeremy found himself going up the path toward that hurricane of noise. The thing was incredible, dream-like. He seemed divided into two minds, one walking that path and the other far off, staring at the figure that went toward its end and wondering at it, shouting silent advice to turn and bolt. He was going slowly and more slowly now. His feet were ice, and it required a conscious effort to lift each in turn and put it forward on the path to destruction. They had turned to lead. His hands, too, dangled heavily, helplessly, at his sides. He ground his fingers together — but the blood would not come. Confused pictures darted across his brain — Manhattan — the great buildings — shadow and sunlight — the ball at Kadetzsky's. What a fool he had been not to stay and face out that small shame and square all with a simple apology to Gorgenheim the next day!

Then a consuming terror gripped him that he might not have the strength to go on into the bunkhouse. He went forward with renewed speed. Terrible speed! He opened the door of the bunkhouse. He stepped inside. It was a long, narrow, low-ceilinged room. Bunks were built onto the wall on every side. Confused blankets lay on them. Two lanterns burned and cast two circles of insufficient light. Hanging in that light were the faint wreaths of tobacco smoke, still rising since the cowpunchers rushed from the house for help.

At one side stood a young fellow, very erect but deadly pale. A naked revolver hung in his hand, and the barrel twitched up oddly now and then — the jumping nerves of the poor fellow. He knew he was condemned, and sentence passed against him, but he would not turn away from the man who was cursing him. His time was drawing short. The door at the end of the room bulged under the shocks as the drunkard flung himself against it again and again, yelling with exultation as the wood began to splinter.

More than he dreaded Tampico Joe, Jeremy Dice shrank from the pale youth. For Tampico might slay him, shame him, but the other would be a living witness of that shame. His lips writhed slowly back: "Get out of here!" commanded Jeremy Dice hoarsely.

He expected to be laughed to scorn, but instead he was astonished to see that an expression of relief swept over the face of the other.

"You order me out, Dice?" he repeated.

"Get out!"

"That's something I wouldn't take from nobody else," muttered the other. "But seeing it's you, Dice, I guess it ain't no shame . . ." And he turned and walked slowly toward the door.

The witness, at least, was disposed of, and Jeremy rubbed a trembling hand across his forehead. His face was burning hot, his fingers ice cold. But oh, fool, fool!

199

Witness? Yonder window was banked with faces. On the other side still others. And a voice behind him from Mary Welling: "Jeremy, you won't shoot to kill?"

The call shook him like a great hand on his shoulder, and at the same time he seemed to be struck behind each knee, unstringing the power of his legs. His hands, too — they would see him trembling. She would see it. He remembered how he had controlled his trembling in the shack when the sheriff broke in on him with the posse. He folded his arms tightly, high on his breast. He spread his feet farther apart and braced them. Was the shuddering of his knees visible? Every time Tampico flung himself against the door, a shock ran through Jeremy Dice.

Someone was calling — many voices. No, they were speaking to one another.

"Look at that! His arms folded! That's to show that he's giving Tampico a first chance to get out his gun. Can he beat Tampico to the draw, starting with his arms folded? It must mean he's going to shoot to kill, eh? Sure, he ain't a fool!"

It was only later that he fully understood what those voices had said. At present it was only a tangle of sound. And now the door staggered — was flung crashing upon the floor — and a red-faced, wild-eyed man stood crouched in the opening, swaying a little from side to side. He made Jeremy Dice think of a mad dog.

"Garry, you dirty skunk! Here's your time come. Go for your gun, you . . ." His voice roared a series of foul oaths. His gun jerked up to a line with Jeremy Dice's breast.

"It's murder! Dice, do something!"

Then a single shrilling cry: "Jeremy! Save yourself!"

He could not even flee. His muscles refused to act. He closed his eyes, and, when he opened them again, he was surprised to find that he was not launched into eternity. The bunkhouse was the same. The same slowly drifting wreaths of blue-brown tobacco mist were moving across the lantern light. The voices were clamoring from the windows. But Tampico Joe was oddly changed. His wild eyes were glazed over, his mouth gaped, and the muzzle of his gun was dropping in jerks.

"You!" he gasped. "You . . . Dice!" His hand rose slowly. The revolver was dropped back into the holster. "The dirty coward . . . he didn't dare face me . . . he had to send you after me." He rubbed his knuckles across his forehead. Then his voice was a whine: "Dice, I guess they ain't any quarrel between you and me. I dunno . . . I . . . I . . . been drunk . . . a fool, I guess."

Slowly, as the wonder to find himself alive lifted like a cloud from Jeremy Dice, he understood. The power of a name had driven the fumes of liquor from the mad brain of the cowpuncher and had overwhelmed him. Suddenly his blood was running once more. He went to the other with short, uneven steps.

"There'll be no trouble, my friend. Just give me your gun."

"Sure, Dice. We're friends, ain't we? Here's my gun."

Jeremy turned away with the weapon in his hand and went back toward the door. The men were boiling through it before he came to it. But the crowd split away before him. He passed awed faces on either side.

One voice: "By heaven, Dice, that was a fine thing. That took nerve."

Outside, he looked around him, dazed. The girl was not there. Yes, here she came. What was this . . . tears?

"Oh, Jeremy, I saw . . . I understood."

It pricked him to the heart with cold. What had she seen and known?

"It was for my sake . . . because I asked you not to kill him . . . that you didn't touch your gun? Because I asked you? Oh, Jeremy, it was a glorious thing to see you, standing there with your arms folded . . . just a step away from death . . . and not afraid."

CHAPTER
THIRTEEN

Calling a Bluff

"Frankly," said Henry Welling that night, "we need you. I am not young . . . the work of managing the ranch is arduous and more and more difficult for me as time goes on. I have to do my work with rough men who need a leader they will respect in order to have the best they are capable of brought out. What I'd like to have you do is to step in as my foreman . . . my manager, if that title pleases you better. You know nothing of the cattle game, but I can supply the knowledge and teach you. In five years I'd like to retire and put the ranch in your hands entirely."

Jeremy refused. In five years? By that time his name would be a jest around the town of Chatterton. If only he could leave the place while his name and fame were established without a blemish, but that was not to be. It seemed that an evil destiny chained him to the spot until in some savage *dénoûment* all the inner truth of his weakness would be known.

But he could not go. There was no place for him to flee. All his past life had become dim. Sometimes it seemed to him that his existence began with that blow of the lantern that had flung him from the top of the speeding freight train. Go back to Manhattan? When he thought of that, he thought also of the morning rides with Mary Welling, with the fresh wind out of the dawn and into their faces. If he thought of the lights of Broadway on certain evenings, he thought also of the living room of the ranch house and the faces of Mr. and Mrs. Welling in the lamplight. He liked even the cowpunchers. At first they had kept away from him, as men will avoid poison, but, since the affair of Tampico Joe, they had undergone a change of heart. Tampico Joe, retained at the express wish of Jeremy Dice, was his most ardent champion. Tampico taught him how to swing a rope. Tampico went over the range with him and taught him intimate bits of cattle lore. Tampico initiated him into the mysteries of the trail, until he began to see how it is that the cowpuncher follows a cattle path as a student reads a book — a constant turning of pages, and every page crowded with new things. He would go out into the bunkhouse at night, and always they welcomed him into the heart of the circle. He played poker with them and lost outrageously, and then won it back, for he was picking up the art of bluffing and betting high. They would also jest and joke with Jeremy Dice — except that in the midst of horseplay no one ever laid so much as the weight of a finger on his shoulder. It was apparently understood that, while one might go a long way in familiarity with Dice, there was a stopping point. When that was reached, one must stand back and give the gunfighter room. He had become an oracle.

When a new gun was to be bought, Jeremy's advice was asked. He had to consult the library and read up furiously to keep ahead of his questioners. If there was a nice question in a dispute, Jeremy was called in to settle it.

He was no longer white-faced. He had grown brown in these few weeks. He had a swing to his gait and a brightness in his eye that had not been there before. But always he felt like a man eluding a certain destiny. He had gotten away from the hounds, but they were circling, and soon they would get the wind of him and come booming down the trail. Then what a hollow heart Chatterton would discover in its newest and brightest of heroes!

He went ahead, blinding himself to the future. He expected that the end would come suddenly — some formidable figure rising in his path — some gunman who would not be daunted by his fictitious reputation. But when the blow fell, it was slowly, so that he could approach his downfall with his eyes open.

Welling came in hastily to his room one day, hardly pausing to rap at the door. He had been in town that morning. He had not even stopped to take off the linen duster as he came into the house. He locked the door behind him.

"Jeremy, my boy," he said with a troubled face, "there's a most unfortunate mess ahead of you . . . Bronc' Lewis is in Chatterton, and it's understood that he's going to send word to you that he's waiting there."

Through the space of two heartbeats Jeremy continued to stare down at the page of his book — the print ran into a gray smear. "And who's Bronc' Lewis?"

The rancher laughed uneasily. "Perhaps he's not very formidable in your eyes, Jeremy. Of course, I know your courage and self-confidence, but Lewis is a man I don't like to have you meet. There's nothing of the thug or the professional badman about Lewis . . . but he's killed his man more than once. Of course, you know all that."

"I never heard of him before. And what's his quarrel with me?"

The rancher gasped. "By the Lord, Jeremy, sometimes you startle me. Never heard of Bronc' Lewis? Why . . . well, he married Shaler's young sister. That's his quarrel with you. As I understand it, he would like to get out of this, but one can understand how it is. I suppose his domestic life isn't very pleasant until he removes the man who killed his wife's brother, eh? And that brings us to the calamity."

Jeremy swallowed. "Something ought to be done," he said faintly.

"Ah," nodded the rancher sympathetically. "I know how you feel. You've been trying to break with your past . . . and now you're dragged into a fight with or without your will. It's hard, Jeremy."

"It is."

"Ordinarily, I know you fellows with the fighting instinct. You'd go a long way for a chance at a man of Lewis's caliber. Of course, he's a more dangerous man to face than Lew Shaler was. And I suppose with his coolness and nerve . . . or lack of nerve . . . he may even have some chance against you. Though personally, Jeremy, I agree with the rest of Chatterton . . . nobody on the mountain desert has a chance against you. However, I wish there were some way of getting out of this infernal scrape. I don't fear for your sake. I only regret that you have to be dragged into the affair."

Jeremy leaned over with a wan face. "Then, Welling," he said huskily, "do something!"

"Eh? But what can I do?"

His complacence maddened Jeremy Dice. "Have him jailed for planning a murderous attack."

The rancher laughed. "You have a sense of humor, Jeremy. I can imagine *you* having an enemy jailed."

Jeremy sank back in his chair. His doom, he knew, was come upon him.

"In a way," said the rancher, "I can't help admiring the nerve of Lewis. He must know that, even if he has the luck to wound you, it would only be signing his death warrant. He'd never get out of Chatterton alive! But, ah, boy, if something *should* happen . . . no, we won't think about the impossible. I don't dare. We'll have to guard against letting this news come to Mary or to Mother. It would torture them and make it all the harder for you. But between you and me, Jeremy, this code of honor that drives men to murder is a horrible thing . . . horrible!"

"Horrible," echoed Jeremy. "I . . . I'd like to be alone, Welling."

The other nodded and went soberly out of the room.

Afterward it seemed to Jeremy that the thing had been a dream. The blow had fallen so casually that it did not seem real. But the truth was borne in on him. Two of the boys came into the house later in the day. They shook hands with him gravely.

"We've just heard. Come in to wish you luck, Jeremy, and tell you that we'll be on hand to watch you drop him."

He managed to smile at them in a sickly fashion, and they were gone.

In the middle of the afternoon the bearer of Bronc' Lewis's cartel arrived. He was shown up to Jeremy's room, a calm, bony-faced, resolute man of middle age. He announced himself as John Saunders, making no effort to shake hands. He plunged at once into the heart of his message.

"I've come from Bronc' Lewis. He asked me to tell you that he'll be waiting in front of the post office at ten o'clock tomorrow morning. You understand?"

The pale eyes of the man fascinated Jeremy, as though this were the face of the angel of death. "Yes," he murmured.

"Of course," went on the other, "we know you won't be there."

"Eh?" gasped Jeremy.

The other became suddenly savage. He made a long stride toward his host. "You skunk," he said through his teeth. "Don't you know that we've seen through you? You've put up a bluff, Dice, or whatever your name is. A mighty strong bluff, but now we're going to call your hand. When we get through with you, you won't have

208

enough reputation left around here to blanket a dog. No, sir, you won't!" He paused, glaring. His wrath seemed to be fed from within. "When I think of a low hound like you pulling the wool over the eyes of Chatterton," he went on, "it makes me sick inside, plumb sick! Why, me and Bronc' figured this thing out a long time ago. But Bronc' didn't want to make trouble. He wanted to let you go . . . only public opinion wouldn't let him stay still. We know you, Dice. You didn't kill Shaler and Arizona Pete. Kill *them?* You couldn't kill half of one of 'em! They fought about the split of the coin and killed each other, and then you come along and make your play. You tear your own clothes, and you have the nerve to cut your head to make the picture look like the real thing. And then you come to Chatterton and make a fool out of a whole town full of sensible men. And now, Dice, I bring you warning. Clear out. Bronc' don't want no trouble. He don't want to dirty up his hands with you. But he'll kill you unless you pull out of Chatterton and don't never show face here again. You can take that for final. Good bye." He stalked from the room.

CHAPTER
FOURTEEN

The Escape

There was no supper for Jeremy Dice that night. He dared not face the eyes of the family, and he sent down word that he was busy in his room to Welling who made sufficient excuses. When the dark had fully settled over the house, the tailor made his preparations for flight. It was a simple matter to escape. A drain pipe from the roof ran directly past his window and down to the ground. Along this he could easily lower himself, and once on the ground he could slip away among the trees and be quickly lost to sight. Then the dark world beyond would receive him, and, cutting across country, he would come after a time to the line of the railroad.

He wrote his farewells. To Henry Welling:

I tried to tell you a number of times. You always stopped me. It was that way from the first. I lied once. That was in the beginning, and the lie was practically put in my mouth by the sheriff. I took it up. I've no excuse to make. I've played the part of a yellow hound, and the best I can ask is for you to forget me as soon as possible.

210

To Mary:

**When you think about me and despise me, I
want you to remember this: that the reason I
stayed on, living this lie, was because I loved
you, Mary. After the first day, whenever I
tried to break away, the thought of you stopped
me. I wasn't worthy of you. Of course, I knew
that, but . . . I couldn't go. I've asked the
others to forget me, but I ask you to forgive
me.**

When he had written and sealed these notes, he
completed his preparations for departure by putting his
hat on his head. Then it was out the window and down
the pipe to the ground. It was even more easily done
than he had anticipated. The darkness of the trees at
once covered him. There was music in the house. Mary
was singing, and it seemed to Jeremy Dice a bitter and
beautiful thing at once that he should leave her life with
this sound of her voice to carry with him.

He skirted past the side of the house, and, coming to
the front among the trees, he paused and looked back
through an opening. As he stopped there, taking his last
long look at the big house, the front door was opened
and the singing of Mary Welling struck out at him.

**What made the ball so fine?
Robin Adair!
What made the assembly shine?
Robin Adair!**

211

And then the voice rose to the climax of the song —
a voice not strong, but thrillingly pure — and it went
into the heart of Jeremy Dice like the point of a knife.
That fiber had never been in her singing before. Or he
had never noticed it. Now it seemed as though, in some
miraculous manner, she were making a profession of
faith. She was calling him back, he, Jeremy Dice, the
tailor, was her Robin Adair.

Jeremy sank upon his knees under the cottonwoods
and prayed for the first time in his life. He prayed
aloud.

"God Almighty, I love Mary Welling. Keep me from
bringing her shame."

The song went on. It seemed to Jeremy Dice to be
giving wings to his prayer and lifting it up past the
treetops to the stars.

Finally he stood up. The house was silent now. The
front door closed — perhaps Henry Welling had gone
out to smoke in the open for a moment and was now
returned. Jeremy went slowly back among the trees,
reached the drainage pipe, and climbed up to his room
once more. It was like stepping into a tomb. He took
the two notes, ignited them, and dropped them on the
hearth. Once, as the flames kindled, he stretched out
his hand to stop the fire, but then he checked himself
and stood with dull eyes until the paper became a red
cinder, then black, then silver, and finally a flimsy ash
rose and drifted up the chimney. He remembered, out
of his childhood, how he had written requests to Santa
Claus and then sent them up the chimney in flames.
There went his last chance to confess.

He could not sleep. Twice he flung himself on the bed, and twice the picture of what would happen on the next morning brought him stiffly up into a sitting posture. He heard the sounds of the family, going to bed. They came to his door one by one, tapped, and said good night — Mary, Mrs. Welling, and her husband last of all.

The deep smooth voice of the man was a grateful thing to Jeremy Dice. Henry Welling was one of those who would have known how to meet death on horse or foot or in the bed of sickness. Sometimes Jeremy wondered what sin had been his, so terrible that he must make expiation in this agony? What was the divine scheme that needed a coward on the earth?

The night was running on with deadly speed. Every time he looked up at the clock, the hands had leaped forward another hour, it seemed. Presently he heard the rattling noises in the kitchen that were telltale signs that dawn was approaching. Indeed, when he looked to the window, he found that it was already gray. He stood up, helping himself with his hands on the table, and, the moment his weight fell on his arms, they shook to the very shoulders.

He went down long before the family was up and got a cup of coffee from the cook. The old Negro tried to make him eat some bacon and fried eggs, but he would not touch them.

"Mars Jeremy," said the old fellow, "I done pray for you las' night. An' heaven keep you today."

So even the cook knew. Even this old Negro would hear the story of Jeremy's death — but would he hear,

213

also, a shameful tale of weakening and cowardice beforehand?

There was not even the strength of the lie to support him now. Lewis and his companion had pierced through to the truth. They would wait until the bullet was fired, and the dead body of Jeremy Dice lay in the dust. Then they would rob the very corpse of its honor. But would Mary Welling disbelieve? No, he had only to die bravely in order to keep her trust.

He went for a brief walk among the trees, and then returned to his room. There was still a coffin air about it. After that, he went through the subtle mockery of looking at his revolver and seeing that the chambers were charged. When he picked up the gun, the muzzle quivered like a leaf in the wind. Jeremy Dice looked down at this phenomenon with a detached, almost impersonal curiosity. It was as if the power of Bronc' Lewis were reaching out and jogging his elbow with imperceptible fingertips. In a flash, it seemed, it was half past eight and high time that he should start for town.

He found his horse saddled, and Henry Welling near the rack came to meet him, shaking his head.

"By the Lord, Jeremy, you look as happy as a boy going to call on his sweetheart. Enough color to do justice to a fever. I'm not going to wish you luck, son. It's too important for that. By the way" — he grew more sober — "I think Mary knows."

"She knows?"

"She's in her room . . . weeping, I'm afraid." He paused. "Jeremy, for all our sakes, come safely back to us."

214

And so Jeremy went down the road. She loved him, then. No, not Jeremy Dice, but a ghost dressed in a lie. He spurred his horse, but fast as he rode he could not outdistance the following thought. It was the walk to the bunkhouse over again, but a thousand times longer and more terrible. He glanced at his watch. It was nine. It was half past nine. At the stroke of ten he entered the main street of the village. Not a soul on either side in the houses — except a pair of urchins playing in a front yard. As he passed, they stopped and stared at him with great eyes. Even the children knew the great Jeremy Dice.

He went on. The horse was walking, but the brute seemed to be covering the distance with gigantic strides. And not a sound in the village. Yes, there was old Jack Thomas, sitting in front of the general merchandise store, playing his wheezing old instrument, drawing it out and pushing it together again and fingering the keys deftly with his withered hands, while he rocked far back in his chair like a connoisseur listening to a symphony. Jack Thomas and his droning old songs were a village curse. Aside from that music there was no sound, however.

Jeremy turned the angle of the street, and there he saw them at last. They were grouped at windows. They filled the doors of the houses opposite the post office. They stood in groups here and there, and at sight of him a murmur went through them like the sound of the wind through distant trees. In front of the post office one man was pacing up and down. At sight of Jeremy Dice he paused sharply and remained standing still.

215

No need to have his name told. It was Bronc' Lewis. Jeremy drew rein. He could not stir — no more than if his muscles had been frozen solid. He could not stir, and now a new murmur went through the crowd. What was it? Wonder? Horror? A suspicion of the truth?

He saw that Bronc' Lewis stood with his arms akimbo, laughing silently. Perhaps he had told his story. Perhaps the truth was already known. Perhaps all these had gathered merely to see the unmasking of the coward, the liar, the cheat who went by the name of Jeremy Dice.

Then a new strain was struck up by old Thomas. It faltered. It moaned and droned through the first few notes, as though Thomas were uncertain of the pitch. Then it gathered strength, became surer. It dissolved into a golden music, pouring like a warm sun into the cold heart of Jeremy Dice. It was "Robin Adair" with the voice of the girl in some miraculous manner, singing behind it.

Jeremy threw himself from the horse, hitched at his belt, and strode forward. As he walked, there was a tingling in the tips of his fingers. His eyes were clearing. He could see clearly for the first time, as though a fog had lifted. He saw the arms of Bronc' Lewis drop from his hips, and the grimace of that silent laughter cease.

Jeremy came on, halted. "Are you Bronc' Lewis?" he called.

Every murmur in that crowd was cut off at the root. A great silence fell upon Chatterton.

"I'm the gent," answered Bronc' Lewis. "But who wants to know?"

216

"I'm Jeremy Dice, and I hear you've been wanting to see me. What about?"

"About the murder of Lew Shaler and the lie you told."

"What way do you talk?" Was this the voice of Jeremy Dice, this strong, clear, ringing utterance? "What way do you talk when you say I lie, Lewis?"

"I talk this way."

The hand of Lewis flipped up and back and came out bearing a flash of steel at the tips of his fingers. Automatically Jeremy found his own revolver in his hand.

Everything seemed to slow down, move haltingly. Perhaps it was because his mind was moving with tremendous speed. It seemed to him that the muzzle of Lewis's revolver rose slowly. He felt like saying: *You're slow. Why don't you hurry, Lewis?* It seemed to him that he circled his finger slowly over his own trigger. He picked out, beneath the chin of the other, the knot of the flaming bandanna. He was saying to himself: *Just the size of the knob of a door. I'm used to that mark.*

And just as there was an explosion from the gun of Lewis, and the muzzle of the weapon jerked up, his own revolver went off. There was a tug at his head, jerking it back, and his hat was blown away. But Bronc' Lewis had dropped his revolver and was spinning foolishly around. He fell to his knees, gasping horribly, and both hands were pressed to his throat.

Now voices broke out, shouting. Every face seemed to Jeremy half glad and half frightened, and all at once he felt that he despised these people. He walked up to the post office.

"Is there a man named John Saunders here?"

His acquaintance of the preceding day halted in midst of his stride, as he ran toward his friend Lewis. He fumbled at his hip.

"Take your hand from that gun," said Jeremy calmly. "Take your hand from that gun, you fool."

The hand of Saunders came away — empty. His face was that of a man who has been stunned by a blow.

"Saunders," said Jeremy Dice, "take your gunfighting friend and get out of Chatterton. He's not going to die. That bullet went through the side of his throat and didn't do more than nick the windpipe. But, as soon as you have him bandaged up, put him in a buckboard and get out. If I see either of you around here again, Saunders, I'll kill you as true as my name is Jeremy Dice. Don't forget."

He turned on his heels. They were swarming across the street at him, shouting. They wanted to drink with him. They wanted to shake his hand.

"Boys," called Jeremy Dice sternly, "go back. I don't want your congratulations. If I'd been at the receiving end of this show, I guess you'd be piling around Bronc' Lewis the same way. Give me room."

They fell back, amazed. He went on. He stopped beside old Thomas, who was standing up, blinking.

"Dad," said Jeremy Dice, "if you ever get tired sitting around Chatterton, come out to Welling's ranch. I'll see that you're taken care of, because I'm the manager of

218

that outfit. And . . . when you come, you can bring along your concertina. So long!"

"But," stammered the old man, "what do you mean by that? What's it for?"

"Because just now you helped me find something . . . and that thing was myself."

THE TRAIL UP OLD ARROWHEAD

A Bull Hunter Story

Frederick Faust wrote a total of five short novels about Bull Hunter, that gentle giant of a man who sees so deeply into the human soul. "Bullets with Sense" was the first, appearing in Street & Smith's *Western Story Magazine* in the issue dated 7/9/21. This was later combined with the second, "Bull Hunter Feels His Oats" in *Western Story Magazine* (8/13/21), to form the book-length novel, BULL HUNTER (Chelsea House, 1924), published under the byline David Manning (even though the stories appeared under the Max Brand byline in the magazine). In 1981 Dodd, Mead & Company reprinted BULL HUNTER, this time under the Max Brand byline, and it is now available in a paperback edition from Leisure Books. In the first two short novels, Bull Hunter is intent on tracking down the notorious gunfighter, Pete Reeve, only for the two to end up becoming partners. In "Outlaws All," the third short novel to feature Bull Hunter, appearing in *Western Story Magazine* (9/10/21) and collected in OUTLAWS ALL: A WESTERN TRIO (Five Star Westerns, 1996), Bull manages to tame the wolf dog known as The Ghost. At the conclusion of that story, Pete Reeve expresses his belief that this combination of the two partners with Diablo, the stallion, and The Ghost "'can snap our fingers at the world, even if the world makes outlaws of us all.'" "The Wolf Strain," appearing originally in *Western Story Magazine* (9/24/21) and collected in THE WOLF STRAIN: A WESTERN TRIO (Five Star Westerns, 1996), continues their story. "The Trail Up Old Arrowhead," as Faust originally titled this short novel, appearing in *Western Story Magazine* (10/22/21) as "Bull Hunter's Romance," concludes the saga.

CHAPTER ONE

Big Decision

"Something has to be done," said big Hal Dunbar, and his handsome face clouded as he spoke. His ranch foreman, listening, swallowed a groan. For nearly fifteen years he had worked the will of this heir to the great Dunbar ranch and watched the headstrong child grow into the imperious, tyrannical man, sullen and dangerous whenever his will was thwarted. But closely as Jack Hood knew his young master, he had never seen Dunbar half so gloomy as today. In his hand, as they stood in the living room, Dunbar held out a small trinket, consisting of a gold chain, broken in several places, and what seemed to be a crushed and disfigured locket.

"You understand?" he repeated, as he dropped the locket into the hand of Jack Hood.

The latter examined it carelessly, finally prying open the locket. Inside he saw the miniature photograph of a woman's face, but hopelessly marred, scratched, and crushed beyond recognition of the features.

"Good heavens!" he muttered presently, "it's Mary's locket. She'll be a wild one when she finds out this has happened." Then he started as another idea came into his mind. "But where, Hal . . . how did you get this? Or am I going crazy? Wasn't this stole from me by that skunk Dunkin, and ain't he half a hundred miles away, and . . . ?"

Hal Dunbar interrupted calmly enough: "Wait a minute. I'll tell you a few things that link up with all this. You remember it was a month ago yesterday that I asked Mary for the hundredth time to marry me?"

"Guess it was about then."

"It was exactly then," reiterated Dunbar. "That was the time she said she would marry me in six weeks to the day."

"Yes, I remember."

"Then, the next morning, that blundering fool, Bull Hunter, appeared, and we chased him."

"Chased him out of sight. I nearly rode the blue roan to death that day." The foreman grinned at the memory.

"But we didn't ride far enough for all that," Dunbar growled. "The hound must have doubled back on us."

"Eh?"

The patience of Hal Dunbar left him. Suddenly his face was suffused an ugly red. He was thundering the words: "I tell you, he must have doubled back, and he saw your daughter while the rest of us were riding our horses to death on a blind trail. That's what happened, and this is how I know. When I got back, Mary was in her room and said she had a headache. When she did come down, she wouldn't say a word about the marriage, and a little while later she said that she couldn't think of marrying me inside of six weeks. She wanted longer. She wouldn't give me any definite answer at all."

"I remember," said Jack Hood, nodding.

"You remember? Then why the devil don't you do something about it? You let your girl treat me as if she was the lady of the land and I a slave, or something." He controlled himself a little and went on: "Well, it never came into my head why she had changed her mind so quick that day. Till this morning. I was out walking in the garden, and I come on this behind a bush. You know what it is?"

"Yep. It's Mary's locket. Plumb spoiled."

"Do you know who spoiled it?"

"I dunno. Some idiot."

"She did it herself!"

"What?"

"I saw a footprint over it. That happened pretty near a month ago, but it was stamped into the ground where the garden mold was soft and where it hasn't been disturbed since. So there was a shadow of a print of the shoe left. And the print was of Mary's shoe."

"Can't be," said Jack Hood, shaking his head.

"Who the devil else around here has a foot no bigger'n a child's?"

Jack Hood was silenced.

"I can tell you just about what happened," continued Hal Dunbar. "Bull Hunter came here to see Mary. He blundered up in full view, and we chased him. He dodged away from us and circled straight back to the house. When he arrived, he found Mary alone in the garden, and he came up and talked to her. What he returned for was to give back that locket. But they talked about other things, too. And in the end Mary was so cut up that she stamped the locket he had brought her into the ground."

Jack Hood sat as one stunned. "I dunno," he repeated again. "I don't understand."

"Sure you don't," said Hal Dunbar with a snarl. "Sure you don't understand what they could have talked about. But one thing is sure . . . they weren't talking about the price of beef on the hoof! Why has Mary been glum this whole month? Why has she had a frown for me every time I came near her? I tell you that Bull Hunter has some sort of a hold on her, heaven knows how."

Her father shook his head. "Then how come she'd leave the locket lying there for a whole month, pretty near?"

"Just another proof that she was all wrought up that day. She was so excited she was blind. She dropped the locket, stamped on it, and then ran away. When her senses come back to her, she goes to the garden to look for it again, but she's forgotten just where she left it, and, besides, maybe a little dust had blown over it and kept it from shining. It was kind of under a bush, too. That explains it easy enough. And sometimes I think, Hood, that your girl is in love with that murdering outlaw."

The attack on his daughter's taste roused Hood to momentary remonstrance. "He ain't a murderer!"

"Didn't he shoot you down?"

226

"Because I got mad about nothing, picked a fight with him, and got what was coming to me. He could have killed me that day . . . he only winged me instead."

"Well, let the murder side of it go. At least you have to admit that he's an outlaw?"

"And what for?" exclaimed Jack Hood with heat. "Because a friend of his that happened to be a robber got stuck in jail? And because Bull Hunter went down to White River like a man and got Pete Reeve out of the jail? They talk about how he done it still. Sure they outlawed him for doing it, but I'd like to have one or two friends that would break the law because they was that fond of me."

"I see how it is," said Dunbar bitterly. "You agree with Mary. You want her to marry him. Well, go ahead and take her to him. Go ahead. I won't stop you."

"Listen," replied Jack Hood, "d'you think I'm a fool? I'd rather see her dead, pretty near, than thrown away on Hunter."

"Yep," said Hal Dunbar, nodding, "you show some sense. You want Mary to own the ranch one of these days. And so do I. She's the one for the place. She's the lady to do it. But" — and here he began to beat out his points by striking his fist into the palm of his other hand — "she'll never marry me while Bull Hunter is alive. Hood, for your sake and my sake and in the long run for Mary's sake, too, that fellow has got to die!"

Jack Hood wiped his perspiring forehead. "Talk softer, Hal," he said pleadingly. "You don't mean what you just said, and, if you do mean it, it's just because you're wrought up over finding this here locket and . . ."

"Send for Mary, and I'll prove I'm right."

"How? By asking her questions?"

"I'm not a fool. I don't pretend to be as clever as she is. That's one reason I want to marry her. Because I'm proud of her, Jack."

The foreman smiled and nodded. He had no real affection for Hal Dunbar, but he had a deep and abiding love for the Dunbar Ranch that he had run for so many years, and the bright dream of his life was to see Mary Hood the mistress of those wide lands.

"If it comes to the pinch, Hal," he said, "I can make Mary marry you. And I'll do it. She's learned one thing . . . and that's to obey me. I'm not a soft man. I've taught my girl to do what I tell her to do. And if it comes to the pinch, I'll order her to marry you. Ain't it the best for her? Could she ever do better? No, sir. She couldn't."

"Maybe she couldn't," said Hal Dunbar, greatly mollified. "And . . . you go as far as you like about persuading her, Jack. I've tried my hand long enough. Here it is three years since I first started to get Mary to marry me, and now I'm further away from it than ever. But I aim to find out where I stand. Will you call her in here?"

Jack Hood looked at him earnestly for a moment, and then went to the door. "Mary," he called.

His voice rang through the hall, and finally the answer came, thin and small, from a distance, swelling suddenly out at them as a door was opened.

"Coming, Dad."

They could hear her feet tapping swiftly down the stairs. At the door she paused before she came in and smiled at them, very beautiful with her dark hair and her dark eyes. Hal Dunbar lowered his own glance quickly. "Jim Laurel just come over from White River way," he said carelessly, "and Jim gave us some news might interest you. You remember the name of the gent that stole your locket from Jack?"

"Dunkin was the name, wasn't it?"

"That was it. You got a mighty good memory, Mary. Well, Jim says that Dunkin's been caught."

"Oh," said the girl, "and did they get my locket from him?"

Hal Dunbar looked up at her in open admiration. For a moment his own conviction that she knew all about the locket was shaken, but he went on. "No, didn't hear Jim speak about any locket. But it's quite a story . . . that yarn about the taking of Dunkin. There was another fellow with him, an outlaw, of course. They got cornered. The other gent was filled full of lead, and Dunkin surrendered."

"Who was the other man?" she asked without too much interest, for many such tales had she heard, and this was by no means violent compared with some.

"The other man?" said Dunbar, apparently trying to remember, but in reality watching her like a hawk. "His name," he finally drawled, "was Bull Hunter."

Dunbar had expected some slight paling, some infinitesimal start, for Mary was always well poised, but the result of his bluff was astonishing. Every sinew in her body seemed to be suddenly unstrung. She dropped into the chair behind her and sat, watching them with a deadly white face and numb lips that kept repeating the name of Bull Hunter soundlessly. There could have been no greater proof than that sudden change of expression. She loved Bull Hunter. Her father bowed his head. Hal Dunbar stared at her as one who has lost his last hope in life.

"It was a joke, Mary," he said gloomily. "It was just a trick to find out where you stood. And it worked a lot better than I expected . . . or a lot worse."

The color struck back into her face in a wonderful manner. "Are you telling true, Hal?" she cried. "They . . . they didn't kill him?"

He shook his head, sick at heart.

"Thank God!" cried Mary Hood.

And then she realized how completely she had betrayed herself. She saw it in the bowed head of her father and the drawn face of Hal Dunbar. She rose to escape, but at the door she turned and faced them.

"It was a cowardly thing to do," she said. "It was a base, base thing to do. But I thank you for it, Hal. Do you know that I've been in doubt of how I really felt about him? But now you've helped me to know the truth. I love him. I'm proud of it."

CHAPTER
TWO

Imprisoned

For a long moment after she left, the two men struggled to recover from the shock, and then Jack Hood rose and began to pace the room.

"I don't believe it," he said. "I can't believe it. Think of throwing her away on an outlaw and . . ."

"You were defending him a minute ago," said Dunbar bitterly.

"Curse him!" said Jack Hood with emphasis. "To sneak in here and take her away from you like a thief . . . why, he hasn't seen her more than three times."

Hal Dunbar writhed as much in shame as in anger, crying: "What did he do? How did he talk to her? That great, stupid block of a man. A child has more sense."

"It's what is called an infatuation," decided Jack Hood. "I'm going up to try to talk her into her right senses. If I can't do that . . ."

"Well?"

"I'll take her away, to begin with. There are ways of teaching girls obedience. I'll find one that will work."

"What would you do?"

"Leave that to me. I guess you want me to go far enough?"

"As far as you like," said Dunbar miserably. "Of course, I ought to give up the fight now, and, of course, I won't. I love her still, Jack. And I've got to have her. Do anything you can. I think you're right. This is an infatuation. Good heavens, how could she live with that penniless scoundrel? He's already under the ban of the law. He'll probably be a robber and a murderer in addition to being a jail-breaker before long. And Mary loves comfort, loves all the things that money can buy for her. Jack, get her for me, and I swear that neither you nor she will ever regret it."

It was the first time in his life, perhaps, that he had ever spoken so humbly. Jack Hood grasped his hand, and then hurried from the room with the will to do or die. Straight to the door of Mary's chamber he went and found it locked. In return for his noisy rapping she finally opened it a fraction of an inch.

"What . . . ?" she began, but he violently pushed the door open the rest of the way and entered.

It was his way of asserting his mastery. He had used it with his wife until her death. He had always used it with Mary. In fact, the foreman had reduced his way with women to a philosophy. It was to give them everything they wanted without question or hesitation. But, when they crossed him on an important point, he suddenly became adamant — more than that, almost brutally aggressive. When he came in, however, he received another shock. His daughter's face was flushed, and tears were on her cheeks. He interpreted this to suit himself, manlike.

232

"I'm glad to see you've got your senses back," he said. "You made a fool of yourself down there. But it ain't so bad that you can't make up for it. Hal still wants you. Heaven knows why, after the way you've acted."

"But I don't want him," she answered disdainfully. "I detest him."

"Eh?" sputtered her father, amazed.

"Suppose it had been true," she gasped out. "Suppose they had really cornered Charlie Hunter. He'd fight to the last drop of blood in him. Oh, don't I know the sort of a man he is? But suppose it were true. How do I know what's happening to him? Dad, we've got to get him away from . . ."

"Look here!" interrupted her father angrily. "D'you mean to tell me that you been up here crying like a baby because of what might happen to Bull Hunter?"

He shook her arm, but there was no resistance. The spitfire he had known as his daughter was gone, and in her place stood a misty-eyed girl he hardly recognized. Some strange thing had happened to change her, and the grim old fellow very shrewdly guessed that it was love, indeed. It abashed him and puzzled him. Also, it profoundly enraged him.

"You've played the idiot once too often," he said sternly. "Hal knows about everything. He has the locket that Bull Hunter brought back to you and . . ."

"Do you know what he did?" said the girl with a sudden transport of enthusiasm. "He took that locket and brought it to me. But he wanted it for himself. I was like a foolish girl. He talked like a knight of the old days. I wanted to try him out. So I told him he could keep the locket if he would capture Dunkin and turn him over to the law. And he did it." She laughed with excitement at the thought. "He captured Dunkin alive and brought him to a jail. Then one of his friends, Pete Reeve, tried to rescue Dunkin and did it . . . but got caught himself. Charlie Hunter didn't know of it until he came back here to tell me he had captured Dunkin as I asked him to do. But, when I told him what had happened, he turned on me and told me he scorned me. He talked to me as no man ever talked to me. He showed me how wickedly vain and foolish I had been. Three men were in peril of their lives because I had asked him to do a thing in which I had no real interest. Nothing but a whim. And, when he knew Pete Reeve was in jail, he swore he would get him out or die in the effort. And that's how he left me. He'll never see me again, Dad. But he did what he said he would do. He went down to the jail . . . he smashed the wall of it . . . he took his friend away and was outlawed for it." She threw out her hands in a gesture of what was both appeal and triumph. "And, when I know a man like that, how can you ask me to love such a fellow as Hal Dunbar?"

Her father bit his lip. It was even worse than he had dared to suspect. "Love is one thing and marriage is another," he said. "You got your children to think about when you marry. How could you take care of children if you married a wild man like Hunter?"

"If I love him, everything else will take care of itself."

"Bosh!" roared Jack Hood.

She shrugged her shoulders.

"Now listen to me," he said, lessoning her with his raised forefinger.

"I'll listen, but it's no good."

"Mary, I've worked all my life to smooth the way for you to this marriage. It means the whole Dunbar estate, girl."

"It means an unhappy life."

"Who is this Bull Hunter? A big, stupid block of a man, as simple as a child."

"He's a man who will risk death for his friends . . . who will ride for weeks and risk his life again to do the foolish thing I asked of him. Do you call such a man a stupid block?"

"I've reasoned enough with you," said her father. "Now comes the time to just tell you what you'll do. You'll marry Hal Dunbar, girl, if I have to drag you to it."

She looked at him with a sort of fierce contempt that changed slowly to wonder and then to fear. "Do you think for a minute, Dad, that even if you would do such a horrible thing, Hal Dunbar would accept such a marriage? Hasn't he the pride of his family?"

"He's got pride enough, but he's in love . . . bad. And he'll do anything to get you. Understand? Look here, Mary. I'm fond of you, but I'm fond of the work I've given my life to. That work has been to make you the lady of the Dunbar Ranch, and you're going to be that, whether you want it or not. Is that clear?"

"Perfectly," she said faintly. "But you don't understand, Dad. There aren't such things as forced marriages these days."

"Aren't there?" he said sneeringly, red with his anger. "I tell you there are a lot of queer things happening in these mountains. I've got men following me would swear black was white any minute, if I said the word. I got men who'd be witnesses and swear you looked happy when you got married. And here's another thing, my lady. Suppose Hal Dunbar took it into his head that the only way to get to you was by removing Bull Hunter? D'you think he'd stop a minute? No, he'd go out and get Hunter and smash him flat. He's bigger'n Hunter. He's stronger. He's a better shot. If you do love Charlie Hunter, think of that a little bit. He's in a sea of trouble now, and you ain't throwing him any life preserver if you get Hal on his trail."

He went to the door.

"I'm not asking you for any promises, Mary. Treat me square, and I'll be the easiest father you ever seen. Cross me, and I'll raise more rumpus in a minute than you ever seen in a year. Understand? Now think this over till morning. That's plenty of time. Take every angle of it and give it a look. It's worth taking your time about."

And so he was gone. It was a very unnecessary touch, but he could not resist it. As he closed the door behind him, he turned the key in the lock and removed it.

The moment she heard the sound, the lips of Mary Hood curled. She had been badly frightened before.

She was badly frightened now, remembering the brutal ways in which he had treated her mother. But, when she heard that turning of the lock that proclaimed her a forced prisoner, she revolted. It was just a little too much.

She went naturally to the window. To climb down would be the simplest thing in the world. There was a drop of ten feet to the ground from the first row of windows, but that would be nothing to her. The main problem was where would she go once she was on the ground? Easy enough to get there, but where flee once she had escaped?

The influence of Hal Dunbar spread over the mountains very, very far, and every soul in the ranges knew that she was expected to become the wife of the rich rancher. No matter in which direction she rode, she would be quickly taken at the first house where she stopped for food or shelter and returned to the ranch. She laughed with angry amusement. It was utterly absurd, and yet it was a little terrible, too. Then she looked beyond the treetops and across the wide domain of the Dunbar Ranch. In the old days what girl would have thought twice if a king had asked her to marry him? And certainly Hal Dunbar, in a way, was a king among men. His word was law. That very fact made her tremble again. His word was law!

Still she could not believe that the whole affair was more than a hoax to break her spirit. She refused to take anything seriously until evening, when there was a tap at the door to warn her, and then the rattle of a key in the lock. Presently without requesting permission to enter, the door swung open, and the old Chinese cook appeared.

Now, the old Chinaman had been the pet and the object of the girl's teasing all her life, and her face brightened when she saw him. But the old fellow placed a tray of food — at least they were not going to try to starve her — on a chair and backed out the door, keeping an immobile expression. She went after him, calling out in anger, but he stepped quickly into the hall, and the door closed in her face.

The grating of the lock had a new meaning to her now. It declared very definitely, that her father had meant what he said. They were going to try force. If the old Chinaman, whom she had teased and petted all her life, could be turned against her so easily, what trust could she put in any man on the ranch?

CHAPTER
THREE

Flight

The men were coming in from the bunkhouse for supper, and very soon she could hear the hum of their voices in the big dining room below. She had been a queen among them for many a year, and now she called up their faces one by one, searching for a friend she could trust. But the faces were grave and hard. Jack Hood was a grim master, and he had chosen grim men to do his bidding, men who would follow him without question. If she had been a queen among those rough cowpunchers, it was merely because she was the daughter of the boss and the prospective wife of the ranch owner. Certainly there was not one among them whom she could take into her confidence.

Also that hum of voices made her unutterably lonely. She was used to perfect freedom. She was used to the open. And now the cold fear of the prison entered the girl and made her quake in her chair. But where could she go? There was only one place, and that was to Charlie Hunter, big and fearless and trustworthy to the end, she knew. Somewhere in the northern mountains he lurked. How she could find a way to him when the posse that was hunting for Bull Hunter and Pete Reeve

239

had failed was another mystery, but the attempt must be made. Otherwise — there was the marriage with Hal Dunbar. She had looked forward to it all her life without repulsion. But now that it was inevitable, it became a horror.

She could do nothing until she was reasonably sure that the people of the house were in bed, for at any time during the evening her father might come to ask her decision. She dreaded that coming, for she feared that she might become weak under another verbal attack.

The long hours wore away, and the noises of life in the house were at last hushed. She waited still longer, hooding her lamp so that not a ray of light could reach either the window or the door. Then she began her preparations. They were comparatively simple. She put on a riding skirt and packed some changes of clothes in a small bundle. Then she strapped the light Thirty-Two revolver with its cartridge belt around her waist and put the big, flaring sombrero on her head. She caught a glimpse of herself in the half-darkened mirror, and the sight of the slender body and the pale face with wide, frightened eyes, disturbed her. She was surely a small force to be pitted against the brains of Jack Hood and the force of Hal Dunbar. Yet, she went on with only the terror now that someone might come before she was out of the room.

She opened the window with infinite pains, lest there should be a squeak of wood against wood or a rattle of the sash. But there was no sound, and she leaned out the window. What had seemed so simple during the daylight now became a desperate thing, indeed. The dark ground seemed a perilous distance below her, and what if her foot should slip as she climbed down toward the sill of the first window from which she was to drop? She lifted one leg over the sill and listened again. The wind was full of whispers like light laughter. Perhaps they were in the garden, the watchers of her window, and laughing at her attempt to flee. Or what if they should see her climbing down and take her for a robber? In that case they would shoot without warning, no doubt.

Yet, she went on, though fear made the grip of her hands weak and kept her foot slipping from its hold as she climbed. She reached the broad molding above the window of the first story. She dropped perilously toward the lower sill and then lost her balance and toppled back. The scream that jumped into her throat swelled to aching, yet she kept it back. It was a short fall, but to the girl, as she shot through the air, it seemed death must come at the end of it. Then her feet struck deeply in the garden mold, and she toppled on her back. She lay a minute with the breath knocked out of her, slowly gasping to get it back, and then picked herself up with care.

She was unhurt, a little muddy from the newly wetted garden soil, but otherwise as sound as when she began the descent. She turned now straight across the garden to the barn. There the mare, Nancy, whinnied a greeting and rubbed a soft muzzle against her cheek. The girl cast her arms around the neck of the horse and hugged the familiar head close to her. Here, at least, was one true friend in a world of enemies.

241

The saddling was a slow process, for every now and then she had to stop to listen to the noises in the barn, little creaking sounds as the horses stirred on the wooden floor and very like the noise of men, approaching stealthily to seize her. But at last the saddle was on, and she led Nancy out the back door of the barn, let down the bars, and stepped onto the muffling grass of the field beyond. Then into the saddle, trembling when the leather stirrup creaked under her weight in mounting. Then down the hollow, fearful lest one of the horses in the neighboring corrals might neigh and bring an answer from Nancy.

But there was not a sound. Looking back, the house on the hill was huge and black, and Mary Hood wondered how she could ever have been happy in it. She had hardly drawn one great breath of relief when the deep night of the trees closed over her. She had ridden through those trees a hundred times before at night, but always in company with others, and now they were changed and strange, and the solemn, small noises of the night were before and behind her.

Her heart began to fail her. She would have turned back to the house of Dunbar and to all that waited for her there, but something made her arm weak to numbness, and she could only let Nancy go as she pleased. The little bay mare went daintily and wisely. She knew every nook and cranny of that wood. Every stump and tree and every root that worked up out of the ground was familiar. Once or twice a twig snapped under her foot, but on the whole she kept to the noiseless ground.

242

She understood that this was a secret expedition as well as if she had been able to understand human speech, and, though like any other horse she was not at all fond of traveling in the dark, she did her best to take care both of her mistress and herself, keeping her head high and her ears pricking as a wise horse will in dangerous country. Once or twice she turned her head and snorted a soft inquiry, wondering at the slackness of her rider's rein, but Nancy was the last horse in the world to take advantage of the loose feel of her bit. She neither lagged nor hurried, and, when they came out of the wood, she poked her head into the breeze and started off at a gentle gallop.

Mary Hood let the horse go as she would. Her way led north. That she knew and little else, for she had heard a rumor that Pete Reeve and Bull Hunter were in the Tompson Mountains. Since the mare had chosen that way by instinct, it began to seem that her ride was fated to succeed. Moreover, the wind of the galloping exhilarated her, and the darkness was no longer complete. Instead, the stars burned closer and closer to her through the thin mountain air.

Dunbar Ranch was whirling away under the hoofs of Nancy, and the old Mary Hood was disappearing behind her. It gave her an aerie feeling, this journey out of one life and into a new one. She could not guess her fate at the end of this trail, except that there would be dangers to pass, and in the end, when she found Bull Hunter, if she were so lucky, she had not the slightest idea how he would receive her. Perhaps he would cling stubbornly to all that he had said in their last talk, and

243

he had spoken bitterly enough. But, whatever his personal attitude might be, she knew that he would help her to go wherever she might choose. How to find Bull Hunter? The Tompson Mountains themselves were huge — an endless wilderness of peaks. And how should she reach them unseen by men who might recognize her?

However, those were questions that would take care of themselves. In the meantime to reach the Tompsons required a two days' journey, and she remembered now with a start that she had taken no provisions with her. Neither had she more than touched her supper that night. She gathered the reins to turn back, but at this moment Nancy shied from a white stone and doubled her speed straight north. All people in danger are superstitious, and Mary Hood took that little incident, coming when it did, as a sign from heaven that she must not double back.

The stars were beginning to fade when she reached the first foothills, and by sunrise she was among the upper peaks, desperately hungry and with an ache at the base of her brain from the lack of sleep. Nancy, too, was very tired. She plodded willingly on, but her head was neither so proud nor so high. She had ceased thinking for herself and, like every tired horse, was surrendering her destiny into the hands of the rider.

At the first small stream they reached, a tiny trickle of spring water, the girl dismounted and bathed her face and throat and let Nancy drink a little and nibble some of the grass near the water. Then she went on again, greatly refreshed. Her sleepiness grew less now that the sun was bright, and with that brightness her chances of success seemed far greater.

But before very long she knew she was coming into a district crossed by many riders, and it would be far wiser for her to lie low until late afternoon or even until the evening. Looking about her for a shelter, she found a grove of aspens, with their leaves flashing silver when the wind struck them and a continual shiver of whispers passing through the trees. So she rode Nancy into the middle of the little wood, unsaddled her, and tied her on a long rope to graze or lie down as she pleased. For her part, she found the deepest shadow, unrolled her blankets, and was instantly asleep.

When she wakened, she was lying in a patch of yellow light. A branch, snapping under the hoof of Nancy as she grazed, had awakened her. Mary Hood sat up, bewildered. She had fallen asleep at about ten in the morning. It was now fully six in the evening, and the sun would be down very shortly. She had been sleeping cold for the last hour perhaps, and the rising sound of the wind promised her a chilly night, indeed.

She went methodically and mechanically about her preparations for the night ride, feeling more and more the folly of this journey to an unknown end. First she looked anxiously to Nancy, examining her hoofs, looking her over with minute care, while Nancy followed her mistress about and seemed, with her sniffing nose, to have joined the inquiry. Nancy seemed perfectly sound. And that was the most important thing just now. That, and the fact that her stomach was crying for food.

Mary was so hungry that her hand shook when she saddled the mare. She mounted and rode out of the wood. She had barely reached the open, however, when she whipped Nancy around and back into cover. Over a nearby hill jogged half a dozen horsemen, and at their head she recognized the formidable figure of Hal Dunbar. Her first impulse was to give Nancy the spur and ride as fast and as far as she could away from the pursuers. But she was already out of the country with which she was thoroughly familiar, and she felt that, even though she out-distanced the horses behind her, she would eventually be caught in a long chase. Certainly Hal Dunbar would not spare money or horse-flesh to catch her.

She followed a second and really braver impulse. She tethered Nancy in the center of the wood and crept back, on her hands and knees literally, to the edge of the copse. There she lay in covert and watched the coming of the horsemen. Her father was not among them, by which she was given to understand that he had taken other groups of men to hunt in different directions. But the rat-faced Riley, the close lieutenant and evil genius of Hal Dunbar, was among those who now brought their horses from a lope to a stand not twenty yards away. It seemed to the girl that, when once any pair of those keen eyes turned in her direction, they would pierce through her screen of leaves and reveal her. But, though many eyes turned that way, and she shrank in mortal fear each time, no one came closer.

"You see, it's what I told you," Hal Dunbar was saying. "She didn't come this way, and, if she did, she'd have ridden a lot farther. That would be her instinct, to jump on Nancy and ride like mad until the mare dropped. No sense in a woman. She wouldn't have the brains to cache herself away for the day and start on again at night."

The girl smiled faintly to herself.

"You're the boss," said Riley sullenly. "But I think she's got more brains than you credit her with, and, if I was you, I'd search every hollow and cave and clump of trees and old shack you can find right about in here. This is the distance she most likely went if she stopped a little after it was full day. If I was you, I'd begin and hunt through that bunch of aspens."

"All right, go ahead and search through 'em."

Mary Hood cast a frantic glance back toward Nancy. She could reach the horse in time to spur ahead of the pursuers, but she found suddenly that fear had stolen the strength from her body, and a leaden heart weighed her down.

"Wait a minute," called Hal Dunbar as Riley started toward the trees. "No use doing fool things like that. We'll ride for White Pine tonight. That'll be a good starting place for us tomorrow. No, I'll go to White Pine. Riley, you'd better take the trail to the hollow. And remember, you and the rest of the boys, when you see her, go out and get her. If you have to be rough, be rough. If you can't stop her without dropping her horse, shoot. I'll be responsible if any danger happens to the girl in the fall. But I'm not going to have that ungrateful slip get away from me. Understand?"

They nodded silently.

"And the lucky fellow who gets her for me will have nothing more to worry about in life. Understand? I'll take care of him."

One by one she watched them nod — sober, gloomy-faced men. If any illusion had remained to her that these cowpunchers were fond of her, that illusion was instantly dispelled. Whatever affection they had for her, they had more for money. And bitterly she recognized in this the result of the hand-picking of her father. Now the group split and rode in opposite directions.

CHAPTER
FOUR

Relief

They spread, as though fate had directed them, to the right and left of the northern course that she had mapped out for herself. Luckily for her that cunning Riley did not have his way. She feared and hated the man for his insight, and, lest he should turn back to take a look at that grove of aspens as soon as the big boss was out of the way, she no sooner saw both groups of horsemen out of sight than she swung into the saddle and sent Nancy flying down the hollow toward the north.

A two minutes' ride brought her into another copse, well away, and, reining there, she turned and saw that Riley had indeed turned back toward the grove with his three companions. He disappeared into it. Presently she heard his shouting. She waited for no more but gave Nancy the rein again and fled on straight north. She had no immediate fear. Riley had found the impression of her body in the soft mold under the trees, and certainly he had found the sign of Nancy. More than that, he would doubtless be able to read her trail running north and follow it swiftly, but he and his men rode tired horses that had been urged hard all through the day, and she herself was on a runner as fresh as the wind. Moreover, the night would soon come and blot out the trail for them.

It was unlucky, of course. It meant that they had picked up the direction of her flight, at least, and they would follow hard, buying new horses when they rode out the ones they were on at present. Yet, too much hurry would spoil her game. Besides, she was weak from hunger and felt that she dared not risk collapse on her own part by hard riding. In thirty hours she had had only a bite of food.

When she dismounted at a water hole to let Nancy drink, she herself went to the pure trickle of water that ran into the pool, and the taste of the water made her head spin. Certainly she must have nourishment before long, or she could not keep the trail. A squirrel scolded at her from a branch above. And the girl looked up at the delicate little creature hungrily. Looking coldly and calmly at it, she forgot that she had always been horrified in the past when men shot these pretty little things out of the trees. Hunger and flight were deeply changing Mary Hood.

But she dared not fire a shot. There was no sound among the hills behind her, no neigh of horses, no clangor of iron-shod hoofs against the rocks. But she knew that the pursuit was coming slowly and surely behind her, and she must not help them along with such sign posts as rifle shots, or even the report of a revolver. The little Thirty-Two that she had balanced in her palm she shoved back into the holster and climbed again into the saddle and went on. Still, as she went, she looked back over her shoulder. The squirrel sat upon his branch, quite ignorant of the fact that he had been a small part of a second from death, and chattered a farewell to her.

Then the evening closed darkly around her, and they began to climb rapidly toward the summit. It was the weariest time in the girl's life. She dared not think of food now, because it brought an almost irresistible desire to weep and complain, and she felt that tears would be a foolish waste of necessary strength. Nancy went valiantly and skillfully about her work, but cat-foot though she was, she stumbled again and again. It was a wretched excuse for a trail that they were following, and, moreover, it was all strange country to Nancy. She was used to the sweeping, rolling lands of the Dunbar Ranch where a horse could gallop with never a care for her footing. She was much at a loss among these ragged rocks.

It must have been about eleven o'clock when they got over the summit and saw the mass of dark ranges, pitching down before them. The loftier masses of darkness against the stars, far north, were the Tompson Mountains. She might reach their foothills in the morning, if she were lucky.

Now, with Nancy laboring down a slope, the eye of the girl caught the wink of a campfire in the midst of the trees. A thousand thoughts of food rushed into her mind. A banquet or a crust of bread? She hardly knew which she would prefer. And straightway she sent Nancy scampering recklessly toward that cheerful spot of light.

All at once the light went out. Mary Hood reined the horse with a groan. She was in country now where she could not be known. But this covering of a campfire at the sound of an approaching traveler was not an auspicious sign. Many a ruffian, she knew, sought a refuge from the punishment of the law among the Tompson Mountains and the neighboring ranges with their intricate tangles of ravines.

Sadly the girl swung her mare's head to the right. In vain Nancy tossed her head. For fear lest the mare whinny, Mary reached over and tapped the muzzle of the bay, and Nancy, as though she understood that silence was desired, merely snorted softly, and went on sullenly with ears flattened. She was a company-loving horse, was Nancy, and she had caught the scent of companions of her own kind, no doubt, for the wind was blowing toward them from the place where Nancy had first seen the spot of light. The wind was coming toward them, and it blew — Mary Hood reined her horse sharply. Of all the tantalizing scents in the world there is none to the hungry man like the fragrance of frying bacon, and that was the odor that came richly down the wind to Mary until her mouth watered and her brain reeled. At once she forgot all caution. She wheeled Nancy and rode straight toward that scent. If there was danger, she would meet it gladly, but first she must have some rashers of that bacon. However grim these men might be, they would not refuse a woman food.

Yet, they might guess her a man, perhaps a pursuer on their trail, and so she began to call as she came

252

closer, hallooing clearly through the woods till faint echoes came tingling back to her from the higher slopes. Still she saw nothing. She was riding through the utter black of the night. And then, under her very nose, someone said: "Pile up the fire again, boys. It's a woman."

A tongue of flame was uncovered — they had framed the fire with a blanket and a dry branch thrown upon it filled the woods around her with uncertain waves of light. It made the whole scene wild beyond description, but wilder than the strange old trees were the three men who walked boldly into the light of the fire. It was not their size that dismayed her. Though they were all stalwart six-footers, they were nothing to the giant bulk of Hal Dunbar or Bull Hunter. But the faces of these men made her quake, and, forgetting all thought of hunger, she wished suddenly to flee. Yet flight would be more fearful than to stay and face the danger bravely. For they were not men to be eluded if they wished for any reason to detain her.

A family likeness united the three men of the mountains. All were of one stature, tall and gaunt and wide of shoulder, powerful and tireless men, she could guess. All had streaming hair, uncut for months, and their lean faces were covered with scraggly beards. But the hair of one was gray — she guessed him to be a man of fifty — and the black-haired fellows beside him were doubtless his sons. All three looked at her from under heavy scowling brows with little bright eyes. They were armed to the teeth with revolvers and hunting knives, and their rifles leaned against the trees around the fire in convenient reaching distance. Habitually their gestures strayed to their weapons, fondling the butts of the revolvers, or toying with the knives, or idly fumbling with the rifles. Even a child would have known that these men did not keep the law. Their eyes were never still, their heads forever turning, and everything bespoke of that restlessness of men who are hunted by men. The fear of an outraged society was upon them.

No matter how much she wished to retreat, now it was too late. The hand of the father fell on the bridle rein of Nancy and drew the mare with her burden toward the fire, and the two tall sons closed in from either side. They seemed doubly formidable at this close range. Mary Hood could not move. Her arms hung limp. Her head sank.

The two boys spoke not a word. But they drew close to her with grins of strange pleasure. One of them took her nerveless hand in his huge, grimy paw, and, lifting it, he showed it to his brother and laughed foolishly. And the other touched her skirt, smiling into her face with eyes that flickered like lightning from feature to feature and back again. She thought them half-witted, or entirely mad.

"Hey, Harry, Joe!" cried the father. "What d'you mean, starin' the lady out of face like that? Been a long time since they seen a girl, and they mostly don't know how they should act. But they'll come around. Don't look so scared at 'em. They ain't going to do you no harm. Here, climb out'n your saddle and sit down and rest yourself."

254

It was the sweetest of sweet music to the girl, these hurried words, together with the sharp reproof to the two big fellows. She got out of the saddle but faltered the moment her heels struck the ground. She was weaker than she had thought. The old man was instantly beside her and had his arms beneath her shoulders.

"Get some water. Don't stand there like idiots," he called to Joe and Harry. "Step alive or I'll skin you. The lady's sick. Sit here, ma'am. Now rest yourself against that log. Wait till I get a blanket. There you are. Put your hands out to that fire. Heaven a'mighty, if you ain't plumb fagged."

The kindness was so unexpected, so hearty and genuine, that tears welled up in the eyes of the girl as she smiled at the wild woodsman. He squatted beside her, patting her hands.

"I know. You got lost. Been riding a couple of days and nothing to eat. Well, these hills would bother 'most anybody. But wait till I get a cup or two of coffee into you and a few slices of . . . hey, Joe, lay your knife into that bacon and get some off . . . and cut it thin. I know the way a lady likes her chuck."

CHAPTER
FIVE

Good News

At least the cooking of Sam, as he said he was called, was better, she was willing to vow, than any she had ever tasted. What matter if the bacon was greasy and cut thick in spite of his injunctions, and the flapjacks unspeakably greasy, and the ample venison steak only half done, and the coffee bitter beyond imagining. It was food, and her blood grew rich and warmly contented again as she ate.

Sam himself sat cross-legged beside her and a little to the front, overseeing all the operations of that meal, applauding each mouthful she took with a smile and a nod, and eagerly following the motions of her hand as though he himself were half starved and the food she ate were nutriment to him.

As for the two gaunt sons, they were kept busy following the orders of their father to bring new delicacies for the girl, or to build up the fire, or to unsaddle her horse, or to cut evergreen boughs for her bed that night to lay in a comfortable place beside the fire. They obeyed these instructions with a sort of hungry eagerness that amazed her. She began to be surprised that she had ever feared them. When they had done something for her comfort, they stole small, abashed side glances at her and flushed under her answering smile. They were like half-wild puppies, fearing the hand of man but loving the touch of it. Her heart welled up in pity for them and their ragged clothes and their fierce lean faces, grown mature before their time.

"Just think of how you near missed us," said Sam as the meal reached an end at length. "When we heard your hoss come up the wind, I had the boys douse the fire. Never can tell in these parts. Wild folks are about, ready to do wild things, and old Sam ain't the one to be took by surprise. No, sir!"

He watched her face keenly and covertly to discover any doubt of the truth of his words.

"I don't think you are," replied Mary Hood. "The fire went out by magic, it seemed to me. And I only blundered on it again by chance."

"You see?" said Sam triumphantly to the two sons. "That's what I tell you all the time." He turned to the girl again. "Joe and Harry always want to leave the fire burning and slip off among the trees. If anybody comes up to snoop around the fire, then it's hunter hunt hunter. And there you are. But my way is best. Never take no chances. Keep away from trouble. Run from a fight. That's my way of doing things. In spite of all that, you'll find trouble enough in this world."

Still, he watched her while he talked. She answered his glance with difficulty, looking gravely and steadily into his face. Presently he laughed, embarrassed.

"Now, we're a rough-looking lot ourselves," he continued. "What might you take us to be, lady? You ain't told us your name yet."

"My name is Mary Hood." *Why conceal the name?* she thought.

"Mary Hood? That's a pretty plain name for a girl like you. But going back where I stopped . . . how might you make us out, Mary Hood?"

She sighed. It might infuriate him if she told the truth, but, if she lied, they would soon suspect her dissimulation. "I only guess, of course," she said softly. "You are men who have been very kind to me, and, of course, I like you for your kindness. You are prospectors, perhaps, in the mountains."

"You make us out that way, eh?" said the old man, rubbing his hands together. "Hear that, boys? This lady has an eye, eh?"

She added slowly: "And I think that, perhaps, you are also fugitives from the law. I don't know. I only guess. But I'm afraid you're unhappy fellows, and the law hunts you."

The three men became three moveless statues, looking gravely at her, not with anger or sullen spite but as men who have been judged and cannot appeal from the judgment.

"You knowed all the time, maybe," said old Sam, sighing. "Well, I guess it sort of shows on a man after a time."

She did not answer but smiled faintly to make amends for her discovery of the unpleasant truth.

"After all, I'm kind of glad you talked straight. It ain't so much to me to be found out, but it's hard on the boys. I didn't know they was marked as plain as that. Yes, it's hard on Joe and Harry."

"I only guessed by the way you hid the fire and because your clothes haven't been mended by a woman for quite a while . . ."

"That won't do, Mary Hood," said the father gravely. "It's more'n all that. It's in our faces, plain as day. If we was all dressed up in fine clothes for Sunday and shaved and got shiny boots on and walked into a town, we'd be knowed just the same. The minute the gents seen us, they'd reach for their guns, and the minute the ladies seen us, they'd let out a screech and cover their faces."

"Did I scream when I saw you?" asked Mary warmly.

"You done your screeching inside, by the look in your eyes. When Harry took hold on your hand, you looked like you was about to die. Like his fingers was claws, maybe. Besides, you got more nerve than most ladies. Good many would've plumb fainted when they seen us. Ain't it happened before?" He smiled gloomily at the thought. "I was made what I am partly . . . and partly I made myself. But the curse I carry around with me, Mary Hood, is my two boys that I've made like myself. But what could I do? Could I give 'em up? I ask you that, with their ma dead, could I give 'em up?"

He laid a frantic hold on her arm. And she placed her other hand over his.

"Of course, you couldn't," she answered, close to tears. "Of course, you couldn't give them up. And nobody with sense would blame you for keeping them with you. You'd have been unnatural not to keep them."

"D'you think so?" he asked earnestly. "You ain't saying that just to make me happy?"

She glanced at the wild, savage faces of the boys and controlled a shudder with difficulty. "No," she answered, steadily enough. "If you love them, it will repay them for anything else they lose."

"Maybe it would," he muttered. "And it helps a pile to hear you say it. A woman knows what's what about kids. They're her business. Sometimes it seems to me like every good woman was sort of a mother to every man, good or bad. That's why I prize you, saying what you do about me and the boys."

Her heart swelled with the pity of it. Perhaps for six months, perhaps for a year, these three had not sat so close to a girl and talked as they were talking now.

"If the boys' mother had lived," he continued, "it would have been different. She would have knowed what to do with 'em, whether for me to leave 'em or to bring 'em along. She looked a pile like you, come to think of it. She wasn't so clean cut around the mouth and the nose, and her eyes wasn't so big, quite, but she was a mighty pretty girl, she was. And she had an eye that looked straight . . . as straight as yours." He went on to ask: "Her being honest . . . that's bound to help make the boys decent in the long run, ain't it?"

"Yes," answered Mary Hood softly. "Oh, yes, oh, yes. It surely will."

The old man sighed deeply. Then a light grew in his eyes, the light of the dreamer. His face changed and softened, and it lifted so that his glance traveled past the dark treetops to the purity of the stars. "One of these days I'll give 'em their chance," he murmured. "I'll get a stake . . . a pile of money. Ten thousand would do it. Yes, sir, with ten thousand dollars I'd send the boys away . . . maybe to Australia. And I'd give them five thousand each. And I'd tell 'em to start a new life, and . . ."

"You could go with them," she suggested.

"Me? Go to Australia? Nope, this is my land. This is where I was meant to die, and this is where I mean to die. Maybe with my boots on . . . I hope so. I know these mountains like faces, and they know me, pretty near. Or they'd ought to. But I ain't going to talk any more about myself. Only seeing you sit there all so quiet and ready to listen and sort of asking me ahead, well, I slipped into this talk sort of nacheral. A good woman is like that. She starts on a gent, explaining how he ain't quite so bad as he seems. After a while, maybe, she makes him be what he tells her he is." He shrugged his shoulders, and then his eyes cleared and became more sharply aware of her. "But how come you to get lost?"

She paused to think. If she told him that she had indeed lost her way, there were nine chances out of ten that he would discover the lie before he had talked with her for five minutes. But, if she confessed everything, she might win him to her side and then whoever followed her trail to these men would get no further clues from them.

"I am running away," she said simply.

At a stride the two tall youths came near with their great shadows standing boldly against the trees behind them. They looked earnestly down into her face as though by her confession she had been drawn closer to them. They, the fugitives, could understand the pursued.

But Sam was chuckling. "You had a little change of words with the gent you're engaged to marry, maybe, and got so mad you figured you'd leave and never see him again? Was that it?"

His random guess had struck so close to the truth that she stared at him.

"Maybe I hit it the first time," he said, nodding. "Yes, I guess I pretty near did."

"Very nearly. But the whole truth is that I have a very stern father."

"Hmm. I've heard tell of such things before, but mostly the fathers I've seen has been stern just to do good to their boys and their girls."

He pointed the moral of his tale with a meaningful glance at the two youths.

"I think so," she confessed. "But sometimes they may be wrong. And this father of mine wants me to marry a man I don't love."

"Hmm," said Sam, nodding. "But maybe you could get to love him? Has he got money and looks and . . . ?"

"Everything," she said frankly.

"But you're kind of fond of somebody else, most like?"

"Yes."

"What sort is he?"

"An outlaw."

The three stared at her, each with parted lips.

"How come?" said Sam softly.

Mary's voice rose a little. "Because a friend of his was in jail, and he went and broke into that jail and brought his friend out."

There was a gasp — of relief, perhaps — from the three.

"He ain't any gunfighter, then?"

"No, he's as gentle as a child."

"But he busts into jails, eh?" said Sam smilingly. "Well, that sounds kind of queer, but they ain't any use judging a man till you've seen him. And it's better to wait till you've watched him work. But you've talked pretty straight to me, Mary Hood."

"Because I think you can help me and will help me," said the girl.

"Maybe," he said, nodding. "To get to this man you're bound for?"

"Yes. Perhaps you know him. A very big man, Charlie Hunter . . . ?"

"Never heard tell of him."

"And a very little man called Pete Reeve."

"Pete Reeve!" cried Sam. "Him?" His face darkened, but finally he drove his angry memories away.

"You do know him?"

"Sure I know him," said Sam gloomily. "Him and me has tangled, and he got all the luck of the draw that day. But sometime maybe . . . ," he paused abruptly. "But this ain't helping you. You turn in and sleep the sleep of your life now. When the morning comes, I'll point out the way to you. I come on the trail of Pete Reeve yesterday."

Mary Hood was sitting up, smiling with happiness. All her worries were on the verge of being solved, it seemed, by this veteran of the wilderness. "How could you tell that it was his trail when you crossed it?"

"By the way his noon fire was built. Fires is made as many different ways as clothes. Some likes 'em small and heaped to a point, and some likes 'em wide, and some lays 'em to windward of rocks, and some is just as happy when they can get a place in the lee of a hill. Well, I come on Pete Reeve's fire and knowed it as well as I know his face. Not having none too much good will for Pete . . . you see, I talk as straight to you as you talk to me, Mary Hood . . . I took the trail on Reeve for a while and seen that he had a big man on a big hoss with him. I just done those things because it was like dropping in on Reeve and having a chat with him without the trouble of talking, reading his trail like that. And I seen the way he was pointing his course before I turned back and took my own way. I think I can point him out to you within a mile of where he'll be in the morning."

CHAPTER
SIX

Bull Hunter

She slept that night as she had never slept before. With the sense of danger gone, the happy end of the trail made her relax in body and mind. When she wakened, the sun was already in the treetops, and the men had been up long since. Nancy came out from among the trees to whinny a soft inquiry after the well-being of her mistress.

Breakfast was a liberal feast, and then Sam took her out from the clump of trees and pointed out her way. She had stolen close upon the Tompson Mountains during her ride of the night before. Now Sam pointed out one bald-headed monster of a peak high above the rest.

"It's named after Old Arrowhead Mountain," he said. "Which is a hard trail and a long trail, but hardest of all and longest of all for another gent to follow. I dunno what's a better way of bothering a sheriff and a posse than to take the trail up Old Arrowhead. But I'll tell you how you'll most like get to Pete Reeve and the man you want. Old Arrowhead is split right in two with a gully about twenty feet wide and a thousand deep, pretty near. Them twenty feet is crossed with a bridge.

And they's only one bridge. The way to it is right up to the top of that shoulder. You aim a straight line for it and ride out your hoss, an' they's a good chance that you'll get to 'em before they cross, unless it comes that they make a pretty early start. Of course, they may not be laying for Old Arrowhead at all. I can't read their minds, but yesterday afternoon, late, it sure looked that was what they was heading for."

He said good bye to her and brushed away her thanks.

"I'm always kind of tickled," said Sam, "to have white folks see me and know me. The next time somebody tells you that Sam Dugan eats his meat raw, you laugh at 'em. And don't you believe 'em when they tell how I kill folks when they sleep. It ain't my way. But the trouble is, I think a lot more of other folks than they think of me. My country don't own up to me no more, but that don't somehow stop me from owning up to my country. S'long, Mary Hood."

So he was gone among the trees back toward his morning campfire. As for Mary Hood, she looked a moment toward the place where this ragged philosopher had disappeared, and then she loosened the rein and gave Nancy her head. The mare ran eagerly to get the chill of the morning out of her legs, and in half an hour they were commencing the ascent of Old Arrowhead.

It was distinct in the range. It was bigger and more barren, a great crag of granite, thrust in the midst of beautiful, forest-bearing summits. It was hard footing for a man and very bad footing, indeed, for a horse.

Even the mountain sheep, those incomparable climbers, were not very frequent visitors in the regions where Old Arrowhead soared above timberline, a bare, black mountain whose stones were polished by the storms.

She kept Nancy true to her work, for now the sun was rolling higher and higher in the sky. Unless Pete Reeve and Charlie Hunter wanted a ride in the heat of the day, they would start from their camp at once — if, indeed, they had ridden this way at all.

Now that she felt she was close to them, she began to wonder more and more how she could face them with her story. Above all, Bull Hunter might be changed from the simple, lovable fellow she had known. The taint of the lawless life he had been forced to lead might be in him, for all she knew. There were a thousand possibilities, and each one of them was gloomier than the other.

But there was no sign of smoke above her that made her more and more certain that Sam Dugan had been wrong, and the two had not ridden this way at all. For the very reason that she doubted, she pressed Nancy the more until the brave little mare was stumbling and sweating in her labor up the steep slope. While the girl worked up the slope in this manner, the first news of Charlie Hunter came down to her. It was nothing she saw, but a great voice that boomed and rolled and thundered above her. It was so great a voice that, when she shouted joyously in answer, her voice was picked up and washed away in the torrent of sound. The singing grew greater, rapidly, as she drew closer. Finally she could make out that the sound was double. A thin, weak, straining voice ran like a rough thread in the huge singing of Bull Hunter. The girl smiled to herself as she hurried on.

She came on a picture that turned her smile to laughter. The campfire was smoldering without smoke to the windward of two big rocks. The breakfast had been cooked and eaten, and the two companions sat together with their shoulders braced against boulders and sang a wild ballad to begin the day. The difference between the volume of their voices was hardly greater than their difference in physical bulk. It seemed that Charlie Hunter, huge of shoulder and mild of eye, could crush Pete Reeve with the weight of a hand. The latter was a little, time-dried man with the agility of a squirrel in body and eye. Yet, it was he who beat the time for the music with an emphatic hand and an arm that swung widely up and down, while the careless giant lolled back and without effort allowed that enormous voice to swell and roll from his throat. The singing of Pete Reeve was a mere sharp edge for the roar of Bull Hunter.

Mary Hood paused to marvel at the carelessness with which these two hunted men exposed themselves. In the first place, they had allowed her to come right up to them, unseen. In the second place, they were not even close to their horses that roamed about, nibbling the grass fifty yards away — one a small cow pony and the other a black giant close to seventeen hands tall and muscled in proportion. Diablo was a fresh marvel to Mary Hood each time she saw the horse.

A moment later, as she swung out of her saddle, the eye of Pete Reeve discovered her. His mouth froze over the next sound, and with staring eyes of wonder he continued for another instant to beat the measure. Then he came to his feet with a shout.

"Mary Hood!" he called, running to her. "By the eternal . . . Mary Hood!"

She let him take both her hands, but her eyes were for the giant who had come to his feet with almost as much speed as his companion. There, on the side of the mountain with only the empty blue sky to frame him, he seemed mightier of limb than ever. Then he came slowly, very slowly, toward her, his eyes never shifting. "Mary," he kept saying, "how have you come, and why have you come?"

"Heavens, man," cried Pete Reeve, stamping in his anger and disgust, "when your lady rides about a thousand miles through a wilderness to see you, are you going to start in by asking questions? If you want to say good morning, go take her in your arms. Am I right, Mary Hood?"

Somewhere in her soul she found the courage to murmur: *You are.* But aloud she said: "I've run away, Charlie, and there was only one place in the world I could go . . . and that was to you."

His bewilderment was changing gradually to joy, and then full understanding came upon that slow mind. He checked a gesture as though he would sweep her into his arms, and instead he raised her hand and touched it with his lips. She loved him for that restraint. He had changed, indeed, from the Bull Hunter she had first

269

known, growing leaner of face and more active of eye. He looked years older, and it seemed to the girl that in his eye there was a touch of that same restless light she had noted in the faces of the Dugan men. The brand of the hunted was being printed on him.

Now he drew her to a place, sitting between them, and the questions poured out at her. So she told all the story, only lightening the blame on her father for shame's sake. But, when she came to the story of the Dugans, Pete Reeve exclaimed: "I never knew he had it in him. I've had the hatchet out for Dugan ten years. Here's where I bury it."

"Heaven only knows," said Charlie Hunter, when the story was ended, "what I've done to deserve you, but now that you're here, I'll keep you, Mary, to the end of things. Not even Hal Dunbar can take you away while I have Pete Reeve to help. I'd given you up forever. We were going to ride north and get into a new country where neither of us is known. But the three of us can do the same thing. Can you stand the hard travel, Mary?"

Mary Hood laughed, and that was answer enough.

"We can't keep on the trail we started," explained Pete Reeve. "I'll show you why."

He took her to the edge of the gulch of which Sam Dugan had spoken. It was a full twenty-five feet across and a perilous drop between sheer walls of over eight hundred feet. Once a narrow bridge had been hung across the gorge, and she could see far below the broken remnants of it.

270

"We've got to go back and climb around to the right. Costs another day's work, the breaking of this little bridge."

"But why do you keep your camp so carelessly?" asked the girl. "Anyone could have surprised you, just as I did."

"No enemy could," answered Pete Reeve. "There's our guard, and he can't be beat."

He pointed to a great, gray-coated wolf dog who lay stretched at full length among the rocks a little farther down the hill.

"The Ghost knew you," said Reeve, "or he would've give us warning when you were a thousand yards away. And now we'll have to pack up and hurry."

"Somehow," murmured the girl, "I don't like the thought of turning back. It seems unlucky."

"We got to," answered Pete Reeve, "because we got to make a big circle and come through Patterson City and get a minister. Then we can hit north again."

And to this, of course, she had no reply.

CHAPTER
SEVEN

Caught in a Trap

When Sam Dugan came back to his camp, he gave quick orders. "Get the shovel, Joe," he commanded, "and cover that fire. We done a fool thing in starting it in plain daylight. That smoke can be seen about five miles away. Get the hosses ready, Harry. We mooch out of here as fast as we can. We sure stayed too long."

Indeed, they had never lighted a fire in broad daylight for many a month at a time, but for the sake of Mary Hood they had broken that time-honored custom. When the father saw that the preparations were well under way, he stepped to the edge of the circle of trees and walked around it, keeping an anxious watch on the hill tops and the big, swift slopes of the mountains. Presently over a southern crest he saw four horsemen, riding straight for the trees.

"Quick!" he shouted to his sons. "We got to run for it!"

As he turned back into the trees again, his eyes flashed toward the west, and he made out a scattering half dozen more hard riders, breaking out of a grove. It was easy to see that they had been surrounded, and that the aim of all those men was the group of trees from which the smoke had been seen to rise. He made his resolution at once and went back to tell it to his sons.

"They got us dead to rights," he said quietly. "They's ten men in sight and maybe ten more coming after them. Boys, we might make a long stand in these trees and hold 'em off, but they could starve us to death. They's just one chance we got again' bad luck, and that is that these gents ain't on our trail. If they don't know us, it's all right. If they do know us, we're lost. Now, go right ahead with your packing up, but take it slow. When they's a bunch of gents around asking questions, it's always a good thing to have plenty to keep your hands busy with. These folks will be here *pronto* . . . they're here now. I'll do the talking."

Even as he spoke, the first of the riders crashed through the shrubbery beyond the trees, and a moment later from every side ten grim-faced men were in view, surrounding the little clearing where the campfire had burned. They discovered old Sam Dugan in the act of tamping down the tobacco in his corncob pipe. He continued that work and even lighted the pipe while the leader of the newcomers was speaking. He was such a man as Sam Dugan had never seen. He and his tall sons were dwarfed by the mighty dimensions of this man. The stout gray horse from which he dismounted was downheaded from the weariness of bearing that load. He had been riding long and hard, and the lines of continued exertion had made his handsome face stern. He looked fiercely up and down at Sam Dugan.

273

"We've come on a trail that points pretty straight toward this campfire you've just put out so quickly," he said. "We want to know if you've seen a girl pass this way? A very pretty girl riding a bay mare?"

Sam Dugan stopped and rubbed his knuckles through his beard in apparent thought. "Girl on a bay mare. I dunno, I dunno. Boys, you ain't seen anybody like that around in sight? Nope, I guess we ain't seen her, partner. Sorry about it. Runaway, maybe?"

His calm seemed to madden the big stranger. But the latter controlled an outburst. "Look here, my friend," he continued, "I'm Hal Dunbar. I'm a little outside of my own country, but, if you were down there, they'd tell you that I'm a man of my word. And I promise you that, if you have seen that girl in passing and can give me any idea where she's gone, I'll make it mighty well worth your while to talk."

"Well," said Sam Dugan genially, "that sounds to me like pretty easy money, and, if I could get a hold on it, I sure would. But what I don't know, I can't very well tell, and I guess that's about all there is to it."

"Hmm," said Dunbar, growling. "It looks that way. But bad luck is certainly following me on this trail. However, we'll keep trying. Heads up, boys. We've got a lot more riding before us, it seems, and I hoped that this might be the end of the trail."

Jack Hood tapped his friend Riley on the arm. "There's something a bit queer about it," he said. "That fire was burning high just a minute ago. Look at that stick, poking out through the dirt. It ain't half charred. That fire wasn't burned out by no means. But inside of five minutes they got that fire covered and their packs about made up. I admit there ain't very much in those packs, but still it's fast work. And now them two long lanky gents are lazing along as if they didn't have any hurry at all in mind. Looks to me, Riley, like the three of them made up their minds for a quick start a while back, and then changed their minds *pronto*. Talk to 'em, Riley."

The latter nodded. Big Hal Dunbar was turning away gloomily when Jack Hood stopped him with a signal.

"Might get down and give the hosses a spell, chief, eh?" suggested Riley to Dunbar, and the latter, receiving the wink from Jack Hood, nodded. Instantly the crew was on the ground, lolling at ease.

"Been long on the trail?" asked Riley, fixing his shoulders comfortably against the trunk of a tree.

"Tolerable long," said Sam Dugan, steady in his rôle of the silent man.

"Been coming down from the north, maybe?"

"Yep, coming down from the north."

"We're up from the south. My name's Riley. This is Jack Hood."

He named all those present. Then he paused. The challenge was too direct to be passed.

"Glad to meet you gents," returned Sam Dugan. "My name's Sam Saunderson, and these are my two boys, Joe and Harry."

The latter turned and grinned at the strangers.

"You been prospecting coming down, I figure," said Riley, glancing at the packs.

"Nothing particular," said Sam Dugan. "Raised color a couple of times. That was all. Nothing particular much to talk about."

"What part you start from?"

"Might say I didn't start from nowheres. Me and the boys have been traveling for so long we don't hardly stop much anywhere."

It was dexterous fencing and done, withal, with such consummate ease that Riley could not tell whether the old fellow was making a fool of him or telling the truth. He shrewdly suspected the former, but pinning down Sam Dugan was like pinning down another old man of the sea. He was slippery as oil.

"Mostly mining?" he suggested.

"Oh, I dunno. Ain't much that I ain't turned a hand to for a spell, take it all in all."

"But liking to follow the rocks, I guess you been around the Twin River Mines, maybe?"

"Sure, I've dropped by 'em."

"How long back?"

"Oh, long about five year back, I guess, or maybe it was only three. I dunno. Dates and things like that get out of my head pretty easy."

"If you was there five year back, I guess you knew Jud Chalmers, maybe?"

"Guess maybe I did. Think I remember having a drink with a gent by that name."

"The Jud Chalmers I know don't drink," said Riley, his eyes brightening.

"Well, well, he don't?" said mild Sam Dugan. "Come to think about it, I guess it was a gent named Jud *Chambers* I had that drink with."

"Maybe you knew Cartwright up there?"

"Cartwright? Lemme see. Well, I'll tell you a funny story about a gent by name of Cartwright. It was back in . . ."

Riley sighed. He had thought a moment ago that he was cornering this ragged mountaineer, but Sam Dugan had skillfully wound out of a dangerous corner and come into the clear again. It was useless to try to corner a man who told stories. It was like trying to drink all the water in a lake to get at a bright pebble on the bottom of it. After all, the man was probably entirely innocent of having seen Mary Hood. Riley gave up, and, in sign that he had surrendered, he rose, yawned, and stretched himself.

"I guess we're fixed, ain't we, Joe?" asked Sam Dugan.

Jack Hood's eye had been caught by something beneath a dry log at one side of the clearing. He crossed to it.

"All fixed," answered Joe Dugan.

"Sorry to leave you gents," went on Sam Dugan. "But I'm leaving you a right good camp. Got good water over yonder, and there's all the wood and forage an army would want. Get my hoss for me, Harry. So long, gents. Sure hope you find the girl, stranger."

And so speaking, waving genially to each of them as he passed, Sam Dugan sauntered across the clearing, leading his horse. The call of Jack Hood stopped him as he was about to disappear among the trees. He turned and saw the foreman of the Dunbar Ranch, standing with his hands on his hips.

"You say you ain't seen my daughter, eh?"

"That girl you was talking about? Well?"

"How long have you been in this here camp?"

"Oh, about a day."

"Then," said Jack Hood, "I got to tell you that my daughter has been here, and she sure has been here inside of twenty-four hours, and she sure couldn't've come without being seen."

"That's kind of hard talk, ain't it?" said Sam Dugan, feeling that a crisis had come.

"It sure is, but it's straight talk. Maybe you got your own reasons for not talking. I dunno what they are, but they sure ain't any good. Here's all the sign I want that she was here."

He raised a hand in which fluttered a filmy bit of white, the handkerchief of a girl.

CHAPTER
EIGHT

Hot Pursuit

With a triumphant yell Hal Dunbar shot across the clearing and caught at the handkerchief as though it had been the girl herself. Then he turned furiously on Sam Dugan. "Now," he said, "will you talk?"

"It kind of looks like I'd been doing a lot of lying that got me nowheres in particular," said Sam Dugan, grinning and quite unabashed. "But still, I don't figure any particular call I got to talk. Not by a pile. So long, gents."

As he turned, Hal Dunbar, with a leap, barred his way. It was a hard trial for Sam Dugan. It was not the first time he had been halted, but it was the first time a rash intruder had escaped unscathed. The odds were too greatly against him. Though Sam Dugan loved a fight above all things in the world, he loved best of all a fight that he had a chance of winning. Moreover, he guessed shrewdly that this man alone would be more than a match for him. Hal Dunbar was no mere mountain of flesh. From head to foot he was the well-knit, nervous type of fighting man, quick of eye and steady of hand. That he was now ready to fight there could be no question. Every muscle in his big body was trembling with eagerness. In his youngest, strongest prime Sam Dugan would have thought twice before he engaged this giant among men.

"Saunderson," said Hal Dunbar grimly, "or whatever your name is, I've been on this trail for a long time, and there are twenty other men riding it with me. And I'm going to keep them riding till the trail comes to an end. That girl is going to be found. Why not speak up like a man and tell me what way she went?"

"You got eyes to find that trail, ain't you?" asked Dugan savagely.

"Mind your tongue," said Hal Dunbar, his eyes instantly on fire. "Look around at these mountains. Chopped up like the waves in a wind. I could spend a month hunting over ten square miles unless I have a lead to follow with my men."

"That sounds like sense," said Sam Dugan, and he spoke more kindly now. He liked the fact that the big man had not yet threatened him with the power of numbers. He liked the big, clean look of Hal Dunbar.

"Why do you cover her trail?" asked Dunbar.

"Because she asked me to."

"If a runaway child of six asked you not to tell where it had gone, would you keep the promise?"

"But she's a pile more'n six, my friend."

"She's not more able to take care of herself."

"That may be true, but she's going to one who will."

"An outlaw," said Hal Dunbar hotly. "A fellow she's only seen three times. It makes me turn cold when I think about it. Suppose she marries him . . . though, heaven knows, how they can ever get to a minister . . . what would come of their life? What of their children?"

This blow shook Sam Dugan to the core. And Hal Dunbar followed it.

"Saunderson, if that's your name, you're saving that girl if you tell me how I can follow her. I've an idea that in certain places you may be wanted, my friend. I think that the sheriffs, any one of them, would be very much interested if I brought in you and your sons. Eh?"

Dugan watched him narrowly, decided that the big fellow could do it if he wished, and then determined that he would make his last stand here rather than be ignominiously captured. Yet, he would avoid the blow as long as he could. He was greatly relieved by the next words of Hal Dunbar.

"I could take you and your boys along. You look suspicious. You must have bought those clothes five years ago, and yet you've been traveling for five hundred miles near towns. Very queer. But instead of forcing you, I'm going to do the opposite. Saunderson, if that girl gets into those mountains with Hunter, she's lost. No man on earth could follow her. For heaven's sake, tell me where she's gone. I love her, I tell you frankly, but I want to stop her in the first place simply to keep her from marrying an outlaw. Is she cut out for camp life like this? Answer that, Saunderson, and you know that camp life in winter . . ."

"Yes, you're right," said Sam Dugan gravely.

"I'll give her a home, and she won't have to marry me for it. I know you're only trying to do what's best for the girl, so, you see, I open my mind to you.

Another thing . . . you and your two boys might need a bit of a stake. I'm the man who can fix that for you."

"How high would you go?" asked Sam Dugan curiously.

"Five thousand . . . ten thousand," was the unhesitating answer.

Sam Dugan sighed. "I guess you're straight about her," he admitted. "I figure, if you'll pay ten thousand just to find her trail, you sure love her, and . . ."

"Part of that sum I'll give you in gold. I'll give you my note for the rest and . . ."

"I don't want the money. I only wanted to find out if you was really fond of her. And you are. And I'll show you the way. But maybe you're too late." He pointed. "Look yonder to Old Arrowhead. Ride straight for the center of the hill, and you'll catch her trail. And ride hard."

A muffled shout from Hal Dunbar and he was in the saddle on the weary gray. His men followed him with less alacrity. Sam Dugan, however, watching them stream out of the grove and across the open country, shook his head as he turned back to his two sons.

"Word-breaking don't generally bring no good to nobody," he said doubtfully. "Maybe I've been all wrong to tell the big chap. But I done what I thought was right."

Meantime, though Hal Dunbar was urging his men on with shouts, the gray could not keep pace. Only fox-faced Riley drew back beside the big boss. "There's a gorge up there and a small bridge across it," he said.

"If they get across that and have time to break down the bridge, we're done for."

Hal Dunbar groaned and returned no answer except by spurring his horse cruelly. The gray, attempting in vain to increase his speed, stumbled and staggered and then went on with greater labor than ever. His head was hanging, his sides working like bellows, and the noise of his breathing was a horrible bubbling, rasping sound. Riley, with a glance, knew that the gray was being ridden to death, but he said nothing. Advice, when Hal was in one of his furies, only maddened him the more. They were working up the hill rapidly.

"They've sighted us!" called Riley at length, "and, if they start for the bridge, we can never stop them."

"Where are they?" asked Hal Dunbar, ceasing for the instant his steady labor of flogging the gray and spurring him on.

"Up yonder. There's their guard!"

He pointed to a gray streak, moving with incredible speed and smoothness across the face of the hill.

"The wolf . . . The Ghost," replied Hal Dunbar with a significant nod. "The beast is their outpost, eh?" He groaned as he spoke. "One last try, boys!" he yelled to his men. "Drive the horses. We've only got seconds left to us!"

He suited his actions to his words by spurring the gray again. But that honest horse had given the last of his strength already and had been running on his nerve alone for some time, crushed under the huge burden of Hal Dunbar. Now he threw up his head as though he had been struck and fell like a clod.

He dropped straight down, and, Dunbar, unhurt, kicked his feet out of the stirrups and ran on, cursing. There was no pity for the horse in him, only a wild anger that he should be hampered at such an hour even by the horseflesh that he rode. But he had not taken a dozen steps when a rifle exploded far up the slope, and a bullet hummed wickedly past him, yet it was far above his head.

"Shall we rush 'em?" he called to Riley.

"Rush Pete Reeve?" said the other sneeringly. "I'd as soon rush dynamite. Get the boys to cover."

He was following his own suggestion as he spoke, and the rest of his men needed no order. They dived from their horses and took up their positions behind the big rocks that littered the side of Old Arrowhead Mountain. Riley found a place close to the ranch owner.

"I dunno what's happened," he said. "They ought to be across that bridge by now, but they ain't. Listen."

The rifle snapped above them again, and one of the men cursed as the bullet splashed on the rock near his head.

"He's just shooting to warn us that he means trouble," interpreted Riley. "When Reeve shoots to kill, he either kills, or he doesn't shoot at all. Ain't many bullets he's wasted on thin air, I can tell you. He's trying to hold us back with his lead, and that simply means that something has happened to the bridge, and they can't get across it."

"Then," gloated Hal Dunbar, "I've got 'em in the hollow of my hand."

284

He shouted a few orders — men scampered from rock to rock until the cordon had been drawn in a perfect semicircle all the way around the crest of the hill. The three fugitives were hemmed in with only one way of escape without a fight, and that way led across a twenty-five foot gorge.

"If you got a white handkerchief," said Hal Dunbar, "put it up on the end of your revolver for a flag of truce, and then go up and talk to them. Tell them that all I want is the girl. The rest of 'em can go. Tell 'em that. Also, tell them that, if money talks to them, I'll hold as long a conversation as they want."

"D'you mean that you'd let both of 'em go, if they give you the girl?"

"Sure I don't," replied Hal Dunbar, chuckling. "But I want to get her out of the way before I finish those two skunks. So make all the promises you want to make. A promise made to an outlaw isn't a promise at all, is it?"

"Maybe not . . . I guess not," conceded Riley.

Straightway he tied a white handkerchief to the end of his revolver and waved it above the rock. There was an answering call from up the hill.

"All right!"

Riley rose and started up the slope.

CHAPTER
NINE

Facing the Enemy

Little Pete Reeve, lying prone among the rocks at the crest of the hill and maintaining a sharp outlook, kept watch for Hunter and the girl. She had lost her courage with the firing of the first shot and sat white and sick of face, leaning into the arms of Charlie Hunter. The big man soothed her as well as he could.

"But if something happens," she kept saying, "it will all have been my fault. I laid the trail that they followed to you."

The voice of cunning Riley came to them from the other side of the knoll, where he had been stopped by the challenge of Pete Reeve before he should clear the top and be able to see that the bridge had actually fallen and that the three were definite and hopeless prisoners.

"Look here, Reeve," said Riley, "we know what's happened. Something's busted the bridge, and you fellows can't get over. Now, the boss doesn't care about you and Bull Hunter. He's got only one thing he's thinking about . . . and that's the girl. He says, if you'll send her come down to him, he'll let you two go clear."

"That's something for the girl to answer, not me," replied Pete Reeve. "Keep back a bit while I talk to them." He turned, walked back up the slope, and then said softly: "You've heard what he said . . . maybe he means it and maybe he don't. I think he'd have his fill of fighting before he got us. But he could starve us out. That's the straight of how we stand just now. I want you to know that pretty clear. I also want you to know that there ain't one chance in a million of you or anyone of us getting away. This is a tight trap. But, if you want to stay, then the three of us stick, and welcome."

"There's only one answer to give him," said the girl, rising to her feet steadily enough. "Tell him I'm coming. But first I want to hear Hal Dunbar swear to let you both go free."

"Shall I tell him that?" asked Pete Reeve.

"No," interrupted Charlie Hunter, speaking for the first time. "Tell him to go back. He gets no sight of Mary Hood."

"She'll talk up for herself, I guess," said Pete Reeve, gloomy, as he saw the one possible chance of escape slipping away from them.

"No," answered Bull Hunter solemnly. "She's come up here to me, and she's mine. I'd rather have her dead than belonging to Hal Dunbar. And she'd rather die than leave us. Is that so, Mary?"

It was the first time that either the girl or Reeve had heard the giant speak with such calm force, but in the crisis he was changing swiftly and expanding to meet the exigencies of that grim situation. He stood up now

— and the little hollow at the top of the hill was barely deep enough to cover him from the eyes of the men down the slope.

"Tell him that," he continued.

"It's a crazy answer," muttered Pete Reeve. "You've got no right to put words in her mouth."

"Every right in the world to," said the big man with the same unshaken calm. "In the first place, I don't trust Dunbar. A gent that'll hound a woman the way he's hounded Mary Hood ain't worth trusting. Suppose we die? I wouldn't live a happy day in a hundred years if I knew I'd bought my life by sending Mary back to Dunbar. Pete, you know I'm right."

The little man nodded. "I couldn't help hoping it would be the other way."

"You can leave if you want to, Pete. They'll be glad to let you through. That'll make their odds still bigger."

The little man smiled. "Leave you in a pinch like this?" he said. "After what we've been through together?"

He turned sharply toward Riley. The latter, during the conversation between Reeve and Bull Hunter, had stolen a few paces farther up the hill until his eye came above the ridge. There, across the gap where there had once been a bridge, was now empty space. Riley shrank back again, grinning and satisfied.

"You seen, did you?" asked Pete Reeve grimly. "And for spying like that you'd ought to be shot down like a dog, Riley. But I'm not that kind. Go back and tell your master that we'll not let the girl go back to him. Tell him we know there's all sorts of prices for a life, but, when a woman is the price, then the man that lets her pay ain't man enough to be worth saving."

It had not been exactly the attitude of Pete Reeve the moment before, but, having been persuaded, he was not one to miss a rhetorical opening of this size.

Riley sneered at him. "That's what you say now," he said. "But we ain't going to rush you, Reeve. We're going to sit down and wait for the heat and the thirst to do the work with you. May take more than today. Then again, it may be that you'll change your mind before night. But we'll get you, Reeve, and we'll get the girl. And we'll cart your scalps in to the sheriff and collect the prices on your heads. So long, Pete."

He waved his hand to them with a mocking grin and strode off down the slope.

"It's going to be a long play," he reported to his men. "The girl won't hear no reason, or rather she lets Bull Hunter do her thinking and her talking for her. We'll have to find the nearest water and start carting it in here. Because the thing that's going to beat them up on the hill before night is that."

He pointed above his head toward the sun. It was losing its morning color and rapidly growing a blinding white. Already its heat was growing every moment, and before noon the effect would be terrible. Old Arrowhead Mountain was a mass of rock that instantly was heated along its surface until the stone burned through the soles of boots and the reflected warmth became furnace-like.

For the circle of guards along the lower slopes the watch through the day was bad enough, though they had the shelter of tall rocks here and there, and one of them was steadily at work, bringing freshly filled canteens. But for the trio imprisoned at the top of the hill it was a day of torture. The small basin in which they were protected was perfect for gathering and focusing the rays of the sun. By ten in the morning the heat had become intolerable, and still that heat was bound to increase by leaps and bounds for five hours!

Mary Hood endured the torment without a word, though her pallor increased as time went on. There was one tall pine, standing on the very verge of the cliff, but storm and lightning had blasted away most of the limbs except toward the top, and it gave them hardly any shade worth mentioning. In the shadow of the trunk there was room only for Mary Hood, and the men forced her to stay there. Pete Reeve, withered and bloodless, endured the oven heat better than the others. Bull Hunter, suffering through all of his great bulk, went panting about the work of fanning Mary, or talking as cheerily as he could to keep her mind from the horror of their situation.

Then at noon, with the sun hanging straight above them and the heat a steady agony unrelieved by a breath of wind, Hal Dunbar came up under another flag of truce and made a final appeal. Their reply was merely to order him back, and he went, trailing curses behind him. That newly refused offer of help made everything seem more terrible than before. It was the last offer, they knew, that would be received from big Hal Dunbar. After that, he would merely wait, and waiting would be more effective than bullets.

There remained a single half pint of hot water in the bottom of Bull Hunter's canteen, and this they reserved for Mary Hood. Twice that afternoon she tried to fight them away, refusing the priceless liquid, but Bull Hunter forced her like a stubborn child and made her take a small swallow. But that was merely giving an edge to the thirst of the girl. As for Hunter and Reeve, their tongues were beginning to swell. They spoke seldom, and, when they did, their syllables were as thick as from drunkenness.

When the crisis of the afternoon came, between half past two and half past three, they made their decision. They could wait until full night, then they would mount their horses and ride down the slope with Mary behind them to be given shelter from the bullets. It was an entirely hopeless thought, they knew perfectly well. Such men as Jack Hood and Hal Dunbar, in particular, did not miss close shots. Those two alone could account, shooting as they would from behind perfect shelter, for a dozen men. But there was nothing else for it. The horses were growing mad with thirst. Mary Hood was becoming feverish, and Bull Hunter was at the last of his endurance.

A wind came out of the north at this moment, but it served rather to put the hot air in circulation than to bring any relief of coolness. The day wore on. The shadows grew cooler and more blue along the sides of the tall mountain above them. There was a haven for them almost within reach of the hand, and yet they were hopelessly barred from it by the small distance across the gulch. All the time they could see the flash and sparkle of silver-running spring water on the slope not a hundred yards from them.

The shadows were beginning to lengthen. It was impossible to find more than one shelter from the sun, and they lay at full length, praying for night. And so Bull Hunter, watching the shade of the great pine tree lengthen and stretch across the cañon, received his great idea and sat bolt erect. Thirst and excitement choked him. He could only point and gibber like a madman. Then speech came.

"Pete," he gasped out, "we've been blind all day. There's a bridge for us. You see? That pine tree can be cut down, and, if it falls across the gulch, we can cross it."

Pete Reeve leaped to his feet, and then shook his head with a groan. "Can't be done, Bull. That wind will knock it sidewise, and it'll simply drop down into the cañon."

"It's got to be tried," said Bull Hunter, and he took his axe from his pack.

CHAPTER
TEN

A Daring Escape

It was an axe specially made for him. The haft was twice the ordinary circumference, and the head had the weight of a sledge hammer. Yet, standing with his feet braced for the work, he made the mighty weapon play like a feather about his head. The girl and Pete Reeve sat silently to watch, not daring to speak, not daring even to hope. The first blow fell with power that almost buried the axe head in the wood. Then the steel was pried out with a wrench, and the second blow bit out a great chip that leaped out of sight in the void of the cañon.

After that the chips flew regularly until the tree was well nigh eaten through, and the top of it swayed crazily in the wind. Bull Hunter stopped. If he continued cutting till the trunk was severed, the tree, as Pete Reeve had said, would blow sidewise in the cañon. So he waited.

"Pray for one breath of south wind," he told the others. "Pray for that. If it comes, we're saved."

They nodded and sat about with their eyes glued to the top of the tree, hoping against hope that they would see the wind abate from the north and swing.

"No hope," said Bull Hunter at last. "We'd be fools to wait for the wind to swing. Mary, lie down there between those two rocks with your revolver. If you see anyone show a head down the hill, shoot as close to them as you can. Pete, get your axe, and as soon as the wind falls off to nothing, you start chopping, and I'll try to give the tree a start from this side."

They obeyed him silently. Reeve stood ready with his axe. The girl, with her revolver before her, lay between the rocks to keep watch. Bull Hunter stood, waiting for the wind to cease before he gave the word. The Ghost, that mighty wolf dog, as though he realized that the girl was taking his own old post of sentinel, came sniffing beside her and lay down with his head dropped on his paws, close to the head of the girl. And big Diablo, the black stallion, apparently guessing that salvation was somehow connected with the cutting of the tree, came with his ears pricking and sniffed the raw wound in the side of the tree. Then he backed away to watch and wait, his eyes fixed in steady confidence on Bull Hunter.

When the wind fell away for a moment, Pete Reeve attacked the slender remnant of the trunk that remained whole, and Bull Hunter, reaching as far as he could up the tree, thrust with his whole weight against it. At that angle he could do little, but the small impulse might decide the entire direction of the fall. And so the trunk was bitten through deep on the one side, and Pete Reeve, stepping around to Hunter's side of the pine, gave half a dozen short, sharp, back strokes. There was a great rending, and the top of the pine staggered and began to fall.

At the same time the unlucky north wind, that had been blowing most of the afternoon, sprang up again and swung the tree sidewise. Yet the impetus of the fall had already been received. The pine fell at a sharp angle, but it spanned the gulch from side to side. Still, it was by no means a comfortable bridge. The Ghost sped across it with a bound and sat down on the far side and grinned back an invitation to follow. The three laughed in spite of themselves, but their laughter was drowned by a shout of rage down the slope. It had taken them this time to realize the meaning of the cutting of the tree, and now, after the first yell of anger, a confused babel of voices swept up to them.

"They know what we're going to try to do," said Pete Reeve, "and they'll press us pretty close."

His words were interrupted by the explosion of Mary Hood's revolver, answered by a shout of mocking defiance.

"Someone tried to edge higher up the hill," she explained through tight lips. "I hit the rock above him, and he ducked back."

"Do you think they'll try to rush?" Bull asked anxiously of little Reeve.

"They don't rush Pete Reeve in broad daylight. Nope, not if they was a hundred of 'em. The price is too high!" He waved to Bull. "I'm the lightest, and I'm next across."

"Good luck, Pete, but wait a minute. Mary goes with you. Mary!"

She came at once but shrank back from the edge of the cañon.

"Don't look down," Reeve cautioned her. "Look straight ahead. Look at The Ghost on the far side, and you'll keep your head. There's plenty of time. Get down on your hands and knees and crawl. I'm here behind you. Now, steady."

She obeyed without a word, casting one glance at Bull Hunter. And then she started with Pete Reeve moving close behind her, waiting for a slip. But the trunk was far more firmly lodged than they had imagined. Once in the center, feeling the quiver of the tree beneath her, the girl paused, trembling, but the steady voice of Reeve gave her courage, and she went on. A moment later she was on the far side, waving back to Bull Hunter.

He waved in return and then, from between the rocks, poured half a dozen shots down the slope.

"They're getting restless. That'll keep 'em for a while," Pete Reeve explained to the girl. "And now comes the hardest part for poor Charlie Hunter."

"Why the hardest part?"

"He has to leave Diablo, and that goes hard against the grain."

"Yes, I know," said the girl sadly, "just as I have to leave Nancy."

"It ain't the same," said Pete. "Diablo is more than just hoss to Bull. He's sort of a pal, too. Combination of partner and slave that's hard to beat. Look there . . . if the hoss don't know that Bull is giving him up?"

For, as Bull Hunter approached the tree trunk, the great black stallion pushed in before him with ears laid flat back and made a pretext of biting him, his teeth closing on the shoulder of his master. Bull Hunter patted the velvet muzzle and stroked the forelock. Then he turned and made a gesture of despair to the two on the other side.

"I've got to go," he said, "but I can't do it. Pete, I'd rather see Diablo dead than have Hal Dunbar ride him."

"There's no other way, Bull," said Reeve sadly. "If Dunbar gets him, you'll get him back before long."

Bull Hunter shook his head, passed his hand for the last time along the smooth, shining neck of the stallion, and then stepped out on the fallen pine. Diablo, fooled by the petting of his master, wheeled and started in pursuit — but Bull Hunter was already beyond reach of his teeth. Holding out his arms wide, he crossed and jumped off to join Mary Hood and Pete Reeve. The stallion reared and struck at the thin air. Then he danced in an ecstasy of rage and disappointment, while Nancy and Reeve's horse backed as far away as possible and, in amazement, watched this exhibition. Next the stallion came to the trunk and placed both forefeet upon it, as though he would try to cross, despite a glance into the depths below that made him shrink. The sunlight trembled along his glossy coat.

"Poor devil," muttered Pete Reeve.

Bull Hunter lowered his head and could not look back.

"Let's start," he said. "Takes the joy out of life to leave that horse, Pete. I'll never see him again. Dunbar won't be able to ride him, and he'll go so crazy mad that he'll kill him. I know!"

He turned away among the rocks, with the girl and Reeve following in silence, but they were stopped by a great neigh from across the gulch. They looked back with a cry of wonder coming from every throat, and that cry was taken up and echoed along the crest on the farther side. There they stood, man after man — Jack Hood, Hal Dunbar, and all their followers. They had rushed the crest at last only to find their quarry gone, but now they stood careless of the fact that they were exposed to the guns of Reeve and Hunter. For Diablo had ventured a step along the trunk with his head stretched out, his legs bent, his whole body trembling with terror. The wind caught his mane and tail and set them flaring. He took another step and shuddered as the trunk, beneath his great weight, settled and quaked.

"Please send him back!" said Mary Hood, catching the arm of Bull Hunter.

"Send him back," shouted Hal Dunbar. "Send him back, Hunter, and we'll stop the chase here. I didn't know such horses were ever bred!"

"How can he turn and go back," called Bull Hunter in answer. "But will you let me try to help him across that tree, Dunbar?"

"Yes," he answered.

Friends and enemies, they stood ranged on either side of the gorge and watched the giant stallion's effort to gain back his master. Each step he made in mortal terror, and yet he kept on.

Bull Hunter waited for no second permission. He was instantly at the far end of the log, and at his call the gallant horse pricked his ears. They flicked back again the next moment as a gust of wind nearly knocked him from his position. He steadied himself and made the next step. But now the trunk grew smaller and therefore less steady, and moreover the central depth of the cañon was straight beneath him.

Then Bull Hunter stepped out on the log. His own weight helped to make the trunk less steady, but the moral effect of his coming would more than counter-balance that. Standing straight up, he placed himself in mortal danger, for the jar of one false step on the part of the horse would kill his master as well as himself. In appreciation of what was happening, Mary Hood covered her eyes, and a deep-throated murmur of applause came from the followers of Hal Dunbar on the farther side.

With short, trembling steps the big stallion moved along the trunk, and now Bull Hunter met him midway over the chasm and with his outstretched hand caught the reins close to the bit. The ears of Diablo quivered forward in recognition of this assistance. Though the powerful hand of Bull Hunter was useless, practically, to steady the great bulk of the horse, the confidence that he gave was enough to make Diablo straighten and step forward with a greater surety.

Within a yard of safety a rear hoof slipped violently from the curved surface of the trunk, and a groan came from the anxious watchers on either side of the gulch. They had been mortal enemies the minute before. Now the heroism of the horse gave them one common interest, and they forgot all else. The groan changed to a great gasping breath of relief as Diablo, quaking through every limb, steadied himself on the verge of reeling from the tree trunk. Here the hand and voice of Bull Hunter saved him, indeed. Another step and he was on the level ground beyond, and Pete Reeve and Mary Hood and all the men of Hal Dunbar joined in one rousing shout of triumph. Diablo stood trembling beside his master, and Bull Hunter let his hand wander fondly over that beautiful head.

The noise fell away as Hal Dunbar stepped forward. He took off his hat and bowed across the chasm to Mary Hood.

"Mary," he said, "I've followed you hard and rough. But I followed for what I thought was your own good. I didn't know Hunter then, as I know him now. But a man whose horse will risk death to follow him, and who will risk death to save his horse, can't be much wrong at the heart. Only one thing, Mary, I want you to know. I could have stopped you here . . . we had Reeve and Hunter under our guns . . . Diablo saved them. And I want to ask you one favor in return. Ask Bull Hunter to cross the gulch and speak with me on this side for a moment. I give him my solemn word of honor that no harm will come to him from my men."

She shook her head. "I've tried you before, Hal. And I won't trust you now. I can't persuade Charlie to go . . . not a step."

Bull Hunter answered: "I don't need persuading. I'll meet you on that side, Dunbar."

There was a faint cry from Mary Hood, but the big man stepped quietly onto the log and recrossed the chasm. A moment later he stood face to face with Hal Dunbar, and a murmur of awe passed over Dunbar's men. For they saw that for the first time their big boss was matched against a man who was his equal in size and in apparent strength.

Pete Reeve had drawn back into the shelter of a great ragged rock, jutting from the mountainside, and now he called from his concealment: "I'm on guard, Dunbar. The first crooked step you take or the first suspicious move you make, I'll shoot and shoot to kill. You may drop Bull Hunter, but you'll never live to talk about it!"

Hal Dunbar bowed in mock courtesy. He had drawn Hunter aside so that their voices could not be heard by the others when they were lowered to a whispering compass.

"Dunbar," said his rival earnestly, "you've played a fair game and a square game today. I'm thanking you. I don't know how you feel about it, but I'd like to shake hands. Are you willing?"

The smile that Hal Dunbar turned on him did not falter in the slightest. But what he said was: "Hunter, I hate the ground you walk on. There's only one thing that keeps me from finishing you today. It's not the gun of Pete Reeve. It's the fact that Mary Hood is watching us. That's why I smile, Hunter, but I'm cursing you inside."

301

Bull Hunter shrugged his shoulders. There was no other answer to be made.

"I haven't asked you over here to make friends," said Hal Dunbar. "And you can rest content that there'll never be rest for either of us until one of us is dead, and the other is safely married to Mary Hood. Just now she's had her head turned by you . . . a little later it may be my turn."

"That turn won't come," answered Bull, unshaken by the quiver of hatred that ran through the voice of the other. "She'll be married to me by tomorrow night."

Hal Dunbar closed his eyes as though a flash of sunlight had blinded him. Then he looked out again from beneath puckered brows. "Tell me, Hunter," he said, "what'll be the outcome of that marriage? You may be happy with her for a few days, but how long d'you think it will last when you and she have to run through the mountains to keep clear of the law that follows you? Are you going to drag her with you and spoil her life because of this selfish thing you call your love for her?"

Bull Hunter paled. "I am not a very wise man, Dunbar," he said, "and I may be wrong, and you may be right, but it seems to me that, if a man and a woman love each other enough, they have the right to take some chances."

"And if you have children?" asked Dunbar, still smiling and still savage.

Bull Hunter sighed. "I don't know," he said. "It looks impossible. But there may be a way."

"That's why I've asked you to come and talk with me. I'll tell you what I can do. I have a little weight with the governor of the state. He needs financial support now and then and ... but it's no use going into politics. The short of it is that the governor will do pretty much what I want him to do. Hunter, suppose I were to ask him for a pardon for you ... and for your friend, Reeve, as well? Suppose I were to do that and leave you free to marry Mary Hood and settle down where you please and live your own happy lives?"

"If you did that," said Bull Hunter gravely, "you'd be the finest man that ever lived."

"But I'm not the finest. I want to know if it's worth taking a risk to get a pardon for yourself and Reeve?"

"Any risk in the world."

"Then listen to me. I'll go back to the nearest town with a telegraph and get in touch with the governor at once. I can have your pardon wired all over the state by tomorrow morning. You can take Mary Hood into Moosehorn before tomorrow night. You understand?"

"It's like a dream," muttered Bull Hunter.

"Here's the part of it that will wake you up again," said Hal Dunbar with his evil smile. "In Moosehorn you leave Mary Hood and come straight back toward Five Roads."

"Why?"

"Because on the road you'll meet me. It'll be after dark, but that doesn't make any difference. If it's dark, we'll fight without guns. For a fight it's going to be, Hunter, without the girl standing by to pity you and weep over you and never forget that I killed you ... you understand?"

"Yes, I begin to," said Bull Hunter. "You get me a pardon from the governor. I take Mary to safety. I come back and meet you. And one of us dies. If it's me, nothing could be better for you. You will be able to pose before Mary as having secured my pardon. It will be proof to her that you had no hand in my killing. If I kill you, you have lost everything, indeed, and I've the guilt of killing my benefactor. Is that it?"

"Is it worth the risk?" asked the other, husky with excitement. "Think of it, Hunter! It means your chance for happiness with the girl. Do you fear me too much to meet me? I'll give you every advantage. I'll come without a gun on me. We'll fight bare hand to bare hand. I've some skill with a gun as you know. But I'll throw that away. Do you agree?"

Bull Hunter sighed. He looked across the chasm at Mary Hood, where she stood watching him anxiously. Never had she seemed so beautiful. Yes, for the sake of her happiness it was worth risking everything. She could not lead that wandering life through the mountains.

"I'll meet you tomorrow night," said Bull Hunter. "On the way from Moosehorn to Five Roads. You have my word that I'll be there."

"Then shake hands."

"Shake hands?" said Bull huskily. "What sort of a devil are you, Dunbar? Shake hands when we intend to try to kill one another?"

"It's for the sake of the girl. It'll make her easier if she thinks that we're friends."

304

Bull Hunter reluctantly took the hand of the other and then went back across the chasm to join his two companions.

CHAPTER
ELEVEN

Setting the Stage

All was done punctually as the ranch owner had promised. Until late that night he kept a telegraph wire to the capital of the state busy. At midnight the pardons of Pete Reeve and Bull Hunter were signed, and the news was being flashed across the mountain desert. Only one person had been with Hal Dunbar while he was doing his telegraphing, and that person was the invaluable lieutenant, Riley. The fox-faced little man blinked when he saw the contents of the first wire sent, but after that he showed no emotion whatever, for he was not an emotional man. He stayed quietly with the big boss until the job was finished.

Then Dunbar went to bed, and Riley slept late. He was awakened before noon by the heavy tread of Hal Dunbar, pacing in the next room of the hotel. Presently the big man came to him and talked while Riley dressed. His ordinary ease of manner was gone. His very walk was jerky and halting. His speech was of the same pattern. A tremendous nervous gloom had fallen upon him. It seemed to Riley that it might be the result of the only generous thing that he had ever known the big fellow to do. He had been truly stunned by the unselfish work of Hal Dunbar the night before. It had made him uneasy. For, having felt during many years that he knew his man so to speak, he was bewildered by this sudden change. As far as he knew Hal Dunbar, there was little good in the big, handsome fellow. He had been a pampered child; he had grown to a spoiled youth and into an utterly selfish manhood. That he should go out of his way to clear the path of his successful rival was beyond the comprehension of Riley.

So he waited this morning, half expecting a confession, with his ratty little eyes continually flashing across at Dunbar's gloomy face. But the latter said nothing until they had finished breakfast, and then he took Riley for a short stroll outside the village.

"How's your eyes these days, Riley?" he asked. "You used to be a pretty fair sort of a shot."

"Never a hand like you with a gun," said Riley modestly, "but I'm as good as I ever was."

"Let me see you try," said Dunbar. "You've got your Colt with you. There's a white knot in that fence post over yonder. Take a try at it."

It was by no means usual for Dunbar to make such requests. But Riley was not in the habit of asking questions. He drew his revolver, lined it with the post, dropped it on the mark, and fired. Dunbar strode forward to examine the results.

"Low left," he said critically when he returned. "You've got a good squeeze when you pull the trigger, but the trigger pull is too light in that gun. And you drop it too far."

"Only half an inch from a dead center," said Riley, somewhat angered by this seemingly carping criticism. "That ain't so bad."

"At a hundred yards it would have given you a wounded man instead of a dead one," said the big man coldly. "When you shoot, shoot to kill."

The other nodded respectfully. There was at least one subject upon which Hal Dunbar was a profound authority, and that was every sort of fighting. From guns to fists and knives there was nothing that Hal Dunbar did not know about battle, and there was nothing he loved more than conflict. He would ride fifty miles to pick a quarrel with a man who was said to be big enough to wrestle with him. Accordingly, Riley accepted his judgment.

"Every time you shoot at a small target, try to think it's the button over the heart of the man you hate most in the world. That's what I've always done, and that's why I've made myself a good shot. I'm not a dead shot. There's no such thing. But I'm very nearly as good as they come. And I'm going to keep on getting better and better . . . if I live."

He uttered this last phrase with such strange emotion that Riley turned and gaped at him. He recovered himself at once, however, and presented the usual blank face to the big boss. Certainly there was something strange in the mind of Hal Dunbar today.

"But," continued Dunbar, "you shoot well enough . . . quite well enough for my purpose, Riley. Long shooting isn't your specialty. At a short distance I think you might do very well."

He paused, and Riley waited patiently for the tale to be unfolded.

"You know," began Hal Dunbar at length, "that I've always loved a fight?"

"I know."

"And tonight I am about to fight, Riley."

"Yes?"

"But for a great prize. For the woman I love!"

"So you're going to fight Bull Hunter?"

"Yes."

Riley breathed deeply. "It will be the greatest fight that ever was fought in the mountains. But I hope not with guns?"

"Why not?"

"Because Hunter was trained to shoot by Pete Reeve, and he's almost as good as the man who taught him. Not with guns, Hal."

"I know everything you know, and that's why I had guns ruled out, but I put it as if I was doing him a favor."

He chuckled at the thought, and Riley grinned in sympathy. This was the Hal Dunbar he had always known, crafty, hard, cunning under all of his apparent carelessness.

"It's to be bare hands, Riley."

"And I'll have a chance to watch?"

"I don't think you care whether I win or not," said Hal angrily. "All you want is to see the fight."

"But, of course, I want you to win," said Riley.

"Never mind. This is the point. With so much at stake I must not lose the fight . . . you understand?"

"You'll trick Bull Hunter?" asked Riley, and he looked down at the ground.

There was one article in Riley's creed, and that was fairness in fighting.

"I'll fight him fairly and squarely," said Dunbar, "and I ought to beat him with fists and hands. He's strong, but I'm still stronger, I think. Besides, I know boxing and wrestling, and he doesn't. It's a finish fight. If I down him, I'll kill him with my hands. If he downs me, he'll finish me the same way. But, even if he leaves me dead on the ground, he must not win the fight!"

He turned and clutched the arms of his companion as he spoke.

"But how the devil . . . ?" began Riley.

"Listen to me," said Hal Dunbar. "I love that girl in a way you can't understand. I've loved her so long that the thought of her is in my brain and my blood . . . part of me. No matter to whom she goes, she must not go to Hunter. He ruined everything for me. If I thought that after my death he was to have her, I tell you my ghost would come up and haunt them. Whatever happens, no matter if he kills me, Hunter must not win. You understand?"

Riley shook his head, bewildered.

"You fool!" gasped out Dunbar, maddened because he had to bring out the brutal truth in so many words. "You're to be hidden near the place where we meet, and, if Hunter wins . . . you shoot him down. You shoot him like a dog!"

Riley blinked. Then: "Where do you meet?" he asked.

Hal Dunbar sighed with relief. "You'll do it? I thought for a minute that I was mistaken in you . . . that you were weak. But you're still my right-hand man, Riley. I'll tell you where. There's a wood between Five Roads and Moosehorn. We're to meet somewhere between those two towns after dark. And I'll leave early and wait for him near the trees. That will give you a chance to stay close to the fight, and there'll be a full moon to help you . . . if you have to shoot. You understand, Riley?"

"I leave this afternoon and get posted?"

"Leave now. I'll follow along after a while. Go around through Five Roads. We mustn't be seen to ride in the same direction. Be sure that, if you have to lie for a long time during the fight, you don't get your right arm cramped." He turned back. "Start now, Riley!"

CHAPTER
TWELVE

The Battle

It was thick twilight when Bull Hunter stood up from his chair in the room at Moosehorn where he and Pete Reeve had celebrated their return from outlawry to peaceful citizenship. Now the big man went to Mary Hood and took her hands.

"When a man's heart gets too full," he said quietly, "he has to go off by himself. I'm too happy, Mary. I'm going out for a ride on Diablo all alone. I'm not even going to take The Ghost with me. Pete will take care of you."

She smiled faintly and anxiously at him as he turned to the big wolf dog, pointed out a rug in the corner of the room, and commanded him to stay there until he was called away. The Ghost obeyed sulkily, dropping his huge scarred head upon his paws and watching the master with an upward glance. Then Hunter turned at the door, gave himself a last look at Mary Hood, waved to Pete Reeve, and was gone.

The door had hardly closed when Mary Hood was beside the little gunfighter.

"Pete," she said, "there's something about to happen . . . something about to happen to Charlie. I feel it. I sensed it in his voice when he said he was going. It was queer, too, the way he watched the coming of the night. Pete, you must go out and follow him and see that he comes to no harm. Will you?"

The little man shook his head soberly. "If you're wrong, and Bull finds that I'm following him, it'll be bad business," he declared. "He hates to be spied on . . . even by me."

"But I know that I'm right," she said eagerly. "I'm cold with the fear of it, Pete. Will you go?"

He rose slowly from his chair. "I'd ought to laugh at you," he answered. "But I can't. There's something spooky in the way a girl gets ideas about things she don't really know. Maybe you're right this time. Anyway, we can't take any chances. I'll saddle up the roan and follow Diablo as close as I can. But that isn't any easy job if Bull starts riding hard."

She thanked him huskily as he left, and from the window of the hotel she saw him lead out his little cow pony, swing into the saddle, and disappear instantly into the dusk.

The black horse was a glimmering phantom in the night far ahead of Pete Reeve, and he spurred hard after it. If Diablo had been extended to three quarters of his usual speed, he would have drawn out of sight at once, but tonight for some reason Bull Hunter was riding merely at a long-ranging gallop, giving the stallion his own way in the matter of taking hill and dale. Pete Reeve, by dint of spurring now and then, was able to keep barely within eyeshot of the rider before him.

Yet it was precarious work to keep barely within view without being seen himself, and he kept his eyes riveted on the shadow in the darkness. The way was leading straight to Five Roads, and, with every mile he put behind him, he became more and more convinced that the girl had been right. For Bull Hunter did not ride in the careless fashion of one who is following a whim. He kept to a steady, purposeful gait, and the little man who trailed him began to suspect more and more definitely that there was a rendezvous ahead.

He rode a little closer now, for it was complete night, and the moon had not yet risen, though the light in the east gave promise of it. Pressing on with his eyes fastened on the form that moved before him, he swung a little from the beaten trail — the next moment the roan, putting his foot into an old squirrel hole, pitched forward on his head. Pete Reeve shot out of the saddle and landed heavily on his back.

When, after a time, he wakened from the trance, it was with the feeling that he had been asleep for endless hours. But he could tell by the moon, low in the east, that it had not been long. The poor roan had broken its leg and lay snorting and groaning. Pete put it out of misery with a bullet, but he did not wait to remove the saddle.

A moral certainty had grown in him that Bull Hunter was, indeed, riding toward a rendezvous, perhaps into danger. Otherwise why such secrecy, such care in leaving even The Ghost behind? No doubt he could not arrive in time to ward off trouble, but, if there were a fight, he might come in time to help at the finish.

Throwing his hat and cartridge belt away to lighten him, and, carrying his naked Colt in his hand, Reeve started running down the road.

In the meantime Bull Hunter had come, at moonrise, to that clump of tall trees by the road, and he had found Hal Dunbar, waiting on horseback. He halted, dismounted, led Diablo to the side of the road, and then advanced. Hal Dunbar — a mighty figure — came to meet him half way.

"Have you kept your word?" asked Hal Dunbar. "Have you come unarmed?"

"I have nothing but my bare hands," said Bull quietly. "But, before we start, Dunbar, I want to make a last appeal to you. You've been . . ."

"You've not only played the sneak, but now are you going to play the fool, too, and maybe the coward?"

On the heels of his words he leaped at Bull Hunter. His right fist, driven with all the power of his body and of his leap, landed fair and true on the jaw of the other, such a blow as Bull Hunter had never felt before — it sent him reeling back and cast a cloud of misty darkness across his mind. Hal Dunbar paused an instant to see the colossus drop. Yet, to his amazement, the other giant did not fall. His slight pause gave Hunter's brain a chance to clear. They rushed together, shocked, and again the heavy fists of Dunbar crushed home. This time he changed his aim, and the blows thudded against the body of Hunter.

It was like smiting ribs of steel. Hal Dunbar gave back, gasping his astonishment. Here was a man of stone, indeed. The first fear in battle he had ever had came to the big man. He tried again and again every trick at his command. Dunbar hooked and swung and drove long straight rights with all the strength of his big body behind them. Half of those punches landed fairly and squarely. They shook Bull Hunter, but they did not topple him from his balance. His face was bleeding from half a dozen cuts — the flesh of his body must have been bruised purple — but there was not the slightest faltering. Yet, he seemed to be fighting a helpless, hopeless fight. The trained footwork of Dunbar kept him easily out of the range of Hunter's unskillful punches, while from a distance he whipped his own blows home and then danced away again.

But at the very moment when Dunbar seemed to have victory in the hollow of his hand, with only time as the question, his terror began to become blind panic. For the strength and endurance of Hunter were incredible. Blows that should have felled an ox glanced harmlessly from him.

Finally a blow landed squarely. It was not a powerful blow, but it sent a jar up the arm of Hunter, and the new sensation excited him. He was a new man. He came in with a low shout, rushing eagerly, no longer dull-eyed but keenly aggressive. He became lighter on his feet, infinitely swifter of hand. At the very time that Dunbar was beating him he had been studying the methods of the tall fellow, and now he used them himself.

It became impossible to avoid him altogether. For all his lightness of footwork Dunbar found terrific punches crashing through his guard. He himself was fighting like a madman, striking three times to every once for Hunter. His arms were growing weary, his guard lowering — and then like a flash, striking overhand, the long arm of Hunter shot across, and his right fist met the jaw of Dunbar. The latter dropped as though hit by a club, and Hunter leaned over him.

In the shadow of the trees Riley raised his revolver, but Hunter was saying: "Dunbar, this is the end. You're growing tired. You're getting weak. I can feel it. Don't force this on. You've fought hard. You've cut me to pieces. But now you're done. And I've no malice."

He stopped. Hal Dunbar had worked himself to his knees, looking up with a bleeding face at the conqueror, and, as he kneeled there, his hand closed on a huge, knotted branch of a tree, torn off in some storm by wind or lightning or both, and flung here beside the road. The feel of the wood sent a thrill of new and savage hope through him. Vaguely he realized, not that his enemy had spared him when he might have finished the battle with a helpless foe, but simply that he was alive and that a chance to kill had been thrust into his hand. He leaped from his knees straight at Hunter, swung the branch, and struck.

The first blow beat down the arms that Hunter had raised to guard his head and struck him a glancing blow, but the second landed heavily, and the big man crumpled on the ground in a shapeless heap. Hal Dunbar, with savage joy, caught him by the shoulder and wrenched him back. He laid his hand on the heart. It beat steadily but feebly and Dunbar, gone mad with the battle, swung up the club for the finishing blow.

He was stopped by a cold, sharp voice from the wood that he hardly recognized as the voice of Riley.

"If you hit him again with that, I'll shoot you full of holes."

The amazement turned his blood to ice. He turned, gaping, and there came little Riley walking from the shadow out of the wood with the revolver leveled.

"I couldn't stand the gaff," said Riley calmly. "All the time you were fighting, I watched. When I seen Hunter knock you down, I pulled the gun to kill him. But he let you get up . . . and then you whale him with a club . . . and want to brain him after you've knocked him cold. Listen, Dunbar, I'm through with you. I ain't a saint, but neither am I a skunk. I'm through with you, and so will be every other decent man some of these days. Step back from Hunter, or I'll kill you."

The giant obeyed, his face working, unable to speak. And the little man followed, making savage gestures with his weapon.

"You ain't worthy of touching his hand," said Riley slowly. "You ain't as good as the dirt he walks on. Now, get on your hoss and ride!"

Dunbar raised his hand: "Listen!"

Far off down the road they heard a voice. "Bull! Oh, Bull Hunter!"

"It's Pete Reeve," said Riley. "He must've guessed at some dirty work. Get on your hoss and ride one way, and I'll get on mine and ride another. It won't do much good for either of us to be found here by Pete Reeve."

"Riley," said Hal Dunbar, "the day will come when you'll drag yourself on your knees to me, and I'll kick you away."

"Maybe, but it ain't come yet. What I'm thinking about just now is that, being so wise as you and me have been, Dunbar, don't always pay. Here's a simple gent, lying here stunned. Well, it ain't the first time that he's beat the both of us. He's lying there knocked cold, but he'll be found by a partner, Pete Reeve. And he'll be brought back to Moosehorn, and he'll marry the prettiest girl we ever seen. How does he get all this? Just by being simple, Hal, and honest. Which, God help our souls, we ain't either of them things. Now get out of my sight!"

Whether he fled from his own shame or remorse, or was moved by the threat of his companion, or dreaded the voice of Pete Reeve coming down the road, the big man mounted, turned his horse, and galloped away. Riley returned to his covert in the woods until he had seen Pete Reeve come and bend over the fallen man. When he heard Bull Hunter sigh, then Riley turned and slipped away into the night. He had lived one perfect day.

About the Author

Max Brand is the best-known pen name of Frederick Faust, creator of Dr. Kildare, Destry, and many other fictional characters popular with readers and viewers worldwide. His enormous output, totaling approximately thirty million words or the equivalent of 530 ordinary books, covered nearly every field: crime, fantasy, historical romance, espionage, Westerns, science fiction, adventure, animal stories, love, war, and fashionable society, big business and big medicine. Eighty motion pictures have been based on his work along with many radio and television programs. For good measure he also published four volumes of poetry. Perhaps no other author has reached more people in more different ways.

Born in Seattle in 1892, orphaned early, Faust grew up in the rural San Joaquin Valley of California. At Berkeley he became a student rebel and one-man literary movement, contributing prodigiously to all campus publications. Denied a degree because of unconventional conduct, he embarked on a series of adventures culminating in New York City where, after a period of near starvation, he received simultaneous recognition as a serious poet and successful popular-prose writer. Later, he traveled widely, making his home in New York, then in Florence, and finally in Los Angeles.

Once the United States entered the Second World

War, Faust abandoned his lucrative writing career and his work as a screenwriter to serve as a war correspondent with the infantry in Italy, despite his fifty-one years and a bad heart. He was killed during a night attack on a hilltop village held by the German army. New books based on magazine serials or unpublished manuscripts or restored versions continue to appear so that, alive or dead, he has averaged a new book every four months for seventy-five years. Beyond this, some work by him is newly reprinted every week of every year in one or another format somewhere in the world. A great deal more about this author and his work can be found in THE MAX BRAND COMPANION (Greenwood Press, 1997) edited by Jon Tuska and Vicki Piekarski.

SPECIAL MESSAGE TO READERS

MEN BEYOND THE LAW

This Western trio opens with "Werewolf", the story of a man fleeing after a gunfight, whose encounter with an ancient Cheyenne in the wilderness changes his course. All is lost to him until he completes a spiritual journey, and confronts the shadow within himself.

In "The Finding of Jeremy", a young New Yorker forsakes his profession to go West. He thinks himself suddenly rich when he sees two bank robbers kill each other over loot, until a sheriff's posse arrives and hails him as a great hero.

And "The Trail Up Old Arrowhead" concludes the story of Bull Hunter, a gentle giant of a man who sees deeply into the human soul. Two previous installments of his story have appeared in Max Brand's books *Outlaws All* and *The Wolf Strain*.